ENDO

A masterful skating fantasy that will entertain readers of all ages. The enduring principles of honesty and fair play win out over the evils of cheating and revenge every time.

—*Oleg Petrov*, Ice dancer and coach,
Russian world senior team member,
principal skater with the Russian
ice theater *All Stars*

Rainbow Rinks is a spellbinding adventure. The tension between Cammie and the witches of the Icy Park is fascinating.

—*Maria Pocheykina*, Freestyle skater and
coach, Russian world junior team member

Come and glide through the many rinks of Skateland with Cammie and Alex. Let your imagination run wild as they experience the good and the bad of their skating trials. In one word: fant-ice-tic.

—*Neal Wood*, Professional ice dancer, coach,
civil engineer, skate sharpener, and
boot fitter for sixty years

Cammie & Alex's
adventures at
RAINBOW RINKS

CAMMIE & ALEX'S
adventures at
RAINBOW RINKS

written by: OLGA JAFFAE

TATE PUBLISHING & *Enterprises*

Published by Tate Publishing & Enterprises, LLC
127 E. Trade Center Terrace | Mustang, Oklahoma 73064 USA
1.888.361.9473 | www.tatepublishing.com

Tate Publishing is committed to excellence in the publishing industry. The company reflects the philosophy established by the founders, based on Psalm 68:11,
"The Lord gave the word and great was the company of those who published it."

Book design copyright © 2009 by Tate Publishing, LLC. All rights reserved.
Cover design & interior design by Lindsay B. Behrens
Illustration by Brandon Wood

Published in the United States of America

ISBN: 978-1-61566-300-2
1. Fiction, Fantasy & Contemporary
09.09.18

DEDICATION

This book is dedicated to Neal Wood, whose creative excellence and love of skating have inspired figure skaters for three generations.

ACKNOWLEDGMENT

Very special thanks to Gary Jaffae, my wonderful husband and best friend. Without his constant help and support, this book would have never been written.

TABLE OF CONTENTS

New Girl

The new girl was absolutely gorgeous. A true skater—at least that was what Cammie thought. Tall and slim, the girl stepped on the ice with the confidence of a professional. As she glided toward the middle of the rink, her long black hair flowed behind her like a bridal train. Cammie leaned against the barrier and waited. The girl stood with her arms lifted gracefully above her head, waiting for her music to begin. The first chords sounded familiar—feisty and rhythmical.

"*Carmen*," a voice came from behind.

Cammie looked around. Coach Louise stood next to her, her eyes on the pretty girl. "The music is from the opera *Carmen*. It was written by Bizet, a French composer."

Cammie nodded. Yes, she had heard the name *Carmen* before.

"This piece is a little overused, but it suits her perfectly," Coach Louise said.

Cammie watched the girl perform a complicated sequence of steps on the ice. Mohawks, double three turns, twizzles. The skater's feet moved across the ice quickly, effortlessly. Cammie wished her footwork were that smooth. The girl spun on the ice, made a quick turn, and lifted her leg in a high arabesque.

Cammie applauded. "Wow!"

"Okay, that's enough!" Coach Louise shouted to the skater.

The girl went into a back pivot and froze in the middle of the rink, lean and graceful. For some reason, Cammie felt disappointed. She didn't want the girl to stop skating.

Coach Louise stepped on the ice and joined the graceful skater. "You had no speed going into that flip. No wonder it didn't happen."

Huh? What did Coach Louise just say? The girl hadn't landed her flip? How come Cammie hadn't noticed it?

"We'll have to work on that." Coach Louise was

all business as usual. "Now next time I want you to..."

For the next five or ten minutes, Coach Louise skated around the rink, the pretty girl by her side. For some reason, the coach didn't look too happy; she looked as though she was criticizing the girl. Well, coaches could be weird sometimes. If Coach Louise didn't enjoy what she had just seen, it was her problem. Cammie, however, was completely enthralled by the new skater's performance. Oh, how she wished she could skate so gracefully! And of course, she would give anything, even her newly acquired axel jump, just to be as beautiful as that girl. Even from where she stood, Cammie could see the skater's bright eyes framed with long thick eyelashes, a small straight nose, and full red lips. *She looks like the real Carmen*, Cammie thought. *Why can't I be like her?*

Everybody had always told Cammie that she was cute, but now compared to the new girl, she felt like Cinderella watching her stepsisters get ready for the ball. Her own brown hair looked drab and mousy; her eyes were too small, and her eyelashes...oh, forget the eyelashes! Did Cammie even have any?

Cammie turned to her friend Margie, who leaned against the boards next to her. There was an unwritten rule at the rink that if somebody's music was playing, the rest of the kids gave the skater the right of way. And because the rink wasn't big enough, it was always better to keep the middle part empty so programs could be practiced.

"Where did she come from?" Cammie whispered.

"Who?"

"Carmen." Cammie pointed to the stunning girl. She was now gliding on her left forward outside edge, her right leg behind her in another perfect arabesque. Some extension she had, just like Sasha Cohen.

"Oh, you mean that girl," Margie said. "She's from California, I think. Her family just moved here. "

"Okay, it's enough for today, Isabelle," Coach Louise said.

Isabelle. *Isabelle?* So that was the girl's name. How nice. It sounded like music, sparkled like rhinestones on a skating dress.

"There she is, my sweet girl!"A slightly accented voice came from behind.

Cammie turned around and saw a tall muscular man wearing a white sport coat and black velour pants. Even before the man hugged Isabelle,

Cammie knew he was the girl's father—that was how much the two of them looked alike. The man had given Isabelle his dark almond-shaped eyes, black hair, and olive skin. Like father like daughter—both looked great.

The man smiled at Coach Louise, who was still on the ice. "May I have a word with you, Coach?"

He turned to Isabelle and said something in Spanish. The girl nodded and headed for the locker room.

"Of course, Mr. Alvarez," Coach Louise said.

Alvarez. *Isabelle Alvarez.* That was even more beautiful. The last name suited the girl perfectly, and the Spanish language went well with her skating style. The flow of Spanish sounds, the chopped *d*'s and rolling *r*'s, reminded Cammie of the thumping sound of the blade connecting with the ice after a double jump—first the sharp *crush* of the toe pick; then the soft *whoosh* of the blade.

Cammie cast another longing look at the locker room door through which Isabelle had just disappeared and stepped on the ice slowly, reluctantly. For some reason, she didn't feel like practicing. With Isabelle gone, the rink had lost its attractiveness.

For the rest of the day, Cammie couldn't get the image of Isabelle out of her mind. Oh, how she wanted to look like her! Gosh, why did she have to be so plain? And why hadn't her parents chosen a better name for her? *Cammie*—some name for a skater, thank you very much! Although ... *Cammie* was only a nickname, a shorter version of *Camille*. *Camille Wester*. Well, perhaps not as cool as *Isabelle Alvarez*, but certainly not too bad. Okay, it was settled: from now on, Cammie would insist on being called *Camille*. She had outgrown her childish nickname.

Her next step would be her looks. She wasn't going to put up with her plain appearance anymore. If she hadn't been blessed with gorgeous dark eyes and full lips like Isabelle's, she would have to use makeup. As simple as that. That was no big deal; all skaters, Cammie included, used mascara and lipstick for competitions. It was allowed; even Cammie's mother helped her when it came to applying makeup properly.

So from now on, Cammie was going to wear makeup to every practice. She was eleven already, and that was old enough. And perhaps ... perhaps, she would look as gorgeous as Isabelle, and Isabelle would notice her. Maybe, one day, they would even become friends. Oh, how wonderful that would be!

That night Cammie fell asleep dreaming of

Isabelle and herself gliding across the ice at their home rink, both looking gorgeous, the eyes of the other girls fixed on them. She woke up in the morning feeling completely happy; she smiled the whole day at school, and she also beamed with joy when it was time to go to the rink.

It was Friday night and time for a cardio class. Cammie always enjoyed the lesson when skaters of different levels came together as a group. For those who skated better, cardio was an opportunity to relax and have fun. For weaker skaters, attempting more difficult moves was a challenge; trying to keep up with better skaters was a continuous endeavor. Today, Cammie looked forward to her favorite class even more. First of all, she knew Isabelle would be there because, for Coach Louise's students, cardio was a mandatory class. And of course, Cammie couldn't wait to demonstrate her new—and very improved—looks to the whole rink.

Cammie had taken a lot of time to polish her appearance. Even the circumstances had worked in her favor. First of all, her mother had gone grocery shopping just a couple of hours before they had to drive to the rink. The timing was perfect because, first of all, it had given Cammie the opportunity to put on her mother's makeup. Second, it hadn't put her in the position of having to hang around the house in full glamour for a long time. That would have been risky: her mother might have noticed something wasn't right.

The moment the door closed behind her mother, Cammie ran to her parents' bedroom and positioned herself in front of the vanity table. She rummaged through her mother's makeup kit. She knew very well what was there because her mother had helped her apply rouge and eye shadow many times before competitions. It was good Cammie had already had some practice putting on makeup.

Cammie giggled as she thought of her friend Diane, who had once decided to wear her mother's mascara to school. Diane hadn't done it right; her makeup was smudged badly. Besides, it had rained heavily. Diane's makeup had streaked down her face, so the poor girl entered the classroom looking like a zebra. Of course, that wasn't going to happen to Cammie; she was quite an experienced beautician.

Cammie started with rouge, which made her pale face look brighter and healthier. She dipped a small brush into dark green eye shadow and put some on her upper lids. Not bad. Right away, her eyes looked larger. Cammie looked through her mother's collection of lipsticks, finally settling on bright pink. She had always liked pink and besides, she was going to wear her new pink sweater to the rink.

Cammie took the hairband out of her hair, letting long brown strands cover her shoulders and chest. All right, she almost looked like Isabelle. Perhaps if she squinted and tilted her head, like that...Cammie gave herself another critical look. Not bad, but something was missing. Oh yes, of course, the eyelashes. Isabelle's were so long and thick, and Cammie's were thin and short. Would mascara do the trick?

Cammie ran her finger against her eyelashes. She didn't want to take a risk. During their cardio class, Coach Louise made the skaters move so fast that Cammie's face was always wet with perspiration. Besides, nothing could ruin your makeup faster than cold wind in your face. Cammie thought for a minute and decided that the best option would be artificial eyelashes. Cammie knew her mother had several pairs—not that she used them often.

"They are very uncomfortable," Cammie heard her mother complain to her father. "It's enough that I have to wear contact lenses, but artificial eyelashes on top of those? Too much, what do you think?"

Cammie's father had agreed, of course. But Cammie's mother didn't skate, so she didn't have to be afraid of cold wind in her face, and Cammie didn't wear contact lenses, so ... okay, how were you supposed to apply artificial eyelashes? Cammie read the instructions. No problem. She quickly attached the lashes to her upper eyelids. Perfect!

"Oh, my gosh. I look incredible!" Cammie squealed. She danced around the room, tried a few arabesques—really good ones, lifted her arms—just like Isabelle—and looked in the mirror again.

Wow, that was exactly what she wanted. It was amazing how makeup could change a person's appearance. Looking back at Cammie from her mother's mirror was a mature, confident skater with sparkling green eyes, radiant skin, and long, thick eyelashes. Cammie ran her fingers through her long brown hair and sprinted to her bedroom to put on her new sweater.

There was one problem, however. How was Cammie going to ride to the rink wearing all that makeup? For surely, her mother would notice how terrific Cammie looked and start asking questions. And of course, she would be really mad to find out that Cammie had used her makeup—especially her artificial eyelashes—without permission. Cammie had to think of something.

Cammie heard her mother come in from the store and met her in the foyer wearing a large pair of sunglasses.

"Why are you wearing sunglasses, Cammie?"

"The sun is too bright today, especially against the snow," Cammie said. She wasn't lying; there *was* a bright glare coming from the snow. Cammie wondered what she was going to do after practice because it would be too dark to wear sunglasses. Well, perhaps she could go to the restroom at the rink after everybody left and wash off her makeup.

Cammie's mother didn't ask any more questions. When they reached the rink, Cammie grabbed her skating bag, muttered a quick, "See you, Mom," and rushed to the door. The engine rumbled behind her, and the car was gone. Good. Her mother hadn't suspected anything.

The first part of the evening went exactly as Cammie had planned. The girls admired her makeup. Margie even said her eyes sparkled like emeralds. But Margie had always liked Cammie. She was kind; not like Susie, who merely grunted and looked away.

"You're just jealous," Cammie said.

Susie shrugged and didn't say another word. Who cared!

But nothing could be compared to Cammie's joy when Isabelle appeared in the locker room looking trim and gorgeous in her black leggings and yellow sweater.

"Hi, everybody. You look really great today, Cammie," Isabelle said.

Isabelle knew her name? She had actually noticed her! Cammie's lips spread into a broad smile, and her cheeks became pleasantly warm.

"We're not supposed to wear makeup for practices," Susie said icily.

Isabelle gave Susie a patronizing look. "I think a good skater should always look her best. Good job, Cammie!"

Cammie had never felt so excited. As all the girls stepped on the ice, Cammie tried to stay close to Isabelle. She followed Isabelle when the group went around the rink in backward and forward crossovers. It was easy, and Cammie was glad she could keep up with Isabelle, even though her new friend was older and her legs were longer.

When time came to execute spirals, Cammie tried to raise her leg as high as she could, to get deeper on the edge. Getting into an arabesque position had never been difficult for Cammie, so she didn't know what happened this time. She didn't even realize that something had gone wrong. One moment she was gliding along the rink enjoying herself, and in a split second, she lay prostrate on the ice, her right knee throbbing. Oops! She must have tripped over her toe pick and fallen. It had never happened before. Cammie got up awkwardly, her cheeks burning, angry tears welling in her eyes.

"Are you all right, Cammie?" Coach Louise asked.

"I'm fine, thank you," Cammie said getting to her feet.

"You should look in the direction you're going, not to the side," the coach said.

Yes, she was right. Cammie had been trying to follow Isabelle with her eyes, forgetting that leaning too far could be dangerous. It would never happen again. Cammie tried to concentrate on the lesson without looking in Isabelle's direction anymore. It must have worked because she didn't make any more mistakes.

Everything went well until the last minute of the lesson. The girls were swirling around the rink chasing one another when Cammie heard a thud and a squeal.

"What?" Startled, Cammie looked back.

Oh, no! Margie sat on the ice wincing. "I tripped over something," she whined, rubbing her thigh.

"Let me see." Coach Louise helped Margie to get up, made sure the girl was all right, then bent down, looking at something on the ice.

"Of course!" Coach Louise finally said, picking something up.

The girls gathered around, and Cammie skated up, squinting at something tiny in Coach Louise's hand.

"Who brought this to the rink?" the coach asked sternly.

"What is it?" Cammie asked, but at the same moment, she understood what it was, and her heart sank. Coach Louise was holding an artificial eyelash—the one Cammie had glued to her eyelid only a couple of hours before. *Oh no, how had it ended up on the ice?* Instinctively, Cammie grabbed her left eyelid. Sure enough, the artificial eyelash was gone. It must have unglued when Cammie had gotten sweaty skating fast. She examined her right eye. The right eyelash was still in place. For a split second, Cammie thought it was good news; but in another moment, she realized how wrong she was. Her only remaining eyelash was definitely a giveaway.

"I see," Coach Louise said. Her cold hazel eyes fixed on Cammie.

Cammie couldn't stand the coach's firm look; she hung her head.

"Cammie, what were you thinking?"

Cammie quivered. There was nothing to say. Surely she couldn't tell everybody that she had applied her mother's artificial eyelashes to look as gorgeous as Isabelle.

"Don't you understand that a foreign object on the ice can get a skater injured?" Coach Louise asked.

Cammie sighed. Of course she knew that. It wasn't her first time at the rink. The problem was that in trying to look glamorous, she had forgotten everything.

"Now I want you to throw this thing into the trash can and never, ever use it again," Coach Louse said.

Totally humiliated, Cammie accepted the crumpled eyelash and walked off the ice. In the locker room, she tore the remaining eyelash off her eyelid and threw both of them away. When Cammie glanced at herself in the mirror, she didn't like what she saw at all. The eye shadow had smudged a little, making her look as though she had bruises under her eyes. Cammie carefully washed off her makeup, making sure nothing was left. Her mother was about to pick her up, and none of the girls cared anyway. Except for Isabelle, of course. Oh, if only Cammie's false eyelash hadn't fallen off! Now Isabelle would probably never even look in her direction.

"Hey, that was funny!"

Cammie looked up, her face still wet. Isabelle stood by her side, grinning.

Cammie shook her head. "What a mess!" She reached for a paper towel.

"Relax. You look fine." Isabelle turned off the water. "By the way, when did you last have your skates sharpened?"

"What?" That wasn't a question Cammie had expected. "Why do you ask?"

"The reason you fell tonight…You know, I think it's because your blades are too dull."

"Well…" Cammie wrinkled her forehead, trying to remember. "I guess Mr. McKingley sharpened them about three months ago. Yeah, it was before I took that pre-preliminary moves-in-the-field test."

Isabelle clapped her hands. "Three months? Come on, girl, you can't let your blades go three months without sharpening!"

Cammie shrugged. "I never thought of that.

Okay, thanks. When Mom comes, I'll ask her to talk to Mr. McKingley. He's probably still at the rink."

Isabelle curved her bright lips. "Who on earth is Mr. McKingley? Are you a competitive skater or what? Don't you understand how important it is to get your skates sharpened by a professional?"

"What do you mean?"

"Listen." Isabelle lowered her voice so Susie, who had just walked in, wouldn't hear them. "The best skate sharpener lives in Skateland. And I'm going there right now. Do you want to come along?"

Cammie's head spun. "Now?"

"Yes. Now."

"Who's taking you there?"

Isabelle rolled her eyes. "We'll go alone. I have a car."

"You have ... your own car?"

"And why not? I'm sixteen."

"I can't believe it!" Never in her life had Cammie hung out with a girl who drove her own car. And surely she would never ever think of going to a skate sharpener without her parents. But the more Cammie thought of Isabelle's suggestion, the more excited she got. Going to Skateland with Isabelle would be fun. But would her mother let her go?

Cammie thought for a moment and decided

that she would only tell Mom that she wanted to go to a terrific skate sharpener with a friend. Surely, her mother would never even think that Cammie's friend would be a sixteen-year-old skater, who traveled to Skateland alone. Of course, Mom would assume that Isabelle's mother was coming too, and that was all Cammie needed.

"So, are you coming or not?" Isabelle asked, this time sounding a little impatient.

"Oh yes, sure. I'll tell my mom, okay?"

Isabelle took the car key out of her red skating bag. "I'll be waiting for you outside. Don't make it too long."

With trembling fingers, Cammie pulled on her boots and zipped up her parka. She ran out of the locker room. Yes, there was Mom walking in her direction.

Just like Cammie had expected, her mother didn't ask too many questions. It wasn't hard to convince her that Cammie needed the best skate sharpener in the area. She agreed to let Cammie go to Skateland with her friend (and her mother!), only asking Cammie not to stay there too long.

"It'll start getting dark soon, Cammie. I want you to be home before eight, all right?"

"Sure. Thanks, Mom." Cammie kissed her mother on the cheek and ran out of the building.

MELVIN REED

S itting next to her new friend in the passenger's seat, Cammie felt completely happy. She looked dreamily at the trees flying past them and the road stretching far ahead. If her friends from the rink could see her now, they would probably die with envy. The sun was slowly disappearing behind the pine trees, and the pale sky looked like a sheet of ice that had just been resurfaced.

"Ever been to Skateland before?" Isabelle asked without taking her eyes off the road.

"Sure. I competed there last year and—" Cammie stopped short. What she wanted to say was that a year ago, she had spent a long, hard day in Skateland with her friend Alex. The two of them had been turned down from the competition because they hadn't mastered the basics of skating. So they had gone to Skateland on their own; and that had been quite an experience. Skateland was a special place where people wore skates all the time. They skated to school, to work—everywhere. And of course, there were many indoor rinks and ponds in Skateland, so residents of that beautiful village had practically unlimited ice time. Cammie loved Skateland!

Unfortunately, dedicated skaters were not the only people Cammie and Alex had met on their trip. As it had turned out, there were evil witches in Skateland, whose only purpose in life was to destroy the careers of promising skaters.

On their way to the Sport Center, Cammie and Alex had run into three scary witches—the Witch of Injuries, the Witch of Pride, and the Witch of Fear. The evil women had almost made them give up skating forever. To break the witches' powerful curses, Cammie and Alex had been forced to complete a series of tedious assignments. They had been asked to do all the four edges, perform several sets of three turns, and demonstrate waltz eights—exactly what both Cammie and Alex hated the most. Boy, how hard had they practiced to finally be able to execute all the moves flawlessly. At the beginning, both Cammie and Alex had thought practicing the basics would be a complete waste of time. And yet, quite unexpectedly, they had both won their competitions.

"Cammie?"

"What?" Thinking about her previous experiences in Skateland, Cammie almost forgot about Isabelle.

"What else did you do in Skateland? You said, you competed and ... "

"Ah, I ... " Cammie didn't know what to say. The truth was that even though Cammie and Alex's adventures in Skateland had been real and exciting, they hadn't really shared them with anyone. First of all, both of them knew that few people believed in witches. So if Cammie or Alex started telling their friends that they had driven the Witch of Injuries to tears, humiliated the Witch of Pride, and intimidated the Witch of Fear, they could expect nothing but patronizing laughter in return. Actually, Cammie had tried to entertain her mom and dad with the exciting details of her wandering about Skateland. Both of them had laughed.

Dad had patted Cammie on her cheek and said, "Good job, sweetheart."

Mom had merely smiled and said nothing. Yet

when Cammie was already in bed, she heard Mom talking to Dad. "The girl's imagination is way too wild; what do you think?"

"She's an artistic type," Dad said.

Huh? How about that? The only person who had believed Cammie was Margie. Her blue eyes got really wide when she listened to Cammie's description of how they couldn't stop executing three turns for two hours.

"I would never be able to do that; I'd get tired!" Margie had whined.

"We were tired too, but we had to defeat the witch," Cammie had said.

"Cammie?" Isabelle said, this time sounding impatient.

"Yes?"

"Come on; talk to me! What else did you do in Skateland? Take tests?"

"Ah? No, I just…my friend Alex and I, we only…walked around Skateland, you know…just to see what it was like."

"Ah!" Isabelle sounded slightly disappointed. "That's nothing. I competed in Skateland four times, and I took five tests there. Now that's a place to skate and compete in."

"Yes, I enjoyed the competition too."

"Well, did you medal?"

"I came in first," Cammie said, unable to conceal her pride. She remembered the cold feeling of the medal around her neck, the flashes of photographers, her mom and dad smiling at her. That had been really the best time of her life.

"Did you win your competition too?" Cammie asked Isabelle.

For some reason, Isabelle didn't answer the question. "And the sharpening," she said, as though Cammie hadn't asked her about the competition. "I once tried to get my skates sharpened in a different place, and the blades turned out horrible. I could barely skate. Hey, do you care for hard candy?"

Cammie smiled politely. "Sure."

From the glove compartment, Isabelle took out a turquoise candy shaped like an icicle. "It's from Skateland."

Cammie nodded as she licked her candy. It had a wonderful fragrance of mango and tangerine. "Yes, I saw those in Skateland."

The car took a sharp right; the tall trees stepped to the side, and a magnificent iron gate appeared in front of them. The entrance to Skateland was decorated with intricate patterns that looked like branches of trees and flowers, but as the car came closer, Cammie saw that those were images of skaters in different positions.

"Okay, let me park first," Isabelle said.

"Oh! Where's the parking lot?"

Isabelle gave Cammie a suspicious look. "You were here, and you don't remember where your parents parked?"

"I came here by bus."

"So? A lot of skating clubs bring their skaters here." Isabelle pointed to two school buses parked at the far end of the parking lot.

Cammie shrugged. She didn't know what to say.

As the two of them walked through the gate, Cammie couldn't contain her excitement at the figurine of a graceful skater in the attitude position. The smiling girl held a snowflake with sparkling multicolored buttons in her right hand and a plaque saying *Instructions* in the left. Cammie squinted and read:

All visitors are required to wear skates. An arrow indicated the location of locker rooms.

Underneath there was a keyboard with further instructions:

If you are here for the competition, press one.
If you consider joining a skating program, press two.
If you are interested in private lessons, press three.
If you are a skating customer, press four.
If you want your skates sharpened, press five.

"How cool!" Cammie said excitedly.

Isabelle was obviously growing more and more suspicious. She pressed five and gave Cammie a meaningful look. "So you don't remember the instruction board either, huh?"

Cammie clasped her hands. "It's just...I was here for a competition and so nervous that I...I didn't notice anything."

"Ah!" Isabelle appeared to be deep in thought. "I guess that's possible. I heard of situations like that. But girl, you should be more observant."

Cammie gave out a forced giggle and followed Isabelle to the locker room. She didn't want to lie to her new friend, but telling the truth might make it even worse. Would Isabelle ever believe that Cammie and Alex hadn't entered Skateland through the main gate but through a secret passage, hiding in the back of a Zamboni machine?

Alex had overheard their Zamboni driver, Mr. Walrus, say that all ice rinks in the world were magically connected. It meant that you could get to any rink if you rode a Zamboni machine. So Cammie and Alex had decided to try, and that was how they had traveled to Skateland. It was not a pleasant experience; it was actually quite dangerous because the secret road to Skateland weaved between deep ravines. One wrong move and…

So even though it had taken Cammie and Alex very little time to get to Skateland, they had decided that they would never reveal the whereabouts of the secret passage to anyone. After all, it wasn't their secret; it was Mr. Walrus's.

Cammie and Isabelle changed into their skates and glided along the narrow path in the direction of Main Square. Cammie realized with relief that the area was familiar to her. She recognized the circular outdoor rink and dozens of small shops around the square. Only the last time Cammie was here, the square was almost empty, so Alex and she practiced their programs. This time there was a tots' competition at the outdoor rink. Cammie and Isabelle stopped to watch. The tiny skaters were supposed to swizzle as fast as they could from one dollhouse to another. The winners got cookies shaped like medals.

"Care for something sweet?" Isabelle asked.

"Oh, yes!" Cammie remembered the delicious pastries shaped like skating boots she had shared with Alex and smiled excitedly.

Cammie and Isabelle entered the Sweet Blades store and took a seat at a small round table next to a window facing Main Square. The tots had already finished their competition and were now skating happily around the rink. The girls ordered Skate Tea that was scalding hot and had a delicious sweet-and-sour flavor.

"It has a lot of vitamin C, and this is what skaters need," Isabelle said.

They sipped their tea, biting off a scrumptious snowflake pie—crisp crust topped with whipped cream.

"How about some shopping before we get to the sharpener?" Isabelle said. "We still have plenty of time."

Cammie agreed gladly. Of course, she didn't have much money; the ten-dollar bill that sat in her wallet was just enough to get her skates sharpened. But even looking at the picturesque skating displays would be fun.

They went to Smiling Skater, the store that, as the owner claimed, featured the best collection of blades, boots, and skating accessories. Cammie walked around the spacious room touching the boots, running her fingers against the sharp blades, admiring the rhinestones on multicolored skating dresses. Perhaps one day, when she was rich, she would buy this ... and that ... and perhaps—

"Here you go!"

Cammie turned around. Isabelle stood next to her with two expensive-looking sweatshirts—red and blue—in her hand.

"This is for me," Isabelle said, showing Cammie a gorgeous red sweatshirt with *Skateland* emblazoned with gold in the front.

"I like gold," Isabelle said. "Even my blades are gold, see?"

Cammie shook her head in amazement. Gold blades, how much could they cost?

"And this is for you." Isabelle handed Cammie the blue sweatshirt. It felt soft and warm, and a silver, sparkling logo *Skateland* glittered in the front.

"I think silver will go well with your eyes," Isabelle said.

Cammie stared at Isabelle. "What?"

"It's yours, silly. Take it!" Isabelle squeezed the sweatshirt into Cammie's hand.

"But I...but I have no money to pay for it," Cammie stammered.

"Oh, forget the money. It's my gift to you."

"But...but I can't. It's so expensive."

Isabelle laughed. "My dad makes more money than he can spend. Believe me. He never refuses to get me whatever I ask him. So if I want to get a gift for my best friend, it's my business."

Cammie's ears turned hot. Her best friend? Cammie was Isabelle's best friend? She couldn't believe it. Still she wanted to ask one more time. "Are you sure you father won't mind? This sweatshirt is so expensive."

"I told you. My dad is pretty loaded. He's a plastic surgeon, you know. He makes people's faces beautiful."

Cammie nodded. "Ah, is that the reason you're so good-looking? Did your father work on your face?"

The minute the words came out of her mouth she knew she had said a stupid thing. Boy, what was she thinking? Plastic surgeons were for old people!

Luckily, Isabelle wasn't offended. She only laughed, showing Cammie her pearly teeth. "Of course, Dad never worked on my face. I don't need it yet. He did Mom's, though. My mom was a top fashion model before they got married. But then she started getting old. So Dad fixed her face, and now she looks youthful again."

"Ah!" Cammie didn't know what to say.

"Anyway, don't worry. Take the sweatshirt."

With trembling fingers, Cammie accepted the gift. Wow, what a gorgeous sweatshirt!

"May I?" She gave Isabelle a questioning look.

After Isabelle nodded with a grin, Cammie pulled on the sweatshirt. It fit perfectly. She looked at herself in the big floor-to-ceiling mirror. She looked terrific, and the expensive sweatshirt made her look really glamorous, just like Isabelle.

Isabelle glanced at the tiny gold wristwatch. "We'd better go. We don't want to be late. Mel is funny about punctuality."

"Who's Mel?" Cammie asked as they glided past small houses in the direction of a park.

"Melvin Reed, the sharpener. You'll see him. He's not my favorite person, I can tell you." Isabelle made a funny face.

Cammie laughed.

The entrance to the Icy Park was brightly lit. The familiar statuette featuring a skater in the attitude position welcomed the girls as they were ready to plunge into the darkness of the alleys. This time, however, the statuette held what looked like an enormous flower with multicolored petals. *Rainbow Rinks* said the sign on top of the flower. When Cammie came closer, she saw that each of the petals represented a rink. An arrow on each of the petals gave skaters directions to that particular rink with a short explanation of its advantages. Cammie found the directions quite funny because the instructions were rhymed.

Follow this link to the pink rink, declared the pink petal. Another petal suggested, *Choose the rink that's big and yellow, where the ice is soft and mellow.* The petal closest to Cammie read, *Not quite sure what to do? I'm the best: my ice is blue.*

"Come on," Isabelle said before Cammie had a chance to study the rest of the petals.

"It's funny," Cammie said as she tried to catch up with her friend. "Are there really multicolored rinks in Skateland?"

"Sure. They sometimes call Skateland *Skating Rainbow* or *Rainbow Rinks.* How come you never heard that?"

Cammie shook her head. Last time she was in

Skateland with Alex, they were so busy; there simply wasn't enough time for a guided tour.

They skated along the winding paths of the park. There were no people around, and the whole place was almost strangely quiet. An owl hooted nearby making Cammie quiver.

"Are you sure this place is all right?" she whispered.

"What do you mean?" Isabelle didn't sound frightened at all.

"Well...it's dark, and we're alone." Actually, Cammie knew what gave her the uncomfortable feeling. It was in this particular park one year ago that Cammie and Alex had met the Witch of Injuries. And even though they had defeated her, who knew what scary creatures might be hiding behind the tall, snow-covered trees?

Isabelle only waved. "Don't worry. Skateland is the safest place on earth."

The path went deeper and deeper into the park. The ice under their feet was hard—perfect for hockey players. Cammie preferred softer, kinder ice that allowed her to feel the edges more.

"How far is the sharpener?" Cammie whispered. She didn't know why she didn't feel like speaking out loud; perhaps she didn't want to wake up the witches. But that was silly. There couldn't be any danger; Cammie and Alex had defeated all the evil creatures in Skateland.

"This way, I think." Isabelle stopped for a second, staring intensely at something in front of her. "Yes, there it is."

Cammie followed Isabelle off the icy path into soft, powdery snow. Her feet sank deep, almost up to her knees. The snow felt like a cold, wet blanket. Cammie shivered. "Is there any ice here?"

"I don't think so. Don't worry; we're here."

The sharpening shop was a small log cabin that hid behind thick trees. Cammie and Isabelle put on their skate guards and clomped up the slippery steps to the porch. They rang the doorbell shaped like a snowflake. A pleasant clanging sound pierced the quietness of the night, but nothing happened. No one came out to greet the girls; the house looked empty.

"What's going on?" Isabelle glanced at her watch nervously. "I thought we had an appointment. Oh, never mind. Mel must still be skating. We'll find him at the Purple Rink. That's where he hangs out."

"Purple Rink?"

"Yeah, sure. You'll see in a minute. This way."

Cammie waddled through the snow in the direction Isabelle had indicated. The trees stood dark on both sides; heavy snow pulled the limbs down almost to the ground. As they approached something that looked like a wide-open area, the moon shot out from behind the clouds, painting everything silvery bright. Cammie saw that they were facing a big pond, almost round in shape, and the ice was the deepest purple she had ever seen.

"Wow!" Cammie exclaimed, unable to contain her excitement. "Have you ever seen a purple rink before?"

Isabelle shrugged. "It's Skateland. Anyway, this is Mr. Reed's rink. And…oh, there he is. Oh, no! Oh, my…"

Cammie looked at the purple glittery surface. What she saw shocked her so much that she had to gasp for air. Right in the middle of the rink, a tall skinny man set himself for a salchow jump. He went into a quick three turn, got on the backward inside edge, and flew into the air higher, higher, and higher. Cammie couldn't believe the height he reached. But that wasn't everything. Having put a six-foot distance between the ice and himself, the man began to spin in the air, faster than anybody Cammie had ever seen. Perplexed, Cammie started counting the revolutions: one, two, three, four…(four!), and…oh, no, five! The man had just completed a quintuple salchow!

"Did you see what I saw?" A very shocked Isabelle grabbed Cammie by the hand.

"I…I don't know. I think he did a…a quad. Wow, what a skater!"

"A quad?" Isabelle grip loosened up. "Uh, is that what it was? Because I thought—"

"There he is about to do it again!"

The man sped around the ice, picking up speed on backward crossovers, turned around, swung his leg, and…

"One, two, three, four, five," Cammie mumbled. This time it wasn't a mistake. She had seen it clearly.

"Five, five!" Isabelle breathed out. "It's not a quad; it's a quintuple."

"Yes, it is."

"But it means…It means—"

"Nobody in the world does those," Cammie said slowly. "Just him. Is he a world champ or something?"

Isabelle shook her head. "Perhaps. I don't know. Maybe years ago. He's old now."

"Is he?"

The moon was shining directly into the man's

face now. Cammie saw a gray-haired head and deep wrinkles on the man's face. "He must have competed years ago."

"Yeah, and he can still do quintuple jumps?"

"It looks like he can."

Down on the ice, the man had just completed a flawless quintuple toe loop.

Isabelle shook her head. "Look, you don't understand. If there's a man here, in Skateland, who can do quintuple jumps, why doesn't everybody know about it? Why aren't all the newspapers writing about him? Because nobody has ever landed a quintuple jump. Ever."

Cammie nodded. "Yes, and why doesn't he go to the Olympics if he can do quintuple jumps? He would beat everybody."

That was something none of them could understand. In complete silence, they watched the older man as he jumped and jumped on the purple surface. His incredible performance made Cammie jealous.

She looked down at the ice that stretched only a foot away from her. "Do you want to try?"

"My jumps?" Isabelle waved her hand. "I'd be embarrassed."

"The ice looks good, though. I want to try it."

"I would be careful if I were you. This kind of

ice will reveal your strengths, but it won't be merciful to your weaknesses," a male voice with a slight English accent said from the right.

Cammie turned around. The quintuple jumper towered in front of her. Cammie realized that he was even taller than she had first thought.

"Welcome to the Purple Rink, though I wouldn't recommend practicing here. My name is Mel Reed." The man stretched his gloved hand that Cammie shook tentatively. "And your name would be?"

"Cammie Wester, sir."

"It's a pleasure to meet you, Cammie. Nice to see you again, Isabelle."

Cammie noticed that for some reason, Mel Reed didn't look particularly happy to see Isabelle again. Isabelle must have discerned it too, because her eyes narrowed.

"I thought we had a six o'clock appointment with you," she said coldly.

"Oh!" Mel slapped his forehead. "I beg your pardon. Of course, we do. You're not trying to say I'm late, are you?"

Isabelle looked to the side, her whole posture showing that that was exactly what she meant.

"Alas! It's three minutes after," Mel said as he

looked at his wristwatch. "All right, ladies, if we proceed into my shop now. After you, please."

Mel followed the girls up the deep snow in the direction of the house.

At that point, Isabelle, apparently tired of showing her disapproval of Mel's being slightly late, spoke up. "Mr. Reed, I think I saw you do quintuple jumps."

"Oh, yes," Mel said casually.

Isabelle stopped so abruptly that Cammie almost walked into her. "Ouch!"

"You did?" Isabelle turned around, blocking Mel's way. "But … but … "

"But what?"

Now that Mel was so close Cammie could see that his eyes were pale blue—like ice—and his nose was long and straight.

"No one in the world can do quintuple jumps," Isabelle said with a note of disapproval.

"Indeed," Mel said with a sparkle in his eyes.

"Can you teach me?" Isabelle said impatiently. "My father will pay you; don't worry."

Mel grinned and walked up the slippery steps to the porch. He pressed the button, which caused the bright sign *Melvin Reed's Skate Sharpening Shop* to light up, and unlocked the heavy door. "Come on in, ladies."

Mesmerized, Cammie followed Mel into the shop. The man turned on the light, and Cammie couldn't contain a gasp of excitement.

Mel Reed's sharpening shop was the most unusual place Cammie had ever seen. It wasn't exactly a shop; it was more like a skating museum. Facing the front door was a shelf with figurines of skaters of different times wearing most exotic outfits: long skirts and hats, tuxedos and cylindrical hats, knee-length skating boots and blades without toe picks, rounded at the top. The skaters' faces were different too; apparently Mel Reed had gathered dolls from different countries of the world. There were white skaters and black skaters, men, women, and children that looked Chinese or Japanese. Another shelf had a display of skates that looked as though they belonged in the nineteenth or even eighteenth century. The blades were dull, and the boots had snowmen, flowers, and snowflakes engraved on their scratched surface.

"Do you like them?" Mel must have noticed Cammie's interest.

"They're fantastic!" she said quietly, unable to take her eyes off the exotic skaters.

"I'll show you more. Come on." Mel led Cammie into a cozy room, where the walls were lined with bookshelves filled with skating books. Skating dresses of different kinds and styles hung from the ceiling. A Christmas tree decorated with blades and snowflakes shimmered in the corner, and the whole area in the middle was occupied by a toy rink. All you needed to do was press the button to set the whole scene in motion.

"I love it!" Cammie laughed as she watched the little dolls representing young kids chase one another around the rink.

"So is it all right, Mr. Reed?" Isabelle asked from behind.

"Isabelle, look!" Cammie pointed to the display.

"It's fine." Isabelle dismissed her with only a brief glance at the toy rink. "Mel, I really, really need to learn how to jump right. I've always been struggling with jumps."

"Back to the basics, back to the basics," Mel sang as he handed Cammie a huge picture book with images of skating princesses on the cover.

"I know about this basic stuff," Isabelle said angrily. "But it's the jumps I need. I'll work hard; don't you worry, Mr. Reed."

Mel winked at Cammie. "Do I look worried to you?"

Cammie didn't want Isabelle to see her grin, so she quickly looked down.

"Mr. Reed, ple-e-ase! Dad will pay anything to the best coach."

Mel shrugged his bony shoulders. "Who told you I was a coach? I've never been one. I'm merely a skate sharpener."

Isabelle stomped her foot. "Don't lie to me! I saw you!"

Mel tilted his head. "And what did you see, Isabelle?"

"You did quintuple jumps. We both saw you. She did too." Isabelle jerked her chin in Cammie's direction, which made Cammie blush. She didn't want Mel Reed to get upset. She liked the man, and Isabelle was rude to him. That wasn't nice. Now Cammie didn't want to disappoint her new friend, but at the same time, being impolite to an older man wasn't a good choice either.

"Did you?" Mel asked Cammie. He looked as though he was enjoying himself, although the whole situation was making Cammie more and more uncomfortable.

"Yes, I did," Cammie said, feeling her cheeks get unpleasantly warm.

"All right, all right." Mel sat down on a soft couch in front of the doll rink. "I think you exposed me. Now here is the thing. The jumps you saw were nothing I did."

"Nothing you did?" Isabelle whispered. "But we saw you—"

"Well, of course, you saw me spin five times in the air before I landed. But I didn't do the jumps; those were the boots."

"W-what?" Both Cammie and Isabelle shouted almost in unison.

"The boots I'm wearing. See?" Mel stretched his long legs, and Cammie saw that the man's skating boots were most unusual: metal instead of leather, very clean and shiny.

"I made them myself; I actually invented them. See, when I was a young skater and still competing…" Mel cast a quick glance at Isabelle, who still stood in the corner looking disappointed. "I wasn't particularly good at triples. Why, I don't know. Maybe, it was my height; most male skaters barely reach six feet, and I'm six three. But I wanted to be the best. I worked so hard, but I never got my triple jumps straight."

Isabelle shifted her feet and coughed. Cammie looked at her, but the older girl said nothing, looking sullen.

"I finally retired. I never won a major competition. But I liked skating so much that I decided to become a skate sharpener. I was still close to my favorite sport. And then...eventually, I had ideas about improving skates. And I came up with these." Mel raised his legs and looked at his boots with admiration. "They have a built-in motor, and it can propel you into the air as though you were an airplane. It helps you to spin too. And of course, you can control your speed, so you won't over-rotate."

Isabelle cleared her throat. "But we saw you do quintuple jumps, not triples."

"Ah!" Mel waved his hand dismissively. "Old man's fantasy. See, for the boots it doesn't matter how many revolutions you do. You can program them for three, or four, or five—whatever. Maybe, even ten revolutions are possible, who knows? I haven't tried more than five, though. It's fun."

"How much do you want for them?" Isabelle said abruptly.

Mel winced. "I beg your pardon?"

"I want to buy these boots."

Mel leaned back and laughed. "Oops, I forgot to tell you the most important thing."

Isabelle frowned. "What do you mean?"

"You can't compete in these boots."

Isabelle looked angry. "Why not?"

Mel spread his arms. "See, it wouldn't be right to use self-spinning boots in competitions. Not fair to other skaters, of course. So when I invented them, I went to the Skateland president and told her about my ideas. Actually, I never meant them for competitions. I rather saw these boots as sort of a harness, a device that would help a skater to get a feel of her jump, to learn to control her body in the air. The president liked my enthusiasm, but she agreed with me that allowing skaters to compete in self-spinning boots would be unethical. Now you can use them for practices, but you need your coach's permission. Unfortunately, most coaches think that self-spinning boots don't do a lot of good for the skater. You need to become comfortable in the air when you jump naturally. That's what counts."

Mel paused and ran his long fingers through his perfectly trimmed gray hair. Cammie glanced at Isabelle. The older girl sulked in the corner.

Mel stood up. "So don't worry about these boots, young ladies. They are nothing but an old man's idea of fun. Come on; let's take care of your skates."

Mel made Cammie take off her skates. He measured her feet, studied her boots and blades, and ran his fingers over the screws that secured the blades to the boots.

"I would remount the left blade a little," Mel finally said. "It will help you with your edges."

Cammie nodded. Good edges were important; she already knew that.

As Mel worked on Cammie's skates, Isabelle walked around the shop casting absent-minded looks at various displays. She looked disappointed.

Poor thing, Cammie thought. *She probably wanted those boots really badly. Why, though? Who cares if self-spinning boots carry you up in the air? The only thing that counts is what you can do on the ice.*

"Hey, look at these!" Isabelle called from a counter in the other room, the one Cammie hadn't seen yet.

In her stockinged feet, Cammie approached the counter where her friend stood looking excitedly at something displayed under thick glass.

"See them?" Isabelle pointed to three sparkling pins—bronze, silver, and gold—each showing a skater in a perfect scratch spin. In the middle of the skater's waist sat a glittering stone that looked like a diamond.

"They're amazing," Cammie said sincerely. There was really something charming, almost magical, about the pins—something that really made you wish you could have them. But they were probably expensive; Cammie could never afford one.

"Hey, Mel! I like those pins." Isabelle was already beside Mel.

The man said nothing. He lifted Cammie's skate, brought it closer to the light, and examined it critically. "It looks fine now. Here."

"Thank you very much!" Cammie accepted her skate. As she was handing Mel the money, Isabelle spoke up again.

"Do you know what I mean? The ones with spinning skaters."

"Ah, those pins." Mel smiled weakly and shook his head. "Sorry, but it's not jewelry. Those pins have magic powers. When you wear them, they give you strength and confidence in your abilities. A skater who puts on a pin before he skates his program is sure to do his best."

"Ah! This is exactly what I need." Isabelle took her wallet out of her small leather pocketbook.

"How much do you want for a pin? I think I want the gold one."

"I can't sell them. See, I haven't bought or made any of those pins. I won them in competitions when I came in first, second, and third. That's why they can't be sold." Mel was looking at Isabelle's skates now.

"Oh, come on!"

"I'm sorry."

"But…but…" Isabelle spread her arms in a gesture that showed how absolutely stunned she was at Mel's unfair treatment. "Look, first I ask for your self-spinning boots, and you tell me they're illegal; now I want a pin, and you don't want to sell me one. Can you give me a break? I've got to buy something."

"I'm sorry to disappoint you." Mel carried Isabelle's skates into his shop. "You can't buy another person's success, achievement, or glory. It is something you have to earn for yourself."

Isabelle smirked. "This is ridiculous. Everything has a price."

Mel shook his head. "There are things you work for, not buy."

"I'm out of here!" Isabelle snatched her skates out of Mel's hands. "How much do I owe you?"

As Isabelle paid for the sharpening, Cammie wondered what had made her friend so upset. Surely Mr. Reed was right. A skater's job was to skate her best. If you won a medal, it counted. But you couldn't buy a medal; it would be like ... cheating.

"Stupid guy," Isabelle said on the way home. "It doesn't matter what you want, all you hear is *no*. What kind of business is that?"

"But why do you want that pin so badly?" Cammie asked carefully.

Isabelle sneered. "Didn't you hear what he said? A skater who wears a magic pin skates her best."

"Ah!" Cammie thought about it. Yes, perhaps, Isabelle was right, and it would be great to have something that would bring out the best in her skating. She could probably use one of those pins too. But if Mr. Reed didn't want to sell them, there was nothing Cammie and Isabelle could do. And besides ...

"You're a very beautiful skater, Isabelle, and you don't need a magic pin to look great," Cammie said sincerely.

"Yeah, right," Isabelle snarled.

Cammie's new friend sulked almost the whole way back, and it was only when they reached Cammie's house that Isabelle finally lightened up.

"I'll see you at the rink," Isabelle said, and the blue Porsche disappeared into the night.

Cammie looked at her watch. It was seven fifty-six. Gosh. She only had four minutes to get home. She ran up the steps and pressed the doorbell hard.

The door swung open. "Well, you made it," Mom said. She kissed Cammie on the cheek. "So did you have fun in Skateland?"

"Oh, wow!" Cammie smiled brightly. "Skateland is the best place in the world."

IMPORTANT DECISION

"**H**ow come you always look the best, Isabelle?" With a sigh, Cammie looked at her own reflection in the mirror. Her new freestyle dress was nice—light blue with rhinestones in the front. In fact, Coach Louise had said it fit her program set to Beethoven's "Moonlight Sonata" perfectly. Well, at that point, Cammie had thought so too. But now, looking at Isabelle's tall, trim figure in a simple black dress with nothing but a red rose in the front, she realized how plain she really looked.

"This costume looks like a cocktail dress, and

those are the most stylish," Isabelle said. She came up to the mirror and gave herself another look. She ran her index finger along her eyebrows and readjusted her lipstick that was now bright red. The lipstick was probably supposed to match the rose.

Looking satisfied, Isabelle glanced at Cammie. "You look fine; don't worry!"

Cammie wasn't so sure. "Don't you think I need brighter lipstick, like yours?"

"No. You're wearing pale blue, so light pink is just right."

"Yes, but the eyelashes…" Cammie was really disappointed that her mother wouldn't hear of false eyelashes.

"Are you out of your mind? You're eleven!" Mom had said.

As though an eleven-year-old didn't need to look her best at a competition.

"It's time to go, Cammie." Coach Louise was in the locker room looking Cammie in the eyes. "Ready?"

Cammie pulled her dress down a little and looked in the mirror again. "Yes, I think so."

"You'll do fine. Remember, don't rush your jumps. Hold the edges long enough. And don't think about the competition. Skate from your heart."

Cammie gave her coach the last smile and stepped onto the ice. She skated to the middle, her eyes scanning the stands for her family and friends. Yes, there were Mom and Dad and some girls from her class.

"Go, Cammie!"

She turned around at the sound, and her heart leaped joyfully in her chest as she saw Alex cheering from the front row. They were still good friends; although at the rink, Alex mostly hung out with boys his age. But he hadn't forgotten that Cammie was competing in this preliminary freestyle event, and he had come to support her. Cammie had already seen him skate and win a gold medal. Well, no surprises there. Alex had never skated poorly in a competition. But neither had Cammie. She had already accumulated a nice collection of medals and trophies that were proudly displayed in her bedroom at home. The pressure of competitions never affected Cammie's performance. Yes, she was always a little nervous, but it only helped her to skate better.

Three minutes later, Cammie put the guards over her blades with trembling hands and disappeared in the locker room to hide from people's sympathetic eyes and their oh-it's-all-right-it-can-happen-to-anyone-just-give-it-some-time-you'll-do-better-at-the-next-competition remarks. Well, perhaps, they were trying to encourage her, but that was not what she needed.

All she wanted to do was to get under the covers in her room and cry. Just cry her heart out. She had never, ever skated so badly in her life.

It was as though someone had stolen her body and pushed another girl—ugly and clumsy—to the middle of the rink to skate Cammie's program. Yes, sure, it couldn't have been Cammie because Cammie Wester would never have fallen on an axel; she wouldn't have missed her double salchow and two-footed her double toe loop. Even the scratch spin—Cammie's favorite move—wasn't centered. Cammie couldn't believe it. What had just happened was impossible. Ridiculous. Cammie didn't really want to cry—being a sore loser was even worse than being merely a loser—but tears rolled down her cheeks, and there was nothing she could do.

"Cammie, what happened out there?" Coach Louise came up and sat down next to her. She took Cammie's trembling hand in her soft, warm one.

Cammie bit her lip. "I don't know."

Coach Louise sighed. "At some point you looked

as though you lost your concentration. Is that what happened?"

Cammie rubbed her forehead. She wished she knew. All she remembered was trying to look her best, not to make any mistakes and then … then she looked at the audience and saw Isabelle smiling at her, and she smiled back and then … And then she glided forward on her outside edge ready for her axel, and that was it. The beginning of the end.

"Where were your thoughts when you were skating your program?" Coach Louise asked.

What? Her thoughts? Well, she thought how great it would be to win another gold medal—that was it. Of course, she was also trying to impress Isabelle. It was important for Cammie. During the past three months, the two of them had become best friends. It was amazing: Isabelle Alvarez, the queen of their rink, and little Cammie Wester. Even Cammie's mother was surprised at Isabelle's choice.

"What I don't understand is why a sixteen-year-old would want you for a friend." Mom had once asked.

Why? Honestly, Cammie had never thought about it. She shrugged and laughed happily. "Because I'm the best skater at the rink, I guess. Who else would she be friends with?"

"Okay, but aren't there older girls at your rink, someone closer to Isabelle's age?" Mom asked.

Cammie furrowed her eyebrow. "Older girls? Well, yes, of course there are some. But Isabelle doesn't like being around them."

"Why not?" Mom still wanted to know everything. Why, though? If Isabelle liked Cammie, that was all that mattered.

"Well, maybe it's because Isabelle doesn't compete at their levels," Cammie said. "She's only in pre-preliminary, and other girls her age are in juvenile and even junior."

"Well, maybe, but you are so much younger than her! What do the two of you have in common?"

Cammie straightened up and curved her lips in a patronizing smile, just like she had seen Isabelle do. "The two of us are future champions, okay? The rest of the girls don't even come close. So naturally we hang out together."

Mom shook her head, and later in the evening, Cammie heard her talk to Dad.

"You know what? I don't think Isabelle is a good friend for Cammie."

"What's wrong with Isabelle?"

"Too princessy, if you know what I mean. She barely talks to anyone; she looks down on other people. In other words, she behaves as though she were an Olympic champion already. And I notice Cammie is trying to imitate her."

Dad began to laugh. "She does?"

"Did you see Cammie batting her lashes all the time? And rolling her eyes? And she doesn't talk to other girls anymore; Isabelle is her only friend."

Dad laughed again. "I wouldn't be worried. Our little girl is growing; that's it."

"I don't know..." Mom didn't sound convinced; though she never talked about Isabelle again.

"Cammie, are you with me?" Coach Louise squeezed her arm gently.

Cammie looked up, startled. She had been thinking about Isabelle, and she completely forgot where she was.

"You need to take it one step at a time," Coach Louise said. "It's important to focus on every single move, every individual jump."

Cammie looked down.

"Okay, you need rest." Coach Louise stood up. "Don't worry; anybody can have a bad competition. You'll do better next time."

She left Cammie alone in the empty locker room. Cammie sighed and stood up. There was no point in sitting there thinking about something she couldn't change. By the way, why hadn't Isabelle come to comfort her?

Cammie looked at the clock on the wall. 5:03. Oh, no! How could she forget?

Cammie quickly changed into her street boots and ran out of the locker room. Isabelle was going to skate in her pre-preliminary free skate in five minutes.

"There you are! Are you okay, Cammie?" Alex cut her off as she ran past the rink where Isabelle's group was already warming up.

"Umm, not quite, but I'll be fine." She didn't want Alex to see her upset.

"Don't worry; just practice your jumps more. It happened to me once."

Cammie frowned at him. "I don't think so. I would remember."

"It was before you knew me."

"Ah! Okay, I'm in sort of a hurry now. I want to watch Isabelle skate."

"Isabelle?" Alex looked at the trim figure in black gliding in a graceful catch foot spiral. "Is she any good?"

"She's terrific!" Cammie said passionately, surprised that Alex hadn't noticed the gorgeous girl at the very beginning.

"Okay, I think I'll watch her too, then," Alex said and joined Cammie as she sat in the third row right across from the judges' panel.

The warm-up was over, but Isabelle remained on the ice. She was the first to skate. Cammie waited, her hands clasped on her lap.

At the beginning, Isabelle looked as though she was going to ace her program. Her crossovers were good; her spins were centered; her spirals were high. The only difficulty she apparently had was her jumps. Even though she only did singles, her jumps were small and tentative, and twice she landed on both feet.

"She isn't that good." Alex sounded disappointed.

Cammie didn't know what to say.

The applause was polite but not overly enthusiastic. When Cammie approached a glum Isabelle, the older girl walked away from her. Cammie didn't follow Isabelle. She understood what her friend was going through.

When the results were posted, Cammie found out that she had placed fifth out of eight. An abysmal result considering that she had never returned from a competition without a medal. Even Margie—the fat, clumsy Margie—had gotten a bronze medal, though she had skated in pre-preliminary. Alex had gotten the gold in his category, which didn't surprise Cammie. Isabelle, however, had come in dead last in her group. Cammie didn't see any more of Isabelle after the competition, nor did she want to.

Cammie's parents took her out to Olive Garden—Cammie's favorite restaurant—to celebrate. When Cammie heard of it, she couldn't contain a sad smile. "Celebrate?"

"Well…" Dad looked a little sheepish. "It wasn't your best skate, but you're still a wonderful performer, and we're proud of you."

Cammie wasn't in any mood to go out, but she had to comply. During the dinner, she was quiet and withdrawn, pushing her pasta around the plate. She wasn't used to losing. She had always been the best.

"You need to eat, honey," Mom said.

Cammie frowned. "I'm not hungry."

"It's not the end of the world, you know," Mom said. "You need to learn from your mistakes and move on."

Learn from her mistakes? Cammie tried to think. Well, on her double toe loop, if she had reached further when she was about to pick with her toe pick, her body would have been straight and—

"Cammie?"

"What?" She looked up.

Her father was smiling at her. "You're still the best skater in the world."

Oh, no! What was Dad talking about? Did he think Cammie was still a little girl who couldn't tell a good performance from a bad one? How silly! Cammie was so deep in thought that she didn't even notice that she had actually said what she had thought out loud.

"That's not a nice thing to say to your father," Mom said, looking unhappy. "If you don't want to talk about what happened, it's all right. All we want you to understand is that fifth place isn't the end of the world. "

Fifth place! After she had been first, second or, at least, third!

Cammie made a face and pushed her plate away.

"We want the check, please," Mom said angrily to the waitress.

They left the restaurant in silence. Mom didn't even look at Cammie, though Dad pulled her ear slightly as he got behind the steering wheel. Cammie tried to smile at him, but her lips wouldn't spread. Cammie wasn't sure her grimace looked too much like a smile, and apparently Dad thought the same because they reached their home without saying another word.

Cammie came to the rink the next day feeling weak and sluggish. She didn't feel much like practicing, although when she walked through the door and saw the familiar sheet of ice in front of her, she told herself that she would do her best. So what if she had had a poor performance? She would practice, and she would improve, and she would still show everybody what Cammie Wester could do.

As Cammie walked past Coach Louise's office, she saw that the door was open. It wasn't surprising; Coach Louise always came to the rink before everybody else. Cammie had already passed the office when she heard a familiar voice. Isabelle? Cammie stopped, surprised. Her friend spoke loudly and impatiently, sounding very upset.

"I've made my decision. I'm going to work with another coach."

What? Cammie stopped in her tracks.

"Oh," Coach Louise said. That was it. Whether she was shocked or upset, Cammie didn't know. Coach Louise's *oh* could mean anything.

"I need a change," Isabelle said.

This time, Coach Louise didn't say a word. The pause was long. Isabelle must have waited long enough for an answer, because eventually she went on talking.

"And of course, the facilities are much better there. I'll have more ice time. And I know I'll finally be able to land my axel."

Yes, that was it. Cammie knew that Isabelle had been working on her axel jump for a year—first at her old rink in California, then, for the last three months at Cammie's rink. She still couldn't land it, although everybody, including Coach Louise, had been trying to convince Isabelle that it was only a matter of time. The axel was a difficult jump.

"There they can help me with it," Isabelle said.

Why wouldn't Coach Louise say something? Cammie felt sharp pain in her left side. That was probably what her grandmother called *heartache*. How come Cammie had never known before that she also had a heart, and it could hurt when she heard really bad news? Isabelle was leaving their rink. Moving to another place. But what about her, Cammie? What would happen to their friendship?

Tears pricked Cammie's eyes when she realized that there would be no more fun, no more gliding around the rink side by side with Isabelle, deep in conversation. There would be no more private conversations about things only Cammie and Isabelle cared about. There would be no more jealous looks from the other girls.

Now Cammie and Isabelle were the most gorgeous girls at the rink, the most popular ones. And it was all because of Isabelle. Without her, Cammie would be just another eleven-year-old skater who still couldn't land her jumps consistently. With Isabelle by her side, Cammie felt as though she belonged in the glamorous world, where pretty girls drove Porsche sport cars and wore bright skating jackets with Skateland's logo.

"So where are you going?" Coach Louise's voice came from her office. It was strange that she hadn't asked the question before, when Isabelle first said that she was leaving.

"To Skateland."

"Ah! Of course."

"And what's that supposed to mean?"

Boy, that Isabelle surely had the guts to talk to her coach like that. No other girl would ever dare to challenge Coach Louise's statement. *What's so special about Isabelle?* Cammie wondered for about the umpteenth time. The funny thing was that within the last three months, Isabelle had somehow managed to become as close to Coach Louise as any girl could ever dream of.

Isabelle often stood at the boards watching other skaters and then whispering something into the coach's ear. Coach Louise often asked Isabelle to demonstrate difficult steps for everybody—mostly moves in the field. Isabelle was pretty good at those. *Queen of the Moves*—that was what Susie had once called Isabelle. Cammie's friend wasn't that good at jumping, but she still was the coach's pet. And Cammie knew it too; but she wasn't jealous of Isabelle. After all, Isabelle was her friend.

"Is there anything else I can help you with?" Coach Louise's voice was as cold as the air at the rink.

"That's it," Isabelle said, sounding defiant.

"Then I want you to excuse me. I have a practice to run." Coach Louise's skate guards clomped against the wood floor.

Cammie barely had time to step to the right and hide behind Susie's father, who had been videotaping his daughter's practice.

Coach Louise walked past her without turning her head.

"Margie! I want you to try that sit spin again."

The coach's voice boomed from the other side of the rink.

Cammie looked around, shocked. How come Coach Louise hadn't even tried to talk Isabelle into staying at their rink? Of course, Skateland was the best place for skaters, and Skateland coaches really had a terrific reputation. But still… leaving like that? Without even talking to Cammie?

Cammie didn't remember getting on the ice. She couldn't care less about the practice that night—Isabelle's last night at their rink. She missed the coach's instructions; she stumbled on her three turns; she couldn't even do a decent spiral. Her mind was definitely not on the lesson. All she could think of was Isabelle. How could Cammie come to the rink if her best friend wasn't there? Skating would lose all attraction to her.

Cammie didn't even stay close to Isabelle that afternoon. What for? If her best friend was leaving anyway, she might as well get used to being alone again. Isabelle must have been watching Cammie, though, because at the end of the lesson she skated up to her.

"You know what? You're getting worse," Isabelle said without even bothering to tell Cammie about her plans.

Cammie frowned. "What do you mean?"

"You heard me. Come on, don't you notice yourself? You blew the competition and today ... boy, I've been watching you."

Cammie had never realized that the ice rink was actually a very hot place. Her cheeks burnt as though she stood under a bright summer sun. "I ... I ... it's not true!"

Isabelle smiled slyly and took Cammie by the hand. "No offense. I only have the best for you in mind. Do you know that I'm moving to Skateland?"

At first, Cammie wanted to pretend she had never heard about it; but then she decided to tell Isabelle the truth. "Yes, I heard."

"My parents and I think it's for the best. I'll be taking lessons from Darrell Johnson, and he's the best coach there is. You must have heard his name; he has prepared several world champions."

Cammie nodded absentmindedly.

"It's all arranged. Dad will be happy to pay all the expenses. I'm moving tomorrow. I'll live in a dorm, and I'll have as much practice time as I want."

Cammie sighed. "I'll miss you."

Isabelle gave her a critical look. She seemed to be thinking of something. Her face brightened.

"Hey, I've got an idea. Maybe you need to go to Skateland too?"

Cammie looked up. "What?"

"Think about it. You're a preliminary level skater, and I know you want to get better. Maybe it's time for you to move on, to get to a place where there are top coaches and nice ice rinks. And we'll be together."

Cammie's heart skipped a beat. Wow, could it be possible? Going to Skateland to train? Being with Isabelle all the time?

"It's actually not that expensive," Isabelle continued. "Not much more than you pay here. I'm sure your folks can afford it. But you'll skate at Rainbow Rinks. You'll see how great that ice is."

"I know. I've been there."

"See? Just tell your folks you want to become a better skater. I'm sure they won't mind."

"Perhaps, they won't," Cammie said slowly. "I hope they won't."

Cammie's mom and dad did mind. Oh, did they get furious when they heard about Cammie's decision!

"Are you out of your mind?" Mom yelled. "You're

doing great here with Coach Louise. I thought you liked her."

Cammie grimaced. "Yes, I kind of do, but…I haven't been landing my jumps lately and—"

"But it has nothing to do with Coach Louise. Come on, anybody can have a bad performance. Just practice more."

"I want to go to Skateland," Cammie said stubbornly.

Mom raised her arms. "I can't believe I'm hearing it."

Dad coughed. "Cammie…hmm, are you sure you're not overreacting? I know coming in fifth in that competition was hard on you, but—"

"It has nothing to do with it!" Cammie exclaimed.

"Calm down now!" Dad raised his hand, obviously expecting Cammie to lower her voice, but she couldn't contain her anger anymore.

"I'm not a little girl. I'm eleven. Many athletes my age move away from home to train. I want to work with top coaches. I need more ice time."

"Okay, we'll do it this way," Mom said. "How about talking it over with Coach Louise? If she really thinks it's time for you to move on, we'll think about it. Okay?"

"Okay," Cammie said defiantly. She felt like a winner. Mom and Dad didn't look too happy, but overall they seemed to understand that Cammie deserved better training.

Cammie turned out to be wrong. Completely wrong. Mom did exactly what she had promised. Next time Cammie and her mom showed up at the rink, Coach Louise was waiting for both of them in her office.

"I believe," the coach said as the three of them sat at the small desk, "I really think this move is a bit premature. Cammie is a talented skater, and she has been progressing well, but she isn't at the level where moving away from home and practicing on a full-time basis would do her much good."

"I'm going to Skateland," Cammie said stubbornly.

"See? This is all I've been hearing the last two days," Mom said without looking at Cammie.

"Cammie, is there anything you're not happy with at our rink?" Coach Louise asked.

Cammie shifted in her seat. Coach Louise's question had made her uncomfortable. Of course, she had nothing against Coach Louise. She was cool. Cammie had been working with her for three years, ever since she first started skating at the age of eight. Coach Louise had taught her everything she could do now. She had choreographed all of her programs. And Coach Louise understood her. If Cammie couldn't do some difficult move, Coach Louise was never harsh with her. On the contrary, she always tried to get Cammie to believe that she was a good skater, that she would get the tough element. Yes, Coach Louise had always been able to understand Cammie, so why couldn't she just tell Cammie's mom that going to Skateland would be a good idea?

Coach Louise's hazel eyes were fixed on Cammie. She was still waiting for her answer.

Cammie shrugged reluctantly. "Everything is fine here. It's just…I need more ice time."

"You practice enough for a skater your level," Coach Louise said. "Besides, if you feel you need to skate more, you can always come to extra public sessions."

"There is better ice at Skateland rinks," Cammie said.

"So what? If you learn all the difficult moves on worse ice, you'll have no problem when you compete on good ice. Anyway, Cammie, I've never heard you complain before. What has changed? Is it the competition?"

Cammie's eyes filled up with tears. She looked to the side.

"I know you were disappointed, but it's time to move on. Forget what happened there; let's work on those jumps. You'll get them; I promise."

A tear slid down Cammie's cheek down to her lips, and she licked it off.

"Okay, now be a good girl and get changed. Let's see how we can improve those jumps."

"I'm going to Skateland," Cammie said, perhaps louder than Mom and Coach Louise had expected.

Mom and Coach Louise exchanged nervous glances.

"Cammie, you're not old enough to live away from home yet," Coach Louise said. "This move will be tough on you. You'll have to change schools. You'll have to live in a dorm. Are you ready for those changes?"

"Isabelle is doing it," Cammie said, trying to stay calm. "If she can do it, why can't I?

She felt a rush of anger. Really, if Isabelle's parents were so supportive, why couldn't her mom and dad understand that Cammie really, really needed to move to Skateland?

"Isabelle's mom and dad aren't giving her a hard

time," Cammie said, fighting off tears. "It's only you, only you!"

She couldn't stand it any longer. Tears streamed down her cheeks.

Coach Louise sighed heavily. "Ah, that's what it is. I suspected something like this, but I wasn't sure."

Mom gave her a quick look. "What?"

"Isabelle. Of course!"

"Isabelle? Cammie's new friend?"

"Yes." Coach Louise slapped the table with her gloved hand. She looked really upset. "Isabelle Alvarez, our new student. She is friends with Cammie, and I've noticed your daughter getting influenced by her. "

"Isabelle's older too," Mom said.

"Exactly. She's almost seventeen, and Cammie is only eleven. What kind of a relationship is that, anyway? And by the way, Isabelle is very manipulative, and she won't stop till she gets her way. Now I'm sure it was she who put that crazy idea about moving to Skateland into Cammie's mind."

"Is this true, Cammie?" Mom asked.

Cammie pressed her lips. She decided to stay quiet. Yes, of course, it was true. But if Mom and Coach Louise believed moving to Skateland was

Isabelle's idea, not Cammie's, they wouldn't want to hear another word about it.

"This is ridiculous," Mom said angrily. "I don't even want to talk about it. Cammie is staying here. End of discussion."

"No, I'm not." Boy, what was she going to do? How could she get the two of them to understand?

"Forget it, Cammie. I won't allow it. Did you hear me?"

Before that Cammie had been crying silently; now she was sobbing. "It's cruel, cruel! You don't understand!"

She grabbed her skating bag and ran out of the office. In the locker room, she put on her skates, her hands shaking. She would show everybody that she wasn't really growing as a skater here. Both Mom and Coach Louise thought she was doing fine, right? Well, they were going to learn how wrong they were.

Magic Icemobile

Isabelle left, and skating lost all of its attractiveness for Cammie. When she came to the rink, she found herself completely lonely. Yes, sure, there were other girls, and if Cammie tried to skate up to them and start a conversation, they probably wouldn't turn her down. But she didn't feel like talking to anybody. She was used to being special, to being Isabelle's best and only friend.

She still wore the stylish skating skirts and jackets Isabelle had given her because she had grown out of them. But Cammie didn't feel attractive anymore. There was terrible emptiness inside her, and nothing could fill it—neither the fun of her cardio lessons, nor the challenging new moves that Coach Louise always showed Cammie at her private lessons. Cammie was bored.

The first Thursday afternoon after Isabelle left, Cammie didn't even feel like going to her private lesson. What was the use anyway? If Mom hadn't warned Cammie that she would pull her out of skating, Cammie might have stayed home altogether.

Coach Louise was her old, cool self as they went over Cammie's program together. At some point, Cammie forgot that she was upset and did her best to concentrate. But her jumps still didn't happen. Her double salchow and toe loop were the worst. She merely couldn't complete two revolutions in the air because she didn't have enough height. Each time she tried a jump, she would crash on the ice. It hurt terribly. At some point, Cammie thought she had had enough.

"I can't do it," she protested. "I'm not a skater."

"Don't worry, the jumps will come back," Coach Louise said.

"No!"

Coach Louise put her hand on Cammie's shoulder. "Tell you what. Why don't you skate your program leaving out the difficult jumps. Do singles instead."

"That's silly."

"Not at all. At this point, it's more important for you to get the joy of skating back. Go ahead."

Reluctantly, Cammie walked to the middle of the ice and took her starting position. The music poured from the speakers, and Cammie wondered why she had liked "Moonlight Sonata" so much before. The melody seemed boring and monotonous—nothing like Isabelle's catchy Spanish music. And so was Cammie's skating—dreary and colorless. And so was she—a stupid little skater who couldn't do her jumps, couldn't do anything.

Tears clouded Cammie's eyes, blurring her vision, keeping her from seeing where she was going. She wiped them off angrily with her glove. That threw her out of balance; she barely held on to her edge. She wobbled, switched to her backward inside edge—a bad mistake because the lutz jump was to be taken from the outside edge—and jumped. Even when she was in the air, she knew her body was tilted. She landed clumsily on both feet, waved her arms to stay vertical, but slipped and ended up on her backside. So much for graceful skating!

"I can't skate," Cammie bawled. "I can't!"

Her music was still playing, but Cammie couldn't care less. She rushed to the exit, grabbed her skate guards, and headed for the locker room. No one, not even Coach Louise would get her to do another run-through of the program. Forget it!

Coach Louise didn't talk to Cammie any more that day. Cammie saw her discussing something with her mother, though. The coach was probably complaining about Cammie's disrespectful behavior during the lesson. Fine, Cammie didn't care.

Cammie's cardio lesson was scheduled for Friday night, and first Cammie thought she wasn't going to attend it at all. Maybe, she would quit skating. Maybe, it wasn't for her. But as the small hand of the clock on the kitchen wall moved closer and closer to five o'clock, Cammie kept casting furtive glances at Mom. Why wasn't she telling Cammie to get ready? Didn't she remember they were due at the skating practice?

Cammie walked by her mother three or four times expecting her to say something, but her mother went through her daily chores of cooking, cleaning, and doing bills as though her only daughter didn't even have to go to the rink.

Finally, with only twenty minutes left before she had to be on the ice for her warm-up, Cammie approached her mother in the living room. "I think we'd better get going."

"Fine," Mom said, sounding as though nothing had happened. "Get your skates."

Just like that. No questions; no comments. They got into their SUV without saying another word. On the way to the rink, Cammie's mother listened to the radio, and Cammie stared gloomily out of the window. When Cammie got out of the car, her mother didn't drive away but followed her daughter to the rink. Cammie gave her a questioning look.

"Go ahead. I'll pick you up after the lesson," Mom said.

Cammie took her bag and headed for the locker room. Before going in, she looked back to see her mother talking to Coach Louise. From where she stood, Cammie couldn't hear what exactly they were discussing. They only thing that caught her ear right before she closed the locker room door behind her was her mother's remark, "She's not going anywhere. We've made our decision." It wasn't difficult to guess what she was talking about.

Feeling even more upset than before—if that was even possible—Cammie walked into the empty locker room. The rest of the skaters were already on the ice; Cammie was the last to show up. Well, that was for the best. She wasn't in the mood to talk to anyone. Even when Alex caught up with her as she was taking off her guards ready to step onto the ice, Cammie was cranky.

"What's wrong?" Alex asked, looking concerned.

Cammie felt herself fuming again. "Everybody is against me. I wanted to move to Skateland, like Isabelle, to train with the best coaches on their beautiful ice, and they won't let me."

"Who won't let you?"

"Who? Mom and Coach Louise, of course. How stupid!" She slammed her skate guards against the boards.

Alex flinched. "Wait a minute. You wanted to move to Skateland? For good?"

"Well, sure. So what? A lot of skaters train there."

Alex looked serious. "I know, but most of them are elite skaters. You're not quite there yet."

"That's not true. There are kids there, and we saw them. Remember Jeff, the injured boy and the scared red-haired girl? And the fat kids—remember?'

Alex frowned. "I guess you're right. But…they didn't look happy. They got terribly attacked by witches, all of them. Skateland is a dangerous place for a young skater; everybody knows that."

"I can handle it," Cammie said angrily.

"But perhaps Coach Louise thinks you're not old enough for all that pressure. You've got to trust her, Cammie. She's your coach, and she has more wisdom."

"She doesn't care, and that's it," Cammie blurted out. "And Mom is siding with her, of course. It's not fair. Why can Isabelle go, and nobody makes a fuss about it, and I can't? And Isabelle is only at the pre-preliminary level. I'm at preliminary."

Alex looked to the side, looking uncertain. "Look, Cammie, I know you're friends with Isabelle, but she's...I don't know how to say it...I just don't trust her."

Cammie straightened up. She was much smaller than Alex, but with her back straight and chin up, she felt as though she were towering over him. "How can you? You don't even know her!"

"That's right. I don't have any specific information. I just feel...she's not a good friend for you."

"You know what? You may think you're Mr. Know-It-All, but you don't understand a thing about Isabelle or me!" Cammie snapped.

She stepped onto the ice without giving Alex another look. Some friend he was! And she hoped he would back her up. Fat chance!

Cammie's cardio lesson was a disaster. She was determined to show Coach Louise that she wasn't going to get any better unless she moved to Skateland. If the woman didn't understand Cammie's words, surely her poor skating would speak volumes. To prove her point, Cammie deliberately disobeyed Coach Louise. Instead of forward crossovers, she went backward; instead of power pulls, she did swizzles.

"We're supposed to do power pulls, Cammie!" Margie whispered, her blue eyes wide open.

Cammie ignored her. What she was waiting for was Coach Louise's reaction. The woman, however, behaved as though Cammie weren't even there. She joked with the rest of the group, shouted instructions to the skaters, demonstrated difficult moves. That burned Cammie up even more. She swirled around the other skaters as fast as she could; she even cut off Alex twice. She expected him to try to fight her—then she would show him! But that didn't happen. Alex merely ignored her—just like Coach Louise.

The cardio lesson ended, and no one had paid any attention to Cammie. Even Margie kept her distance. Whether Coach Louise had mentioned anything to the skaters or they felt something was wrong, Cammie found herself alone. The skaters stepped off the ice and headed for the locker room. Cammie didn't follow them. She didn't feel like talking to anyone. She did two laps around the rink, moved to the middle, and tried backward crossovers. The ice was bad: scratchy, with deep ruts and holes from where the skaters had picked to do their jumps.

Someone had dimmed the light at the rink. From the middle of the ice, Cammie could hear skaters' voices saying good-bye to Coach Louise and to one another. The door slammed. The music stopped playing, and the complete silence almost deafened Cammie. She stopped and looked around.

The building was empty. Hmm. Normally that was the time when Mr. Walrus came to the rink in his Zamboni to resurface the ice. But Cammie knew Mr. Walrus wasn't at the rink today. She had heard Coach Louise say to someone that the man was home with the flu. No wonder no one had chased Cammie off the rink. Mr. Walrus never allowed anybody to skate after the official practice time was over. But now there was no Mr. Walrus around, so Cammie was free to do whatever she wanted.

She circled the rink one more time. The ice was bad—no, she didn't like it. She cast a look at Coach Louise's locked door, then at the exit. There was no one. How weird. Was it safe to be alone at the rink like this? And where was Mom? From the glass door that led outside, Cammie could see that it was already dark. Mom had to be here by now. What was keeping her? Maybe Cammie should go to the pay phone and dial her mother's cell phone number.

Just when Cammie was about to step off the ice, she heard a familiar noise of the Zamboni gate go up. Aha, so Mr. Walrus had come to the rink after all. If so, Cammie had better leave the ice, or she would have to face the man's displeasure. It wasn't that Cammie didn't like Mr. Walrus. The kids had given him that nickname because of his bald head and long gray mustache that went far below his chin. He was a nice guy, a terrific skater, and when Cammie and Alex fought with wicked witches in Skateland, the Zamboni driver had rescued them several times. But even their common experience in Skateland hadn't made Mr. Walrus less strict.

Cammie hurried to the exit to walk off the ice before the Zamboni machine appeared from the gate.

"Cammie!" A familiar voice called from the gate.

Cammie looked around and froze in her spot. The Zamboni gate was really open, but the vehicle that had come from behind the gate was nothing like the familiar battered black-and-yellow Zamboni machine. Right in front of Cammie stood a big silver sled. Inside, seated comfortably in what looked like a soft white couch was a big middle-aged woman and next to her was ... Isabelle.

"Isabelle!" Cammie could hardly believe her eyes.

Isabelle laughed and stepped off the sled on the scratchy ice, looking chic in her black leggings and a black and yellow leather jacket. "Ugh! This ice is horrible—just as it has always been. No surprises here, Auntie."

The big woman laughed. "What can you expect from a small rink like this? It's not Skateland for you." Her voice was deep and throaty, as though she smoked a lot.

"Cammie, we're here to get you," Isabelle said excitedly.

"What?"

"Hi, Cammie, nice to meet you," the big woman said. "I'm Isabelle's aunt. You don't have to know my name; it's rather difficult to pronounce. Just call me *Auntie*—that's what Isabelle calls me anyway."

Isabelle and the lady exchanged excited glances.

Cammie shrugged. "Okay." It was weird. Why didn't the lady want to reveal her real name? As Cammie shook the woman's hand, her pointy fingernails scratched her palm. Cammie recoiled.

"Oh, I'm sorry," Auntie drawled. "I sometimes forget my fingernails aren't my blades." She turned to Isabelle, and it gave Cammie a good opportunity to look at the woman. She was tall and bulky, but at the same time, everything about her was pointy: her chin, her nose—long and narrowing at the end. The woman's eyes were black and cold. Cammie had a faint feeling she had already seen the lady somewhere. But where? Surely not at her rink. At a competition, perhaps? Or maybe in a dream? Somehow she remembered the bushy, reddish-brown hair that almost covered the lady's face, her sharp nose, and almond-shaped eyes. Well, whoever the woman was, she surely looked very classy in her ankle-length mink coat, with gold and diamond rings glittering on every finger.

"I live and work in Skateland," Auntie said.

"You never told me you had relatives in Skateland," Cammie said to Isabelle.

Isabelle clapped her hands. "I didn't have time to tell you. But I do have Auntie. And we've come to take you to Skateland with us. Auntie has arranged for you to get a scholarship. Your folks will only have to pay a very small amount. Isn't that awesome?"

Cammie swallowed. "Really?"

"But of course! I saw you at the last competition. You're good," Auntie said.

Cammie's ears turned hot. "But I skated terribly."

Auntie shook her head. "What happened there doesn't matter. I've seen many skaters in my life. You have a great potential. You can be a star one day. But it looks as though you have been at this small rink too long. You definitely need a change of scenery. Under a good coach, you will flourish and do triples in no time."

"I can't even do a double toe loop consistently." Cammie felt very embarrassed.

"Things will change once you get to Skateland. It's a perfect place for a skater of your caliber," Auntie said.

Cammie clasped her hands. Oh, how she wished she could say yes. But how about her parents? Just today she had heard her mother say, *"Absolutely not."*

"Don't worry about your parents. Everything can be arranged," Auntie said. "Your mother and father aren't skaters, so they don't understand how important it is for you to get the best possible training. But they will come along. Once we get to Skateland, I'll call your parents, and I'm sure I'll be able to get them to understand what is best for you."

"Oh, will you?" Cammie exclaimed.

"But of course. Don't worry, dear." Auntie put her hand on Cammie's shoulder, and again Cammie remembered something in connection with this sudden feeling of bitter cold that rushed through her body. The same thing had surely happened to her before. But where? And when?

"Why don't you come with us now?" Auntie said.

"Now?" Cammie's head spun. Yes, she wanted to go. Boy, it was unbelievable. Today she would be in Skateland already. And tomorrow she would start working with the best coach, at the best rinks. Only…

"But what if my mom says *no* when you talk to her?"

Auntie waved her hand. "She won't. No mother has refused what's best for her kid yet. Don't worry, dear. I'll be able to explain to your mother that you need to train in Skateland now. See, I was a skater too one day. I moved to Skateland when I was about your age, and I've been happy ever since."

"Oh, were you a champion?" Cammie asked, eyeing the lady with admiration.

The woman's tanned cheeks turned burgundy. "Oh … well … I was a good skater. But never mind. You have your skates on, don't you? That's important. Your mother can ship you the rest of your things later. Come on, let's go!"

"Yes, but—"

"Hop on!"Auntie stretched her hand to help Cammie climb into the silver sled. As Cammie grabbed the massive hand clad in a sparkly white glove, another shot of cold rushed through her. She ignored it. It was natural to feel cold at the rink.

Cammie sank into the soft leather couch beside Isabelle, who gave her an encouraging smile.

Auntie positioned herself in the front of the sled. She rubbed her hands. "Want a skate shake?" she asked Cammie.

Cammie didn't know what Auntie was talking about, but whatever she was offering sounded good. "Sure."

Auntie handed Cammie a huge mug picturing a girl in an arabesque position. Cammie sipped the steamy liquid and felt her doubts disappear in the delicious cherry flavor of the drink. "It's yummy!"

"Yes, like everything else in Skateland," Auntie said. "There's nothing better to warm you up after a long practice than skate shake."

Auntie bent down and spoke into a tiny built-in microphone on the dashboard, "Skateland."

Immediately the sled took off moving in the direction of the Zamboni gate. As Cammie looked back to her home rink, excitement rose up in her. It was really happening. She was on her way to Skateland with Isabelle. The gate went up, and in they went. However, before Cammie's eyes had enough time to register the familiar outline of the Zamboni machine, the massive gate slid down again, leaving the three of them in complete darkness.

"Never mind, never mind," Auntie muttered.

Cammie felt the sled jerk forward, then stop, as though undecided where to go.

"Where on earth is that directory?" Auntie mumbled nervously. "Ah, there it is!"

Just then Cammie saw the faint outline of a plaque on the stony wall. The woman's long fingernails scratched the surface, and it lit up with numerous buttons representing different rinks. And there it was, the right button—Cammie recognized it right away—round and crystal, with a tiny rainbow inside, and the name under it said *Skateland*.

Auntie pressed the button, the sled lit up instantly, and shadows erupted around them. As they moved forward—faster, faster, and faster, Cammie looked at the dark walls with locked doors on both sides. The sled took a sharp turn. Cammie clasped its cold metal side, trying not to look down.

From her previous trip to Skateland, she knew that most of the trail ran across a deep ravine. But now she was much more comfortable than during her first trip. Last time, Alex and Cammie had sat cooped inside the Zamboni machine, trying not to make any noise—not even breathe, lest Mr. Walrus notice them and send them home. This time, Cammie was ensconced comfortably in a soft leather seat, sipping her skate shake, with Isabelle by her side.

"What a terrific sled; it's much better than a car." Cammie didn't realize she had spoken the words out loud.

Auntie grinned. "Yup. Actually, it's not a sled; it's called *icemobile*. See the blades instead of wheels? They only make those in Skateland, and even there not everybody is allowed to use them. Even top skaters are encouraged to skate everywhere. They say it's good for their stamina. Well, perhaps. Personally, I don't like to waste my energy this way. Anyway, the only people who can use icemobiles in Skateland are the president, coaches, judges and…other important people."

Cammie looked at Auntie with growing respect. She had to be a very important person, then. How lucky Cammie was! Surely when her parents talked to this stately woman, they would have no choice but to allow Cammie to stay in Skateland.

"Skateland is a cool place, but I can't imagine myself skating around on those twisty paths," Auntie said nonchalantly. "For a veteran like me, it's quite an ordeal. So it's only fair to leave all the torture to you young skaters. We old folks, we've had our time. Haha."

Cammie wondered why the woman kept calling herself old. To Cammie she looked very young and strong. And yet, when the sled reached a spot that was well lit by a lantern, Cammie examined Auntie's face closely and realized that the woman was probably right. The areas around her eyes and lips were carved with deep wrinkles.

"I went to the nationals in 1975," Auntie said. "I almost got a medal. Almost. But you know how it's done, don't you?"

"What?"

"I mean, you understand this whole skating business, don't you?"

"Huh?" Cammie didn't understand a thing.

"Ah, never mind!" Auntie snapped. "It's great to relax and enjoy time with my precious little children now."

From the corner of her eye, Cammie saw Auntie wink at Isabelle. There seemed to be a secret the two of them shared, but Cammie really didn't think much about it. As the sled moved smoothly along the dark corridor, she kept thinking of the beauty of Skateland that stretched somewhere ahead of her, and it filled her with the happy sense of anticipation. She couldn't wait to get there.

Finally the dark passage became wider, and the familiar sign *Zamboni Parking Lot* emerged from the darkness.

"Aren't we parking?" Cammie asked, as Auntie apparently showed no intention of slowing down.

"Why should we? I'm not driving a Zamboni, am I? Besides, there's no time to waste. I'm going to take you girls straight to your house."

"We'll live in the same dorm," Isabelle said. "Isn't it exciting, Cammie?"

"Yes!" Cammie clapped her hands.

"So Auntie, when you talk to Cammie's mom, tell her she has nothing to worry about. I'll take care of her daughter," Isabelle said.

"Mamma Isabelle," Auntie said in a high-pitched, little girl's voice.

Both Isabelle and Auntie giggled.

It was weird how Isabelle and Auntie behaved as though they were best friends, girls of the same age. Cammie also had an aunt—her mom's sister, who lived in Oklahoma—Aunt Patty was her name. And boy, whenever she came to visit, all Cammie heard from her was what a good girl should do and what was totally inappropriate. Isabelle and Auntie's relationship was so unusual!

"Auntie, are you Isabelle's father's or mother's sister?" Cammie asked.

Auntie turned around, and Cammie saw the woman's almond-shaped eyes beam angrily at her. "What are you talking about?"

Cammie felt uncomfortable. Was her question rude? "I was just curious. You're Isabelle's aunt, so—"

"Ah, that!" Auntie laughed somewhat unnaturally. "Well, let me see. It must be your mom who's related to me; right, Isabelle?"

Isabelle grinned. "I would think so."

Another bout of laughter came from the two of them. Cammie frowned. It seemed as though Isabelle and Auntie were playing some kind of a game with her. Was there something she didn't know?

The sled bypassed the Zamboni parking lot and approached a massive wood bridge with skating scenes carved on the railings. The bridge stretched across a ravine with raging water. Cammie rose in her seat. Oh, how well she remembered the ravine!

"Last time I was here, I had to do a waltz jump to get to the other side," Cammie said. Right away she wished she hadn't mentioned her dangerous experience. Would Isabelle and Auntie believe her?

Auntie didn't flinch, though Isabelle looked as though she didn't believe a thing.

"Yes, Cammie is a terrific jumper," Isabelle said politely.

"That's good. Good jumpers are a real asset to Skateland," Auntie said. "And if you can cover a good distance on your waltz jump, it will help you with your double axel."

Double axel? What was Auntie talking about? Cammie had only started working on her double jumps.

"You're in Skateland now, so dream big. And you, kiddo," Auntie said, turning her pointed nose in Isabelle's direction, "you need to finally land that single axel."

"I will," Isabelle said.

"Good. Remember, the best coaches in the world live here, in Skateland. Even an old woman like me can give you some good tips."

Cammie nodded, looking at the familiar beauty of Skateland unfold around her. They passed Main Square that was now ablaze with lights. They glided by the Icy Park, dark and mysterious, moved along several streets past small houses with closed shutters, and finally stopped in front of a three-story house. The sign on the door said *Juvenile Skaters' Dorm.*

Cammie's cheeks burnt. "I'm only in preliminary." She felt it was important to tell Auntie the truth. What if she was asked to demonstrate her skills to a panel of judges once she entered the house? That would be an embarrassment.

Auntie laughed and squeezed Cammie's arm. Cammie ignored the familiar cold feeling and waited for the woman's answer.

"It doesn't really matter. I told everybody the two of you were promising skaters. So you're allowed to live here. Okay, ready to see your new home?"

Home? For Cammie, the word *home* always

meant her brick house in Clarenceville, where she lived with her mom and dad. For a split second, she wished she were back home, where a huge pine tree grew right outside her window. She was about to walk up to her small bedroom and jump on her bed. Her old teddy bear with one of his back paws sewn back together would wink at her.

Isabelle took Cammie by the hand. "Hmm, I think you won't get lost now. Here's the door; just go inside. Mrs. Page will show you your room. I have some things to do before I crash tonight, okay? I'll see you later."

Before Cammie could say a word, Isabelle got back in the sled and waved at Cammie. Auntie waved too, and the sled disappeared around the corner. Cammie was left alone on the narrow, icy path in front of the dorm. That wasn't quite what she had expected. She thought Isabelle would be with her all the time. For a split second, Cammie felt lonely and rejected; then she shook her head, mad at herself. She was in Skateland, and wasn't it what she wanted? She was a big girl; she could take care of herself.

Cammie picked up her skating bag and walked along the narrow pathway and up the steps to the house that was now going to be her home.

SKATERS' DORM

Inside the skating dorm everything was white— perhaps to remind the skaters about ice and the whiteness of winter. A plump, smiling woman greeted Cammie at the front desk.

"Hi, sweetheart. My name is Mrs. Page. I'm the dorm supervisor and the cook at the juvenile dorm. I hope you'll like my cooking."

Cammie smiled politely.

"Here's your key. You'll be staying in room thirty-two with Sonia Harrison. A charming girl she is, Sonia. I know you'll like her."

"Sure." Sonia Harrison might be nice, but oh,

how Cammie wished she could stay with Isabelle! Somehow she had been sure Isabelle and she would share the same room.

Cammie walked up the steps to the third floor. A long windowless corridor with doors on both sides stretched in front of her. Most of the doors were decorated with skating stickers and posters. Cammie put the key in the lock of the door with nothing but number 32 on it and walked in.

A small, skinny girl raised her head from the book she was reading. Cammie saw a pale narrow face and red curls falling on the girl's shoulders.

"Hi, my name is Cammie Wester," Cammie said. "It looks like I'm going to live with you."

The girl's blue eyes lit up. "Cammie! Is that you?"

"Do you know me?" Cammie looked at the girl with growing interest. Yes, she had definitely seen that short nose covered with freckles, and the girl's slightly bashful smile. But where? And when?

"It's me, Sonia from the Witch of Fear's rink. Do you remember me?"

"Ah, yes!" Now Cammie remembered. Of course. When Alex and she walked across Skateland to the Sport Center, where their competition was to take place, they had to pass the rink that belonged to the Witch of Fear. The evil gaunt woman had attacked a girl—now Cammie knew that her name was Sonia Harrison—so viciously that the poor little redhead couldn't even stroke, let alone do jumps and spins. In order to skate past the witch's property and deliver the girl from the evil woman's clutches, Cammie and Alex had had to perform a series of waltz eights at the witch's rink. They had completed the assignment successfully, and the girl had been set free. And now she was in the same room with Cammie.

"So you're back to skating?" Cammie asked.

Sonia's pale cheeks turned pink. "Yes! Oh, thank you again, Cammie; if it hadn't been for you and Alex … I don't know. Remember, I could barely walk on ice."

How could Cammie forget?

"Yes, and it took me a year to completely overcome fear and to get my skills back. I had to take it one step at a time. Can you believe it? I would come to the rink and do nothing but stroke for two straight hours. Then I tried my edges, and I could do them; then the three turns … and now I can jump and spin again."

"But how about the Witch of Fear?" Cammie asked. "Did she ever try to attack you again?"

Sonia's face became serious. "Well, of course. Remember what Mr. Walrus said? Witches never leave skaters for good. They attack them throughout their careers. But you can't give up, and you need to have your basics nailed. And of course, it's important to practice hard."

"I'm so happy for you!"

"Thank you!" Sonia beamed. "I'm working on my double axel now. It's a tough jump, but I know I'll get it one day."

"Double axel!" Cammie felt a twinge of jealousy. She wasn't even close to starting to work on it. Her double salchow and toe loop were still very inconsistent, and the axel had an extra half revolution. How could Sonia do it?

Cammie looked at her roommate's skinny arms and legs. She would never have thought that the girl was strong enough to land such a difficult jump.

"Jeff is here too," Sonia said cheerfully. "Do you remember him? Alex and you delivered him from the Witch of Injuries."

"Oh, yes. Is he all right?" Cammie thought of the boy, whose wrists and ankles had been broken because he had skated at the rink jinxed by the Witch of Injuries.

"Jeff is just fine. He landed his double lutz yesterday."

"I haven't even started working on it," Cammie said, feeling more and more inadequate. What if she was the worst skater in Skateland? She was used to being the best.

"Don't worry; you'll land it soon. Jeff worked on it for several months."

"Okay." Maybe Sonia was right. Cammie was in Skateland to work, so she'd make the most of it.

"Where's Alex?" Sonia asked.

"He's not here."

"Why not?"

"I don't know." Cammie felt sad again. Really, why hadn't Alex agreed to join her in Skateland? It would be so much fun. But no, it was all right; she had Isabelle with her.

"I came here with another friend, a girl," Cammie said. "She's a terrific skater, and she's gorgeous too."

"Oh! What's her name?"

"Isabelle Alvarez."

"Oh!" Sonia wasn't smiling anymore. In fact, she looked unhappy.

"What? You don't like her?"

"Hmm. No, I guess she's okay," Sonia said tentatively. "I don't know her that well."

Cammie had a feeling that Sonia was hiding something from her, but she decided not to push it. Instead, she asked Sonia how long she had been in Skateland.

"All my life actually," Sonia said with a weak smile. "I was born here. My parents skated pairs themselves. They were even world champions once, and they named me *Sonia* in honor of Sonja Heine. She was a famous skater."

Cammie nodded. She had heard the name somewhere.

"I started skating when I was two. I lived with my parents here for many years. But now Mom and Dad have moved to Colorado to coach. I wanted to go with them, of course, but they think Skateland is the best place for me. Plenty of ice time and no distractions. See, my parents want me to become a champion, and they won't settle for anything else."

Cammie sat down on her bed, careful not to miss a single word. "It must be great to train here."

Sonia shrugged. "Sure. But it's also demanding. Everybody is so competitive here; nobody will help you if you struggle with something. And of course, there are also witches."

Cammie's heart beat faster. "I thought Alex and I defeated them."

Sonia closed her book and jumped on her bed across from Cammie's. "That's true, but you only faced three witches, and there are many more. Besides, even the ones you have defeated will never give up on you. In fact, I see the Witch of Fear all the time."

Cammie wrinkled her forehead. "What do you mean, 'see her all the time'? Where? I thought witches weren't allowed at practices."

"Well, officially they aren't, but you can't always stop them. I saw the Witch of Fear several times— in the audience during competitions and even on the street."

"Wow!" That wasn't what Cammie had expected. "If it's so, how do we protect ourselves?"

"I already told you. Work hard and practice the basics."

The door opened.

"Knock knock," Mrs. Page said happily as she walked in carrying a big suitcase. "These are your things, Cammie."

Cammie jumped off her bed. "What? Where're they from?"

"They came here by UPS. Your parents must have sent them."

"My parents? But how? They didn't even know ... " Cammie shuddered. She wasn't going to tell Mrs. Page or anybody else that she hadn't asked her parents' permission to move to Skateland, that she had run away from home to join Isabelle. She had been so happy to see her friend in the Auntie's silver sled that she had completely forgotten that her parents hadn't let her go to Skateland. Were Mom and Dad really upset now that they knew she was gone? Would she be in trouble for disobeying her parents? Gosh, what if they came to Skateland and demanded that Cammie return home immediately?

"There's also a letter, and I'm sure it explains everything." Mrs. Page gave Cammie an encouraging smile. Cammie smiled back, though she felt very nervous.

"Don't forget to pick up your milk and cookies in twenty minutes," Mrs. Page sang as she closed the door tightly behind her.

Still in shock, Cammie opened the envelope. The letter was written in her mother's familiar handwriting.

Dear Cammie,

I'm very disappointed with you. I still don't think you are old enough to train away from home, and I'm sure your father and I made it very clear to you. Tonight, when I came to the rink and didn't find you there, I was worried sick. I called your father; we even thought of contacting the police…

Oh, no! The letter slipped out of Cammie's hand as she pictured her mother's eyes, wide open with fear, and her father pacing the lobby nervously. How could she get so excited about the icemobile ride that she completely forgot about her parents? With trembling hands, Cammie picked up the letter and forced herself to read further.

…How could you leave home without even saying good bye? I thought your family meant more to you. Honestly, Cammie, I was about to jump in the car, drive to Skateland, and bring you back home. Perhaps this is what I should have done…

Oh, please! Cammie looked through the window at the darkening sky. Would her mother really knock on the dorm door now and tell her to follow her back home? She shook her head and kept reading.

… But then Isabelle's aunt stopped by with good news about your scholarship and a bunch of forms to sign. She told us you have real talent, and it would be a shame to let it go to waste. I hope she is right. Anyway, Cammie, your father and I have decided to let you train in Skateland. There is one condition. You will work hard and when we come to see you at the next competition, you will show us that this move was worth all the trouble. I will call you every day, and I want a detailed report of your practices. I am enclosing some spending money for you, but don't spend it all on candy; keep it for emergencies. Remember: you are in Skateland to work and to become a good skater. We love you and wish you all the best. Call us if you need something. Good luck! Love, Mom and Dad

Cammie read the letter, looked at the other side of the page, and found nothing. Read the letter again. Sniffed it. The letter smelt vaguely of *Miracle*, her mother's favorite perfume. She couldn't believe what she had just read. Her mother, the one who had been so dead set against Cammie moving to Skateland, had actually wished her luck? Unbelievable.

Cammie opened her suitcase and rummaged through her things. Her mother had filled the suitcase with Cammie's skating clothes, several pairs of tights and wool socks, two pairs of jeans, three warm sweaters, her schoolbooks, and Cammie's old teddy bear, Mr. Skate, the one who always sat on her bed at home. Still surprised that her mother had changed her mind so fast, Cammie put the bear on her bed and dragged the suitcase to the closet.

"You look kind of … upset," Sonia said.

Cammie forced a smile. "No, not really. But I don't understand what happened to my mother. See, she didn't want me moving to Skateland."

"Did anyone from Skateland talk to your mother?"

"I think Isabelle's aunt did."

"Isabelle's aunt?" Sonia grimaced. "Who is she?"

"I don't know. Just some lady. She looks classy, though."

"Well, it doesn't matter. I think what she told your mother was that you were a very talented skater, that Skateland would take care of all the expenses, and that one day you would become a world champ—this sort of stuff."

"How do you know all that?" Cammie asked, feeling excited. So somebody did think that she could become a champion one day. Some woman she was, Isabelle's aunt! In about an hour the woman had managed to accomplish what Cammie had been trying so hard to do for a week: getting her mother's permission to move to Skateland. Wow, was Isabelle lucky to have a relative like that!

"That's what they always say," Sonia said sadly. For a split second she looked older than eleven; then she shook her head as though chasing the sad thoughts away. "Oh, forget it. Do you want me to help you unpack?"

Together they hung Cammie's clothes in the closet that was already half filled with Sonia's things.

"There was another girl in this room with me; Krista was her name," Sonia said. "But see, the Witch of Injuries got her, and her ankle was shattered."

Cammie quivered. "Can't the bones grow back together?"

"Sure, but Krista doesn't want to skate anymore. She says she's had enough of it. Her parents feel the same. So she moved out."

Cammie felt fear creep into her heart. No, she wouldn't think of anything scary. Nothing would happen to her; she would surely make it as a skater.

Cammie put her schoolbooks and notebooks in the nightstand. "Will I have time for school here?"

Sonia giggled. "But of course! You'll go to Skateland School. We're in the same grade, I guess."

"That's good." Of course, it was great to know somebody from the same school, but how Cammie wished she could live and do things together with Isabelle! There was nothing wrong with Sonia; she was nice, but she wasn't as cool as Isabelle.

"There are cookies and milk in the dining room," Sonia said. "Want some?"

Only now did Cammie realize that she was hungry. She hadn't had any dinner, and since lunchtime, she had had nothing in her mouth but a glass of skate shake.

Together Cammie and Sonia went down to a cozy room with small tables. Sonia introduced Cammie to other girls at her table: Dana and Liz. Both of them were pretty—Dana, a tall blonde with enormous blue eyes; and Liz, a tiny Chinese girl. It also seemed to Cammie that both girls looked a little aloof. Cammie sipped her milk and took a bite from a big chocolate chip cookie that had a very unusual shape.

"It's a glove!" Cammie exclaimed after giving her cookie a thorough examination.

Dana smirked. "You got it. Mrs. Page wanted something that would remind us of skating; she wouldn't settle for anything else. And of course, Sweet Blades bakery already has blades, boots, and snowflakes."

"As though we need to be reminded of skating," Liz said haughtily.

"Yeah, right, I almost forgot what I was here for," Dana said.

Both girls laughed. Sonia smiled politely. Cammie looked at the three girls, not quite knowing what to say.

"Just eat it," Sonia said softly. "Mrs. Page is a great cook, really. Sweet Blades won't hire her because they have enough bakers, but I think her cookies and pastries are the best."

Liz raised her finger. "Sure, eat it, but remember: nothing will make you fat faster."

Cammie knew she wasn't fat, but the cookie didn't taste that good anymore.

"By the way, have you landed all of your double jumps yet?" Dana asked.

"No." Cammie stared at her unfinished milk.

No one talked to Cammie anymore. Apparently Dana and Liz had lost all interest in her. Cammie and Sonia finished their milk, thanked Mrs. Page, and went up to their room.

"Why are they like that?" Cammie asked Sonia.

Sonia's blue eyes opened wide. "Everybody is businesslike here. People compete all the time, not only during official competitions. Do you want to take a shower first before bed?"

After the shower, Cammie changed into her pink pajamas with small teddy bears looking just like Mr. Skate scattered all over the soft flannel. Sonia wore an oversized T-shirt that said *Skateland 2002 Annual Competition.*

"It was then that I got my first gold medal," Sonia said. She must have noticed the surprise in Cammie's eyes. "I was four years old, and Dad was so proud that he got himself this T-shirt. Of course, it's too old and faded now to wear outside, so I sleep in it. And each time I put it on, I remember Dad."

She must miss her parents, Cammie thought. *I won-*

der what it's like to be on your own. She felt a little insecure. Never in her life had she gone to bed without her parents kissing her goodnight. How would she manage without Mom taking care of her all the time?

Sonia turned the light off. Cammie stretched in her bed, looking at the dark ceiling. Maybe it was better this way. *I'll work hard, and I'll become the best skater in Skateland,* Cammie thought. She closed her eyes, but her bed felt unfamiliar, and she couldn't go to sleep. She tossed and turned; she counted sheep like her grandmother had once taught her. Nothing helped.

A distant sound of bells reached Cammie's ears. She sat up in bed. There was something—or somebody outside the building. Careful not to wake up Sonia, Cammie got out of bed and tiptoed to the window. There, right in front of the dorm, Auntie's silver icemobile sparkled in the moonlight. A tall, slender figure jumped out of the vehicle, and Cammie recognized Isabelle. Her friend blew a kiss at Auntie.

"See you tomorrow then, sweetie," Auntie croaked and then boomed "Home!" into the microphone. The icemobile took off, and Isabelle ran up the steps into the dorm.

As Cammie got back to bed, she wondered where Isabelle had been that late. But she didn't have time to find the answer because sleep finally came upon her.

Is This What Skateland Is About?

Cammie woke up way before daylight. She opened her eyes and stared at the unfamiliar surroundings. Sonia had already turned on her bed light and was hastily getting into her tights.

"Oh, no, what time is it?" Cammie yawned as she looked out of the window, expecting to see the sunrise. It was completely dark.

"It's five o'clock," Sonia said calmly.

"Is this when you get up?"

"Sure if you want to be in time for the six-o-clock practice."

"Hmm." Somehow when Cammie had thought of moving to Skateland, she hadn't considered the fact that she would have to attend morning practices. Back home, she always went to the rink in the afternoon, after school.

"Why do we have to start practicing so early?" she grunted as she strolled into the bathroom to brush her teeth.

"School starts at eight-thirty," Sonia said.

"How about after school?"

"After school there's another practice."

Cammie looked out of the bathroom, her toothbrush in her hand. "Two practices a day?"

There was nothing but surprise in Sonia's blue eyes. "Why, of course. Moves in the field in the morning, and a freestyle session in the afternoon."

"Ah!" Now Cammie wasn't quite sure if she actually liked Skateland that much. Practicing twice a day? *Stop it*, Cammie said to herself. *You're a future champion, remember? That's what Auntie said to your mom.* Somehow the memory of Auntie's compliment encouraged Cammie, and she didn't mind the early morning hour anymore.

Their skating clothes on, Cammie and Sonia

walked down the steps to the dining room. Mrs. Page was already there pouring tea into big white mugs with skaters in different positions painted on the side. The early morning hour didn't seem to affect Mrs. Page at all; she looked as fresh and cheerful as at night.

"Morning, sweeties," sang Mrs. Page as Sonia and Cammie took their seats next to Dana and Liz, who were already finishing their breakfast.

"You're late," Dana said to Cammie and Sonia as she put the last piece of toast into her mouth.

Liz took a gulp of tea and stood up. "Let's go!"

"See you at the rink!" the two girls said in unison, and a second later the door slammed behind them.

"We'd better hurry," Sonia said.

Cammie looked at the food. There was a steaming bowl of oatmeal in front of her and a small slice of toast with orange marmalade. And a cup of tea, of course. No eggs.

Mrs. Page must have read Cammie's thoughts. "I know it's not enough. You girls work super hard. But what can I do? Regulations—I have no power over them. But if you come to my house one day…oh!"

Mrs. Page patted her round belly. "I'll serve you the best breakfast you can ever dream of."

The big grandfather clock in the corner chimed. Five thirty.

"We'd better go," Sonia said as she picked up her coat.

"Cammie, you're at the Green Rink with Sonia," Mrs. Page said. "Here is the map of Skateland. Think you can find the rink?"

"She's coming with me, so no problem here," Sonia said.

"Good luck!"

They headed for the exit. Before pulling the heavy oak door, Cammie cast a regretful look at the warm dining room. For some reason, she felt cold already—perhaps due to the lack of sleep. Surely she had put on enough clothes. There were two pairs of tights under her leggings; she wore a long-sleeve T-shirt, a sweatshirt, and her red parka complete with a scarf and gloves.

Outside it was so cold that Cammie could barely breathe. As she tried to inhale some air, she felt ice in her nostrils. She had to rub her nose hard to open them.

"Let's move fast; we won't feel the cold that much," Sonia said.

They crossed the lawn, snow crunching under

their feet, and stepped on the icy path. The ice was hard and slippery.

"You're at the Green Rink, so you'll need a green practice dress and green skate guards," Sonia said. "Problem is, we don't want to be late for practice, and the stores are still closed. Perhaps you can go to Smiling Skater after school and get everything there, all right? Do you know where it is?"

Cammie could barely move here lips. "Sure."

She remembered visiting the Smiling Skater store with Alex, and her own fascination with the white skating dress. So she needed a green one now. No problem, it was always exciting to get a new skating dress.

"Hey!" Cammie remembered something. "How about Isabelle? Is she at the Green Rink too?"

"Isabelle Alvarez? No, actually, she's at the Blue Rink. She's in pre-preliminary, I guess."

"Oh! Is this what those rinks are all about? Different levels?"

"Sure. If you look at the map, you'll see that there are eight big official rinks in Skateland. Of course, there are dozens and dozens of small out-door rinks; nobody counts those. But there're eight official ones: pink, green, blue, yellow, and white—those are practice rinks, and then there is the Silver

Rink at the Sport Center; this is where skaters compete."

"Pink, green, blue, white, yellow, and silver—that's six," Cammie muttered. "But you said eight."

"Yes, there are eight of them. But two rinks are restricted; I mean, we're not allowed to go there."

"Oh! Why not?"

"Well, there's the Purple Rink, and actually it's the only official outdoor rink in Skateland. But it's sort of experimental. Mr. Reed, the skate sharpener, works there. He doesn't want skaters practicing there; he says it's dangerous. The ice is…well, not regular there."

"Ah, I see." Cammie remembered the eerie feeling she had had as she watched Mr. Reed do his quintuple jumps on the bright purple surface. "And what's the eighth rink?"

"Ugh!" Sonia looked hesitant, as though she wasn't sure whether Cammie needed her answer or not. "Last on the list is the Black Rink. It's over there, in the Icy Park. But Cammie, never, and I mean it, *never* even think of going there."

"But why not?"

"The Black Rink is the witches' rink. This is where they hang out."

"Ah." That was something Cammie understood

well. Naturally, she would never want to go to a place filled with wicked witches. "I wouldn't even think of going there."

"Perhaps you wouldn't, but other people tried. And they got attacked."

"But why did they go there? Weren't they afraid of witches?"

Sonia slowed down so Cammie could catch her breath. As fragile as Sonia looked, she could develop tremendous speed on ice. Cammie realized that she would be way behind if Sonia weren't trying to stay close to her.

"Not all people believe in witches. A lot of them think that you simply fall down and get hurt or refuse to work hard. They say it's stupid to blame everything on the witches. But I know better."

"So do I." Cammie tried to skate faster. "I saw three witches. I fought with them."

"I've heard about witches since I was a little kid. There's even a poem we learned in preschool here:

Children, never think of skating
In the Icy Park.
For there are wicked witches waiting,
Lurking in the dark.

I remember it. But still a lot of people think only little kids believe in witches. Okay, here is our rink."

The building housing the Green Rink had a triangular shape. Inside, the walls were painted green, and the benches in the locker room were green too. Right away, Cammie noticed that the skaters also wore clothes in different shades of green. She wished she had known about it before. Why hadn't Isabelle warned her? Cammie remembered that Isabelle skated at the Blue Rink. *Why can't I be with her?* she thought. *It would be fun, and I look good in blue.*

When Cammie stepped on the ice, she saw that it was also greenish in color, perfectly smooth, not too hard and not too soft. Excellent ice for practice.

The session was supervised by a slim, athletic-looking woman, her blond hair fastened in the back of her head with a green barrette.

"This is Coach Ferguson. She'll be giving you private lessons. She's kind of strict, but she's very good. She won the nationals twice," Sonia said.

"Attention, skaters!" Coach Ferguson clapped her hands, claiming everybody's attention. There were about fifteen skaters at the rink—most of them girls, though there were three boys. Everybody except Cammie wore something green. She hugged herself, as though by doing it she could become smaller, her inappropriate clothes less visible.

Cammie was sure Coach Ferguson would make some comment about her looks, but the woman's eyes merely brushed Cammie and moved to another skater. "Basic stroking counterclockwise, please."

The skaters lined up at the boards on the right and followed one another around the rink. Cammie skated after Sonia, desperately trying to catch up. Boy, how come she had never realized how slow she was? Come on, she had always been the fastest skater in her cardio class. So why was she behind now?

"Change direction," Coach Ferguson said.

Everybody turned. Cammie didn't react fast enough, got on her toe pick, and almost fell.

"Good save!" Coach Ferguson barked.

Cammie felt her cheeks burning. Was the coach teasing her? She cast a quick glance at the woman. No, Coach Ferguson didn't look upset; she was actually smiling.

They moved to forward crossovers; faster and faster they went. It was funny how Cammie had never found that particular step difficult. She felt her legs getting tired. She clenched her teeth and tried harder—like never before.

Backward crossovers felt easier; Cammie even let herself relax a little. Their next assignment was three turns (easy), brackets (not quite that simple), rockers and counters (uh-huh, Cammie could really work on those).

Coach Ferguson was moving from one skater to another, correcting their steps. Cammie's face burnt; she felt sweaty. She skated to the boards, pulled off her sweatshirt, took a sip of water from her bottle. *Funny how something so simple can make you tired*, she thought. But it was still early in the morning. Cammie wasn't used to getting up at five o'clock. She stood and watched the other skaters. All of them were good; almost everybody was better than her. She would catch up. Cammie Wester wasn't a person to give up so easily.

"What do you think you're doing?"

Cammie flinched and turned around to see Coach Ferguson study her face with cold, gray eyes. "I'm a little tired."

"I understand. It's your first practice in Skateland. However, standing and watching others skate will lead you nowhere. You can't be idle. Keep moving. Do something that's easy for you."

Coach Ferguson skated away. Cammie sighed heavily and let go of the board. She moved to the middle and did a series of forward three turns. There. Those were easy for her, perhaps since Alex and she had practiced them for hours at the Witch of Pride's rink.

The rest of the practice was as well organized as the beginning. Cammie could see that everybody in Skateland was really serious about skating. There was no hanging at the boards, no chatting, and no joking. Just work.

Finally, at eight in the morning, they were done. In the locker room, Cammie changed into her school clothes. She thought it would be great to take a break from skating until she remembered that school was far away, and she was supposed to skate, not ride there. There was nothing Cammie could do though, so she followed Sonia reluctantly.

Outside the sun had already risen, but it was still cold. The way to school seemed endless.

"How much time does it take to get there—an hour?" Cammie asked, panting.

"Forty minutes," Sonia said, sounding apologetic. "There's a shorter way through the Icy Park, but we'd better go around it."

Cammie smirked. "Because of the witches, right?"

"Cammie, they are real, and you know it."

"I know." Cammie thought for a moment and decided against skating through the Icy Park. Each time she had met a witch during her first visit to Skateland, she had been forced to do several skating assignments, and she didn't feel in the mood to do any more moves in the field.

Cammie was happy to get to school because that was where she could finally get out of her skates. She changed into sneakers, enjoying the warm feeling in her toes.

The first person she saw when she entered the sixth grade classroom was Jeff—the boy whom Alex and she had delivered from the Witch of Injuries.

"Cammie! Wow!" Just like Sonia, Jeff was really excited to see Cammie.

"How are you?" Cammie looked at Jeff, noticing how much the boy had changed. He was still small—shorter than her—but he no longer looked weak and sad but perfectly healthy and happy. His brown eyes lit up with joy.

"I'm doing great, Cammie. I started working on my double axel this morning. Can you believe it? I fell six times, but I didn't break anything. Actually, we skate at the same rink. Only I was so busy that I didn't recognize you."

Cammie laughed. "I know. But a double axel? Wow, I wish I could—"

"Good morning, class!" The teacher had just entered the classroom and was giving Cammie and Jeff a meaningful look.

As quickly as she could, Cammie took her seat at the desk next to Jeff's.

"For those who don't know my name or forgot it, I'm Mr. Rocker." The short, dark-haired man wrote his name on the blackboard with big capital letters.

Cammie's mouth dropped open. It was unbelievable. Even the man who taught English in Skateland had a skating name.

"As I promised you last time, we will have a spelling bee this morning," Mr. Rocker said. "Do you want to come up front, Nikki?"

Cammie watched as a small girl with very short hair walked forward and stood next to the teacher.

"Here you go: *twizzle!*"

"*T-w-i-z-z-1-e. Twizzle,*" Nikki said.

Mr. Rocker beamed. "Excellent!"

Cammie stared at the teacher in amazement. How could it be? Even at their English lessons, they were going to spell skating terms.

She was right. The next student—a boy by the

name of Steve—had to spell the word *mohawk*. Cammie flinched. She wasn't sure she would be able to spell it right. Steve, however, completed the assignment successfully.

"Jeff, your turn," Mr. Rocker said.

Jeff went forward, looking excited. He winked at Cammie. She smiled back.

"All right, how about s*alchow*."

Jeff shifted from one foot to another. Cammie didn't feel comfortable either. She had never thought of writing down the names of the jumps.

"*S-o-w-c-o-w. Salchow*," Jeff said softly.

Mr. Rocker slapped himself on the lap. "No! The correct spelling is *s-a-1-c-h-o-w. Salchow*. And what was that you said? *Sow cow*, right? Well, well, you probably look like a cow on ice."

The students roared with laughter. Jeff didn't look offended; in fact, he joined everybody else eagerly. Cammie also smiled.

"Now how about you, new girl? What's your name?"

Cammie sat up straighter. Mr. Rocker was looking at her.

"Cammie Wester, sir."

"All right, Cammie, come here."

Cammie took her place next to the teacher's

desk, feeling a little worried. What kind of word was she going to get?

"Could you spell *axel*, please?"

Cammie sighed deeply. Great, that couldn't be too difficult. The word only had four letters.

"*A-1-e-x. Axel*," she said loudly.

There was a short pause, and then the students laughed.

"*Axel*, not *Alex!*" somebody said.

What? Oh no, they were right. What had Cammie been thinking? She had really spelled *Alex* instead of *axel*. How stupid!

Mr. Rocker was laughing as loudly as everybody else. "Alex, huh? He must be your boyfriend."

That was the worst thing the teacher could have said. Cammie felt her whole face getting hotter and hotter; then the heat spread to her neck and her hands, then—

"It's all right, you'll get it next time," Mr. Rocker said. "You may take your seat now."

Cammie hung her head. She sat down, afraid to look around.

Jeff reached for her hand from his desk. "Hey, is Alex here too?" he whispered.

She shook her head.

Jeff nodded sympathetically. Cammie stared at

the blackboard. Alex wasn't her boyfriend; just...a friend. And yet she missed him. He should have come to Skateland.

Their next lesson was science, and the teacher, Mrs. Stevenson, told them about different kinds of ice—soft and hard—and what it took to make ice surfaces just right.

At the math lesson, they worked on ice geometry. The teacher told them about different kinds of circles with radii and diameters and also about triangles, like isosceles (Cammie was afraid someone would ask her to spell that term). At the end of the lesson, the teacher encouraged them to try those figures on ice at their next practice session.

Mrs. Collins, their English literature teacher, gave the students a list of books about skating, most of which were biographies of famous skaters. Cammie made a mental note to go to the library so she could start reading some of them.

Cammie ate her lunch at the school cafeteria— a turkey sandwich with a small salad. She wanted something sweet, but they were selling nothing she liked. Okay, maybe she could stop at Sweet Blades on her way to their afternoon practice.

After lunch, they studied the history of figure skating at their history class, and during the music lesson—the last one of the day—they listened to different genres of music, from classical to rock and rap. The teacher explained the difference to the students and encouraged them to think what kinds of music were good for skating.

The lessons were over, and even though Cammie wanted to take a short walk to Main Square, Sonia told her there wasn't really that much time.

"You'll get tired if you go to those different stores," Sonia said. "Don't you want to go home for a short nap? Afternoon practice doesn't start till four."

Cammie looked at her watch. It was two thirty. "I have to buy a green skating dress anyway."

Sonia nodded. "That's right. Will it be okay if I don't go with you? You know the way, don't you?"

"Sure!" Cammie said enthusiastically. Of course she could find her way around Skateland. Well, of course, it would be better if someone went to Main Square with her. Doing things alone wasn't that much fun. Cammie looked around the lobby, hoping that Jeff was around and he might want to go with her. Nope. He was also gone. Funny how kids in Skateland thought of nothing but skating practices.

Double Loop

C ammie went to Main Square alone. Once she got there, she forgot that she was tired and that she had another practice session that day. Main Square was so picturesque. The stores around the perfectly round rink flashed with multicolored signs; little kids played tag on the ice, and people of different ages whooshed past Cammie, apparently trying to make their appointments.

Cammie went to Smiling Skater and bought a green practice dress. The racks were filled with skating clothes and tights of all possible sizes and colors, but Cammie decided she had no time to try them on. Instead, she crossed the street and entered the Sweet Blades bakery. Boy, she was hungry! Her stomach was rumbling like a hungry bear, and she still remembered the delicious skating pastries she had feasted on with Alex.

"Can I have a skating pastry, please?" Cammie handed three dollars to the saleslady.

"Dark or white?" the woman asked excitedly.

Cammie wanted to say *both*. She was so hungry; she felt as though she could eat an elephant. But she had to be reasonable. She only had about forty minutes before her afternoon practice, so filling up with sugar wouldn't be a good idea at all. But how could she make the right choice? Both kinds of pastries were terrific; the dark ones were made of dark chocolate and filled with vanilla cream. The white pastries were covered with white chocolate and had chocolate cream inside. Attached to the pastries formed in the shape of skating boots were blades made of hard candy. Yes, and of course, customers were allowed to pick out bootlaces of the color and flavor of their choice: cherry, orange, blueberry, and many, many more. Everything was delicious, and if only Cammie could eat all the sweets she wanted!

Cammie sighed and asked for a dark pastry with a cup of tea. She sat at a small, round table in front of the window that offered a perfect view of the little kids playing at the Main Square rink. A little girl wearing a red scarf and matching gloves was chasing a boy in a blue hat, both laughing and screaming with joy. For a moment, Cammie wished she could join them and skate for fun, without paying attention to her edges or balance. But it was impossible. As tired as she was, she had to make the practice. She sipped her tea. It was hot, and it made her whole body feel pleasantly warm. She closed her eyes ... just for a minute.

When Cammie opened her eyes and looked at her watch, it was a quarter of four. Her practice would start in only fifteen minutes, and she had to get to the rink and change. She stuffed the rest of her pastry in her mouth and ran out of the store. As fast as she could, Cammie crossed the circular rink and glided along a hard, icy path. At least the Green Rink wasn't too far away from Main Square.

Cammie didn't remember ever skating that fast, but she made it to the rink with seven minutes to spare before the official practice time. *At least I won't need to warm up. I feel pretty warm already*, she thought as she changed into her new green dress. *Not too bad*, Cammie concluded as she gave her reflection in the mirror a thorough look. A pink dress would probably be better, but green would do too. Cammie remembered that her first private lesson with Coach Ferguson was scheduled for that afternoon. She'd better get on the ice.

As Cammie had expected, the other skaters were already in the middle of the rink. Unlike Cammie, they had come to the building way before the practice began so as not to waste a minute of the precious time. Cammie felt a twinge of remorse. Next time, she would do the same.

Cammie barely had time to go over her jumps and spins, when Coach Ferguson approached her. "Ready?"

Cammie nodded, feeling her knees shake. She knew how important it was to make a good impression on the new coach.

"All right, show me what you can do," Coach Ferguson said.

Cammie started with her spins—scratch spin, sit spin, and camel spin—and the coach nodded in approval. No surprise there; spins had always been easy for Cammie. She demonstrated her spiral position—not bad—went into an outside spread eagle and did an Ina Bauer. Everything was going well so far.

"Let's move to jumps," Coach Ferguson said. "I want to see your single jumps first."

Of course, that wasn't a problem at all.

"You have good technique," Coach Ferguson said.

Cammie felt a rush of excitement. How cool! She wasn't the worst skater at the Green Rink after all. She would still show everybody what Cammie Wester could do.

"Axel, please," Coach Ferguson said.

Cammie managed to land her single axel just right. The jump was secure with a good ride out. Cammie's hard work had paid off. She remembered how difficult the axel had once been for her. Of course, it was half a year and many, many hard falls ago.

The coach suggested that Cammie try her double jumps, and that was when problems began to emerge. Cammie started with the double salchow— the easiest double jump for her. She tried hard, and she landed it right, well … almost. Her landing was a little shaky, but at least she didn't two-foot the jump.

"Not bad; I'll take that," Coach Ferguson said.

So she wasn't that bad. Whoopee!

Cammie landed her double toe loop successfully.

"Good. Now about your double loop?" Coach Ferguson suggested.

Cammie had only started working on her double

loop a month ago, and she wasn't even close to landing it. But she felt so strong and confident now.

Cammie glided across the rink with as much confidence as she could master. She did a forward inside three turn, got on her backward outside edge, bent her knee…a split second later, she sat on the ice, her new skating dress splattered with snow.

"Do it again," Coach Ferguson said.

Cammie clenched her teeth and went through the same routine. She fell again, this time, on her thigh. Immediately it began to throb.

"Don't muscle your way up; let the edge take you up in the air," Coach Ferguson said.

Cammie moaned, making sure the coach wouldn't hear her. The loop was a tricky jump. There was no toe to pick with and no natural spinning motion like in the salchow. Cammie merely didn't have enough momentum that would get her high enough to do two revolutions. Even the single loop had once been very, very hard for Cammie.

"Bend your skating knee more," Coach Ferguson said.

Cammie obeyed, but all she could manage was a very shaky single loop.

"I can't believe it," Cammie whined. "I have been working on it for so long!"

"Don't worry; some jumps are simply more difficult than the others."

"But why?"

"It's all about your muscle memory," Coach Ferguson said. "Sometimes it takes your body months to remember how to do a certain element right. Do you want to try that jump again?"

Cammie tried several more times. Twice she completed two revolutions in the air but landed on both feet.

"It's fine; you're getting the feel of the jump," the coach said. "Try it again."

Cammie swung her arms around as hard as she could. Bang! There she was on both feet again, and she even had a hard time to keep herself from falling.

"You over-rotated it," Coach Ferguson said. "All right, I think it's enough for today. You need your rest."

Cammie stared at her. "But how about my double flip? We haven't even started working on it."

"It's all right. You need to be able to do your double loop consistently before we move to the flip."

"But I can do it. I actually landed it and not just once, several times."

That's not quite true, a small voice whispered in Cammie's ear.

She flinched. "Well, actually, I fall on it all the time, but … but it's almost there."

Why couldn't the coach understand that Cammie simply had no time to waste? Jeff was of the same age, and he was working on his double axel!

A weak smile touched the coach's lips—the first one Cammie noticed on the woman's stern face. "Let's not rush it. Now here is one more thing. I don't see why we can't get you ready for Skateland Annual Competition. We still have almost two months to prepare for it, so I'm sure you'll be all right."

"Oh, that's great!" Cammie said enthusiastically.

"Now what level are you on? Preliminary I presume?"

"Yes, but … I competed in pre-juvenile, but I haven't taken my tests yet."

"All right, so this is what needs to be done first. I want you to concentrate on your pre-juvenile moves in the field and free style. The next testing session is only in a month, so you'll have to work hard. No slacking off!"

Coach Ferguson's voice sounded stern, especially when she warned Cammie against slacking off.

And yet, when Cammie looked the woman in the face, she saw that the coach was actually smiling. It was a nice change from all the criticism Cammie had been getting so far. Unable to contain her excitement, Cammie grinned.

She spent the rest of the session practicing her double loop. There was hardly any improvement, but Cammie remembered the coach's advice to give it time. Well, she would do exactly what her coach had told her, and one day, she would surely become a champion.

Closer to the end of the practice, Cammie was so exhausted that she could barely jump. Not willing to take a break lest Coach Ferguson rebuke her again, she stroked around the rink watching other skaters.

In the middle, Sonia was working on her triple toe loop, looking very serious. She kept falling, but each time, she got up and tried again. Jeff did a series of split jumps across the rink and winked at Cammie. She winked back. *Should I try those?* she thought. *No, I'm too tired.* Her greatest desire was to get out of her skates.

Finally the practice was over, and they skated home—another half hour of gliding on hard ice.

The last block was the worst. Cammie tagged behind, her legs screaming with pain.

Sonia stopped to wait for her. "That's it. Put on your guards now."

Oh! It was good Sonia had reminded her about the guards because Cammie would have walked in with her blades unprotected. She slipped on her guards and clomped up the steps to the third floor. Once they reached their room, Cammie fell on her bed, unable to move.

"Go soak in the bathtub. It will help," Sonia said sympathetically.

"I can't," Cammie moaned. All she wanted to do was to close her eyes and drift away.

"You'll get better; I promise." Sonia went to the bathroom, and Cammie heard the sound of water filling the bathtub.

"Get in first. You need it."

Reluctantly, Cammie took her skates off and wobbled to the bathroom. Her body hurt. She took off her clothes and lowered herself in steaming hot water. "It's too hot!"

"It has to be hot. It will help your muscles to relax!" Sonia's voice came from the room.

Sonia was right. A couple of seconds later, Cammie's body got used to the hot water, and she felt very, very nice. Her eyes closed by themselves. She felt warm and comfortable; she was gliding, gliding away…

"Cammie, don't sleep in the bathtub."

Cammie opened her eyes. Sonia stood next to her, Cammie's pink robe in her hand. "Put it on, and let's go down to dinner."

"No!" Cammie groaned. "I'm not hungry at all. I just want to sleep."

Sonia's blue eyes narrowed in concern. "But you can't live without food. You won't have energy for skating or anything. Come on!"

Feeling like a victim, Cammie climbed out of the bathtub and got into her robe. Could she really go to the dining room wearing her bathrobe? Well, if she couldn't, Sonia would have told her.

Cammie was right; many girls in the living room wore their bathrobes.

"First thing you do after practice is take a hot bath," Sonia said. "We often don't have enough time to put on anything else."

"How about you? You didn't take a bath. I was in the bathtub all the time," Cammie said as she noticed Sonia's jeans and sweatshirt. She felt mad at herself. She had fallen asleep in the bathtub, and poor Sonia couldn't even take her bath.

Sonia waved her hand dismissively. "Never mind. I'm used to it."

They sat down at their table. Mrs. Page brought them their dinner: steak, mashed potatoes, and green beans. Before Cammie smelled the food, she didn't think she was hungry; but when she started eating, she ate and ate and couldn't stop.

"Going to ballet class?" Dana asked Sonia.

Sonia nodded.

Cammie put down her fork. "A ballet class? Tonight?"

"Tonight," Liz said, giving Cammie a mocking look.

"It's optional," Sonia said quietly. "Don't worry; it's only your first day. Better do your homework."

Cammie groaned. "Oh, no, I forgot we also had homework."

"No slacking off in Skateland," Dana and Liz said together in a low croaky voice, apparently mimicking someone.

That wasn't fair. Cammie had been working so hard the whole day! Her face burnt, and she lowered her eyes so that the mean girls wouldn't see her tears. By the way, where was Isabelle?

"Does Isabelle ever eat here?" Cammie asked the girls.

Liz chewed on her green bean. "Hmm, sometimes."

"She probably thinks she's too good for this humble little place." Dana giggled as she sipped her water.

"She hangs out with very important people," Liz said in a deep and dignified voice.

Everybody except Cammie laughed. Even Sonia smiled.

The important person must be Auntie, Cammie thought. She decided to find Isabelle tomorrow and ask her why she was rarely in the dorm.

Back in their room, Sonia changed into ballet tights and a leotard.

"You're still going to that ballet lesson? After all the skating practice you've had?" Cammie shook her head. She didn't think she could make her body do one single dancing or skating move.

Sonia smiled. "Don't worry, it will get easier. Once you are finished with your homework, go to bed; don't wait for me."

Sonia left. Reluctantly, Cammie took her schoolbooks and notebooks out of her bag and sat down at the desk. She would do her math problems—the most difficult assignment. Her body was too tired; she couldn't concentrate. Perhaps she should start with something easier, like history. She opened the thick volume of *Figure Skating History*. There were too many names and dates. On top of everything else, her chair felt very uncomfortable. She crossed her legs, folded them, let them dangle freely—nothing helped. *Why do they have such hard chairs in the skaters' dorm?* she wondered. It would be better if she sat on her bed; at least she would feel nice and soft. She moved to the bed. Yes, it was much more comfortable. She got under the covers to feel warmer, put her head on the pillow. Yes, that was nice. Now what was she reading? *Figure skating is believed to have started as early as 10,000 b.c. in The Netherlands.* In The Netherlands? Where was The Netherlands? Cammie didn't remember, but it didn't matter. Okay, so figure skating started in The Netherlands and then...

The room spun around Cammie, and she followed, going faster and faster in her scratch spin until she found herself in The Netherlands, skating with people wearing long skirts and cylindrical hats, but she couldn't land her double loop. Oh no, what was her problem?

When Cammie woke up, the lights in the room were dimmed. Only the small table lamp on the desk was lit, and Sonia sat at the desk, her head bent over her schoolbooks.

Oh no, I haven't even finished my homework, Cammie thought. *I've got to get up.* But her bed felt so soft that she decided she would rest another minute, just one more minute, and then she would study.

Next time Cammie woke up, it was dark in the room, and Sonia was asleep in her bed. Another sound of a bell came from downstairs, and Cammie realized that was what had woken her up. Apparently Auntie had just brought Isabelle back to the dorm. *I need to go talk to Isabelle now,* Cammie thought. And she almost, almost got up; but her eyelids were heavy, so she fell asleep again. The next time she woke up, it was five o'clock in the morning.

PUBLIC SKATING

Cammie's second day in Skateland was pretty much like the first—long and hard. Her third day felt a little easier; the fourth was even better. By the end of the first week, Cammie didn't even understand how she had lived before without two practices a day, without skating everywhere. She also realized that coming to school unprepared was completely unacceptable. After Mr. Stevens, her skating history teacher, rebuked her in front of the whole class for not knowing what the Dutch waltz was, Cammie made a point of studying hard every evening.

Training in Skateland was rigorous. Now Cammie understood why not that many skaters her age wanted to move there. In addition to two two-hour daily practices, skaters were expected to go to school, take ballet classes, and work out in the gym. Of course, Sonia had told Cammie that ballet was optional, but Coach Ferguson apparently didn't agree with that.

"You're doing well in your ballet classes, I presume," the coach said during Cammie's third private lesson.

Slightly surprised, Cammie repeated what Sonia had told her.

"Optional!" Coach Ferguson smirked. "Skating is optional too; have you ever thought of that? There's no law saying that skating is mandatory for children."

Hmm. Perhaps skating wasn't something Cammie was required to do, but she loved it very, very much.

"Anyway, I expect you to take ballet, and you'd better be good. Now, how about trying this spin again?" Coach Ferguson hadn't even waited for Cammie's response. The matter was settled. Now Cammie didn't even have time in the evening to do her homework.

"Listen to the teachers during classes and try to memorize what they say. I don't have to study at all," Jeff said when Cammie complained to him that she absolutely had no time to study.

It was easy for him to say. Jeff was a straight-A student, the best in Cammie's class. Unfortunately, things weren't that easy for Cammie. She tried to concentrate and listen to her teachers, but her mind was always somewhere else. How could she master that double loop without landing on both feet? And why did she keep falling from her double salchow? When Cammie lived at home, she never thought that much about skating.

"I'm not very attentive in class either," Sonia said when Cammie complained she didn't remember a thing of what their history teacher had been saying. "I have to study before I go to bed."

"Aren't you tired at night? Don't you want to go to sleep?"

Sonia finished lacing her skates and gave Cammie a sad look. "You'll get used to it. Are you ready to go now?"

Cammie tapped her feet against the floor. Her laces were tied just right—not too tight, not too loose. "Let's go."

It was Saturday, and Cammie and Sonia were

on their way to the Silver Rink, the biggest rink in Skateland, the official competition arena. Cammie had already skated there once, during her very first competition, and she had won the gold in her category. She remembered how luxurious the rink was. It would be fun to go there and skate on the best ice in Skateland.

On Saturday, they didn't have school or official practice sessions. Instead, everybody went to the Sport Center, which housed the Silver Rink, for a three-hour session.

"It's actually a public skate, but everybody likes those sessions," Sonia said. "We don't have to do our programs or practice our moves."

"So what shall I do there?"

"Whatever you want. Have fun. You will meet people from other rinks and see how they are doing. And you don't have to wear your rink color. You can pick out any clothes you want. "

"So there will be many people at the rink," Cammie said. They stroked in the direction of the Sport Center. Cammie was in a really good mood. They had been allowed to sleep in. Breakfast was served at nine o'clock, and until then, Cammie had snuggled in bed enjoying the softness of the pillow and the warmth of her down comforter. She would open her eyes, look at the sky outside getting lighter and lighter, close her eyes again, drift back to sleep, and wake up again. After breakfast, Cammie and Sonia worked out in the gym, so by the time lunch was served, Cammie felt strong and ready to skate. Perhaps she would see Isabelle at the rink? It was unbelievable. Cammie had spent a week in Skateland, and she still hadn't had a single opportunity to talk to her friend.

"Yes, there'll be quite a few people there," Sonia said. "But it doesn't matter. The rink is huge, and it's fun to see how other skaters have progressed, what new moves they have learned."

My jumps aren't that good yet, Cammie thought anxiously. But she told herself to calm down. After all, she was going to a public session, not a competition.

They changed into their skating dresses in the locker room. Tired of her green outfit, Cammie put on her favorite hot pink sweater with a black skirt. She stepped on the glossy ice that sparkled like silver and glided forward. Oh, what a feeling it was! Cammie spread her arms, got on her right outside edge, and went along the boards in a spiral position. Now that she was taking ballet, she was sure her posture was even better. Cammie completed the move, circled the rink in fast backward crossovers, and took a closer look at the skaters who were already there.

Sonia was right; there were people of all ages at the rink—from tiny tots to adults, and everybody was wearing nice clothes. Cammie looked at a teenage boy executing one triple salchow after another. She smiled at a tiny girl who was practicing her swizzles with concentration. Cammie watched an older woman rise from a low sit spin and then … oh, yes! A tall slender girl moved across the rink practicing circular footwork. The girl's shiny black hair whirled around her face. The girl turned around, and Cammie saw the perfectly straight nose and thick eyelashes.

"Isabelle! It's you!"

Isabelle stopped midway. Cammie rushed to her side. "Where have you been all this time? I've been looking for you everywhere!"

Something like annoyance flickered in Isabelle's dark eyes, but a split second later, the older girl was all smiles. "Hey, Cammie, it's great to see you. So, how are you doing? Do you like it in Skateland? Cool place, isn't it?"

"What? Yes, of course, it's great but … but—"

"Listen, I really need to practice now," Isabelle

said. "I have very important tests coming in only a month."

"What? Tests? Oh, yes, I'm going to be tested too. What level are you? I'm taking pre-juvenile tests."

Isabelle pressed her lips as though she didn't like the question. "Pre-preliminary. But as soon as I land my axel, I'll get higher."

"Oh, yes; how's your axel?"

Isabelle tossed her hair to the back. "It's great, actually. I've landed it several times in practice, so all I need is more consistency."

"Oh, I'm so happy for you. Listen, could we—"

Isabelle interrupted her before Cammie suggested going to Sweet Blades, Smiling Skater—any place just to be together. "I really have to practice now, Cammie. I'll see you later, okay?"

Without saying another word, Isabelle skated away. She got to the opposite side of the rink, took a starting position, and went into her footwork again. Cammie remained where she was, her mouth wide open. Huh? Was that all? Isabelle didn't even want to talk to her? She was too busy. No, that couldn't be true. Wasn't it Isabelle who had insisted that Cammie come to Skateland, promising her they would spend lots of time together? And now, not only had Cammie not seen Isabelle during the week, her friend couldn't even find time for her on Saturday.

Well, it's not that Isabelle doesn't want to hang out with me; she just wants to practice, Cammie thought.

A black girl wearing a bright yellow dress went into a high waltz jump, almost cutting Cammie off. "Sorry!" she yelled as Cammie dashed by her.

Cammie waved at the girl, signaling she was okay. She had to keep moving; it wasn't a good idea to stand in the middle of the rink with everybody else practicing. She tried to work on her moves, but she couldn't concentrate. What was going on? Why didn't Isabelle want to talk to her? Had Cammie hurt her? Isabelle's sudden enthusiasm for skating didn't look like a good excuse. Hadn't Cammie and Isabelle stuck together during cardio and public sessions back home? Next to her older friend, Cammie had always felt special. She wanted that feeling back. She needed it so badly!

Cammie looked in Isabelle's direction. Isabelle looked as though she was done with her footwork and was trying to execute an axel. She jumped, under-rotated, and landed on both feet. Cammie grimaced. She knew what Isabelle felt. The axel was tricky; you were supposed to jump forward and start rotating while you were already in the air. It was very confusing.

Isabelle tried again; then again and again. No luck. For about ten minutes, Cammie watched her friend; then she skated toward Isabelle.

"Isabelle, try waltz jumps—loops and waltz jumps—back spins," Cammie said. "That's what Coach Louise always recommends. It helped me."

Isabelle stopped and looked at Cammie with annoyance. "Why don't you leave me alone, Miss Coach?"

Stunned, Cammie stepped back, lost her balance, and fell hard. "Ouch!" She got up rubbing her butt.

"Exactly!" Isabelle sounded almost happy. "Before teaching others, why don't you learn to stand on ice yourself?"

Before Cammie could say a word, Isabelle skated away leaving Cammie where she was—in total shock. What had she done? She had only been trying to help. Why was Isabelle so nasty?

Unable to fight tears, Cammie lowered her head. She rubbed her nose and cheek with her glove. Tears welled in her eyes, blurring everything in front of her.

Stop it! She told herself. *You can't fall apart like*

this. You're a future champion, remember? Determined to get the most out of her practice, Cammie glided forward on her left foot, went into a mohawk, backward crossovers, and entered into a fast scratch spin—her best move.

Bang! She didn't understand what had happened. She spun, and the next moment she was on the ice, and her left thigh was sore. Wincing, she got up. Falling from a spin? That was unusual. Although … no, she hadn't fallen by herself. Because she remembered a strong blow right before she went down, as though someone had collided with her.

"It was her!" a childish voice said next to Cammie.

"What?" Cammie looked down at a tiny girl not older than five wearing a black velvet skating dress.

"It was that girl who skated into you," the little girl said, pointing to someone on the other side of the rink.

Cammie followed the direction of the little girl's hand and felt as though blood had frozen in her veins. The little girl was pointing to Isabelle, yes, to Isabelle, her charming friend, who was now doing a terrific scratch spin. It was she who had collided with Cammie.

Cammie sighed deeply trying to calm down.

The little girl was still looking at her, her brown eyes rounded with concern.

"Well," Cammie said, trying to look composed, "it can happen to anybody. You, little one, be careful too because there are many skaters at the rink, so someone may accidentally skate into you."

"It wasn't an accident," the little girl said, looking Cammie straight in the eyes.

"What?" Cammie's left thigh still hurt. She probably needed a break.

"That girl skated into you on purpose," the little girl said. "I saw everything."

"Keep that ice pack on your thigh as long as you can, and you'll be all right by tomorrow," Sonia said.

"It's too cold!" Cammie sat on a bench in the locker room, an ice pack on her left thigh.

"If you don't, you'll have a big bruise tomorrow, and it will be hard to practice. Boy, that Isabelle is nasty!" Sonia stood up shaking her head. "I don't think you should skate any longer today. Let's go home."

"What're you talking about?" Cammie raised her eyes from the icepack. "Isabelle just collided with me."

"She wanted you to fall," Sonia said softly.

"It's silly!"

Sonia shrugged her skinny shoulders. "Everybody saw it. Jeff did and Mary and Jeanna—you probably don't know them; they're from the Blue Rink. But they know Isabelle; she does it all the time."

"And I'm telling you, it was an accident," Cammie said angrily.

Sonia looked away. "You don't have to believe me, but it's true. Isabelle was trying to attack you. And there's one more thing…"

Cammie waited for Sonia to go on, but the girl merely shook her head, looking scared.

"What thing?"

Sonia straightened her skating skirt and ran her hands against her sides, casting a nervous look at the door.

"What? Come on; tell me! Sonia!"

"You see… When we were skating, I think I saw the Witch of Injuries hiding in the bleachers."

"What? Are you sure?" Cammie's heartbeat accelerated.

Sonia nodded. "I'm positive. Jeff recognized her too."

"But maybe… it was someone else? Just… some strange woman?"

"She held Jeff captive for a year. Do you think he could miss her?"

"But why does the witch keep coming to the rink? They shouldn't have let her in."

Sonia grinned bitterly. "And who's going to stop her?"

"Security? I don't know."

"Don't you remember what we talked about? Nobody here believes witches even exist."

"Oh, that's just too stupid!"

Ignoring Sonia's warnings, Cammie dropped the icepack on the bench and ran out of the locker room. She headed right to the exit, where a security guard, a tall black man in a uniform, stood staring impassively at the setting sun outside.

"Sir? Can I talk to you for a minute?" Cammie asked. She was slightly out of breath.

The guard looked at her. "What is it, miss?"

"The Witch of Injuries is here!" Cammie blurted out.

The guard's facial expression changed from indifference to concern. "What? What did you say?"

Cammie told him about the witches that inhabited Skateland, about their ferocious attacks on skaters. "And I heard they couldn't be asked to leave Skateland forever, so at least they have to be stopped from coming to practices. You must have seen the Witch of Injuries come in. A tall skinny woman walking on crutches, all bandaged."

The man's lips spread, showing his perfectly white teeth. Now he was laughing openly, without trying to hide his amusement. "Listen, young lady. What's your name, by the way?"

"Cammie. Cammie Wester."

"Listen, Cammie Wester. I know everybody who comes to this rink. And let me assure you, I would never let in anybody who could potentially harm a skater. Do you believe me?"

"Yes, but the witch—"

"Yes, and speaking about witches, I know, you—skaters—have a very rich imagination. It must come with the sport." The man laughed again. "When I was a little boy, I believed in the Tooth Fairy too. You'll get over your fear of witches."

"No, no, you don't understand! Those witches are nothing like the Tooth Fairy. They are real!"

"Yeah, sure. Just like old Santa."

"Look, let me try to explain—"

"Cammie, why don't you go home and relax?" the man said. "I promise you you'll be all right. If you want to play those witch games, how about doing it in the dorm? I'm really not supposed to talk to people."

Disgruntled, Cammie went back to the locker room. Sonia wasn't there anymore. Most of the skaters were still on the ice. Cammie looked at her thigh, sighed, and decided she'd better call it a day. She picked up her ice pack, tied it around her thigh, and skated back to the dorm. Perhaps she could catch up on her homework.

She sat bent over her books when the familiar sound of the Auntie's sled bell reached her ear. Yes! So Isabelle was home early. Good. Finally she would be able to talk to her friend. Cammie rushed to the window. The silver sled stood in front of the dorm. Auntie sat in the front seat in a relaxed posture, one leg crossed over the other, explaining something to Isabelle. Isabelle seemed to be listening very attentively; Cammie even saw her nod a couple of times.

What are they talking about? Cammie wondered. It had to be something important because Isabelle's face looked serious; the old expression of aloofness seemed to have gone. *I'll go downstairs and talk to her,* Cammie decided. *It's now or never.*

She pulled on her parka and grabbed her gloves, casting another quick look outside. Auntie and Isabelle were still deep in conversation. Cammie walked out of her room and ran down the steps and out of the building. It was there that she felt the first twinge of doubt. What if Isabelle refused to talk to her? She had been so cold and distant at the rink. And Auntie … she was so sweet and nice to Cammie at the beginning, but had she talked to her even once since Cammie moved to Skateland?

Cammie took a tentative step in the direction of Isabelle and Auntie. They were still talking passionately, without looking around. Not really knowing why she was doing it, Cammie stepped to the right and crouched behind a snow-covered shrub. At that moment, she wasn't thinking of eavesdropping; she simply didn't feel like facing Auntie and Isabelle right away. Whatever they were discussing seemed important to them, so if she interrupted the conversation, they might get mad.

I'll wait for Auntie to leave, Cammie decided, *and then I'll talk to Isabelle. I'll ask her why she doesn't like me anymore. And if I've done something wrong, I'll apologize.* Once Cammie came to the decision, she felt less scared, more relaxed. She made herself more comfortable getting off her feet and sinking in the soft powdery snow. She knew she wouldn't last long in the crouched position; her legs hurt too much. Okay, when was Auntie going to leave? Cammie surely couldn't sit on the snow too long. She'd get cold. Yet at the same moment, Cammie realized that from where she was she could hear Isabelle and Auntie perfectly.

"I can't. I've been trying hard, you know. It's a tricky jump," Isabelle whined.

"Look, you think I don't know it? Everybody has problems with the axel. Landing it brings a skater to a higher level. It's a big step. Be patient, you'll get it."

"All you say is *be patient*," Isabelle wailed. "It's been over a year. I need help."

Cammie heard Auntie give out a deep sigh. There was a moment's silence.

"Okay, so what do you suggest?" Auntie finally said.

"You see, I kind of landed the axel once or twice. So I can basically do it; I'm just inconsistent. So I was thinking... if I could get some extra help... just a little... I might be able to land it during the test session."

There was a scratching sound of an icemobile blade scraping against the ice as Auntie shifted her weight from one leg to the other. "And you absolutely need to move up to the juvenile level, is that right? Anything lower is beneath you."

"Auntie, you don't understand!" Now Cammie heard tears in Isabelle's voice. "I'm almost seventeen. I have to test and compete with six-and seven-year-olds. How would you feel?"

"Skating is not about age; it's about skill," Auntie said quietly.

"Come on! I know that's not what you think."

"That's what the rulebook says."

"Forget the rulebook. I need help."

Cammie looked through the white, icy limbs and saw Auntie stretch. In her white fur coat and white leather pants, she looked like a big spoiled cat sitting comfortably on the couch.

"You know I'm always ready to help," Auntie said. "What exactly do you need?"

"You know what I need. The lucky pin."

Cammie frowned. What?

"So what's stopping you? As far as I know, your dad is rolling in dough." Auntie yawned and took a white thermos out of the glove compartment. "Want a skate shake?"

"No. And my dad would be willing to pay, but Mel says those pins aren't for sale."

Ah, that's what it was! Now Cammie remembered. Isabelle was talking of the lucky pins Mel Reed, the skate sharpener, had in his shop—the bronze, the silver, and the gold. Those pins could bring you luck—that was what Mel had said. So now Isabelle couldn't land her axel, and she thought one of those pins would help her.

"You know anything can be bought," Auntie said. "You probably didn't offer him enough."

Isabelle smirked. "Would ten thousand dollars be enough for you?"

"Ten thousand dollars for a pin?" Auntie shrieked. "And your daddy would be willing to pay that?"

Hidden under the shrub, Cammie shook her head in amazement. Isabelle's father had to really love his daughter to be willing to pay that much money for a skating pin.

"You know what, Isabelle?" Auntie said. "I simply don't understand why a girl like you—someone who would never have to worry about money—would even think of going through all that pain of becoming a professional figure skater. All those hours of hard work, the injuries, the disappointment...surely, you don't need it. Go back home and enjoy life."

"I didn't ask you for this kind of advice!" Now Isabelle's voice was ice cold. "How could you even suggest that? I love skating more than anything else in the world. And I'll make it no matter what. I don't care what happens, and if it means stealing the pin, I'll do just that. Are you with me or not?"

"Now, lower your voice, dear. We don't want to be overheard." Auntie looked around, and Cammie squeezed into a tight ball behind her bush.

"There's nobody here," Isabelle said without turning her head.

"I'll help you, all right? Your father has been so generous. I always keep my promises." Auntie giggled.

"Good." Isabelle seemed to have calmed down a little.

"So it all comes down to that lucky pin; do I understand you right?"

"I can't win without it. And if I have to steal it—"

"Don't even think of that! You'll be caught right away. I'll think of something, okay?"

"I'll need the pin for my test next month."

"You'll have it. Now do you want to give me a kiss?"

Cammie saw Isabelle hug Auntie; then the sled glided away. Forgetting that she wanted to talk to Isabelle, Cammie sat behind the bush staring at her friend, trying to digest what she had just heard. So things weren't going too well for Isabelle. She still couldn't land her axel, so she was doing her best to get the lucky pin from Mel Reed—the only thing that would help her to pass her test. Wow! How great it was that Cammie didn't need any help to land her jumps. She knew that it didn't take luck to succeed; it took work.

Cammie waited for Isabelle to disappear inside the dorm building; then she got out from behind the bush and walked back to her room.

PRE–JUVENILE TESTS

Cammie spent the whole month preparing for her moves-in-the-field and free-style pre-juvenile tests. Doing well on those tests was important to her. If she wanted to be a serious skater, she would have to do her best. Coach Ferguson was of the same opinion. Day after day, she drilled Cammie on mohawks, backward three turns, and power pulls—Cammie's least favorite moves. Of course, now Cammie understood how important it was for a skater to have good edge control. It wasn't like a year ago, when Cammie hadn't even been allowed to go to her first competition—only because her edges and three turns were bad.

Like most skaters, Cammie enjoyed jumping and spinning, not doing small turns and changing edges on the ice. And yet, facing three scary witches had helped Cammie to understand the importance of the basics in skating. So now she worked hard on her backward three turns, even though she still wasn't particularly crazy about them. Back home, Cammie could do all of the four backward three turns all right. They were really good—well, almost. Never in the world would Cammie have admitted that she rushed them slightly and the edges weren't always clean. When she skated at her home rink, Cammie had only worked on moves in the field under Coach Louise's strict supervision or, in other words, when she hadn't had a choice.

Here in Skateland, talking about choices wasn't even an option. There was a special session devoted to moves in the field—the early morning session. Coach Ferguson was always there, following Cammie's moves with her unblinking gray eyes. Nothing escaped the coach's gaze—not slipping off the edge or putting the free foot down. Coach Ferguson would make Cammie do the same move over and over again until Cammie got it right. And because Cammie hated those endless repetitions, it sometimes took her the whole practice session to get one little move. It was boring.

And yet today, when Cammie would finally show her achievements to a panel of judges, she was glad that Coach Ferguson was so strict. When she had taken her pre-preliminary and preliminary tests back home, she had been so nervous that she could barely hold her edge. She had thought she would fall for sure, and even after the tests, she still couldn't stop shaking. Now, whenever she thought of her moves-in-the-field test, she only smiled knowing that her edges had never been so secure and her three turns had never been so flawless. Well, perhaps, only when she had had to face the wicked witches—she had been perfect then. But what skater wouldn't do moves in the field flawlessly if a witch threatened to injure her or force her to retire from skating?

I'll do great today, Cammie said to herself as she pulled on her tights and her green skating dress. *I've done those moves like a thousand times already, so what's the big deal? Besides, judges are nothing like witches. They aren't going to hurt me.*

Cammie's parents called to wish her good luck. They had thought of coming to the test session to support their daughter, but Cammie talked them out of it.

"There'll be nothing exciting about watching me do moves in the field. Besides, there is no music," Cammie said to her father.

"You look terrific even without music," Dad said. He sounded a little disappointed.

"Skateland Annual Competition is less than two weeks away. Why don't you guys come to cheer for me then?"

Cammie heard her father chuckle on the other end of the line. "You sound so grown up, honey. Now you're telling us what would be the best time for us to come see you."

"Dad!"

"Okay, okay. Just skate your best."

Cammie hung up smiling. Of course she would do her best today.

She stayed in the dining room longer, sipping her tea and chatting with the other skaters. It was Sunday, so all of them had slept in and looked refreshed.

"What time is your free skate test, Cammie?" Dana asked.

"One o'clock, right after my moves-in-the-field

test," Cammie said. "Free skate is easy. No double jumps, just singles."

Dana nodded. "True. Intermediate free skate isn't too bad either. Just one double jump and a single axel—no problem. It's the moves-in-the-field test that I hate."

"Come on, you can do those moves," Liz said as she put strawberry jam on her toast.

"I know, but they're boring. I'm tired of doing hundreds of brackets every day. So no more brackets after today's tests." Dana smiled happily.

"I wish we wouldn't have to wait till four in the afternoon," Sonia said with a sigh. "You're lucky, Cammie. You'll be done by two."

Yes, and then I'll really relax, Cammie thought as she closed the dorm door behind her. *I'll go to Sweet Blades and have a huge cup of hot chocolate with marshmallows and two—no, three—skate pastries.*

The familiar octagonal building of the Sport Center that housed the Silver Rink looked smaller today, perhaps because there were so many people inside. There were skaters everywhere Cammie looked—scared girls clutching their mothers' hands, confident girls walking with their chins up, busy boys moving with concentration. As Cammie was leaving the locker room, she thought she saw Isabelle looking pretty in her blue skating dress. Cammie wanted to come up to her friend, but the crowd swallowed Isabelle before Cammie could even call her name.

Cammie's moves-in-the-field test was scheduled at twelve fifteen. It was ten thirty now, and the skaters who were to be tested were given practice time at the White Rink that was located in the same building, only on a higher level.

Cammie followed other skaters to the second floor. She had never seen the White Rink before, and she liked it instantly. It wasn't as big as the Silver Rink, but it was cozy, with Christmas trees in the corners and imitation snow scattered around white leather armchairs and couches, where spectators could sit and watch the skaters.

"Cammie! I knew I'd see you here!"

Cammie looked up and couldn't contain a shriek of excitement. Standing beside her was Alex. The one with whom she had wandered around Skateland a year before; the boy who had helped her to defeat three wicked witches.

"Alex! What're you doing here?" The moment Cammie asked that question, she realized how silly it was. Of course, Alex was in Skateland for tests. Why else would he be at the Sport Center?

"I wanted to see you!" Alex's eyes flickered mischievously.

"You didn't! You're here to take a test."

"Well, sure. But I also wanted to see how you were doing. So how is your skating and the … witches?" Alex made the last word sound very scary, lowering his voice and drawing out every syllable.

Cammie laughed. "I haven't seen a single witch here. Well, I mean … " She remembered Jeff and Sonia telling her that they had seen the Witch of Injuries. Still, because Cammie personally hadn't noticed her, it surely didn't count.

"So how're you doing? Have you landed your double axel yet?" Alex asked.

Cammie pouted. "Why is everybody asking me about the double axel? For your information, no, I haven't landed it yet. I'm working on the rest of the doubles, okay?"

"Whoa, take it easy!" Alex raised his arms as though in surrender. "Why are you so uptight anyway? Are you nervous about those tests?"

"Ah, the tests!" Cammie waved her hand dismissively. "I've been working so hard on those moves in the field, I think I can do them in my sleep. So no problem there. And of course, the free skate test is way too easy. And how about you?"

"Same here." Alex smiled confidently. "Look, I'd better do some practicing. My moves-in-the-field test is in half an hour. Do you want to hang out after you're done?"

Cammie's heart leaped excitedly in her chest. "Sure. I'll be done by two. Can you wait for me at the Silver Rink?"

"I'll be there."

Alex waved at her, skating away, and Cammie felt very happy. How awesome! She would take her tests, and then the two of them would go out and celebrate together. Cammie would tell Alex about Skateland, and Isabelle, and everything; and Alex would give her all the details about her home rink. *I wonder how Susie is doing,* Cammie thought, *and Margie? And Coach Louise? Is she still upset with me? I hope not. After all, I've learned so much in Skateland. I'm not even afraid of the tests.*

Cammie's practice went well. When they were asked to leave the ice, she felt perfectly warmed up and even excited at the thought of skating in front of the judges. She glanced at the clock on the wall. It was twenty after eleven. She still had an hour before her moves-in-the-field test, and she felt her feet getting tired in her tight skating boots. Perhaps she could take the skates off and give her feet a break.

In the locker room, Cammie got rid of her skates and put on her thick wool socks and sneakers. Uh! What a relief. She did a couple of stretches and decided to go to the Silver Rink to watch Alex getting tested. Boy, she hadn't seen her friend skate for a long, long time.

Alex did great—even better than Cammie had expected. His edges were deep and secure, and when he turned on the ice, he did it so effortlessly that Cammie was sure if she closed her eyes for a split second, she would miss the turn.

I'm not that good, she thought bitterly but rebuked herself immediately. Why wasn't she good? She had been practicing hard, and she would do great.

Alex's free skate test went even better. Again, Cammie couldn't help feeling jealous as she watched her friend's powerful jumps. *But mine will be as good one day too*, she said to herself. *I'll be working very, very hard.*

When Alex stepped off the ice, Cammie waved at him, gave him a thumbs-up, and hurried back to the locker room. Her own test would start in only ten minutes, so she'd better get ready.

Cammie changed back into her skates, slipped on her guards, and waited at the boards. When the two girls who were ahead of her were done, she bent down to take off her guards.

"All right, now relax and think of nothing but your moves."

Cammie looked around. She hadn't noticed Coach Ferguson approach her.

"You'll do fine," the coach said with an encouraging smile. Cammie didn't even remember if she had ever seen Coach Ferguson act so kindly.

"Cammie Wester!"

Yes, it was time to go. Cammie took a deep breath then slowly let out the air and stepped on the ice. She pushed off, but instead of the familiar feeling of gliding forward, she got stuck in the same spot, and her blade screeched against the ice.

I'm on the flat! Cammie realized, desperately trying to get back on the edge. Skating on the whole blade instead of either the outside or the inside edge was the worst mistake a skater could make. Not only did it look bad, the blade usually made a nasty scraping sound, and everybody at the rink could hear that.

Cammie bent her knees and pushed gently into her outside edge. The result was the same. The blade scraped the ice, refusing to move. Unable to stop her momentum, Cammie fell forward, landing hard on her knee.

I must have forgotten to take off my guards! Cammie thought. Her head began to spin. How silly! What would the judges think of her? She bent down to take the guard off her left blade, but to her great surprise, she saw nothing but the steel surface. She hadn't forgotten to take off the guards after all. But if not, what was the problem? Why couldn't she skate properly?

Her eyes full of tears, Cammie put her left foot back on the ice. She shuffled her feet. No, something definitely didn't feel right.

"Cammie, come back here!"

Startled, Cammie looked back straight into Coach Ferguson's angry face. "Get off the ice!"

Why? What had she done? Fighting tears, Cammie hobbled back into the stands. "I don't know what's wrong. I—"

"Be quiet!" Coach Ferguson said. "Over here!"

She led Cammie to a bench. "Lift your left foot. Okay, now your right. I see."

Coach Ferguson left Cammie where she was, standing with her mouth wide open, and walked in the direction of the judges' table. Cammie watched her say something to the judges—five women and two men—and saw them nod. The gray-haired man who announced the skaters' names brought the microphone to his mouth and called out the name of the next skater. Tears streamed down Cammie's cheeks. What was wrong? So she wasn't going to be tested at all?

Coach Ferguson came back. Her lips without a trace of lipstick were pressed tight; she looked as though she were trying to stay calm.

"Did you leave your skates unattended?" Coach Ferguson asked softly, but Cammie could see how upset the coach was.

"Ah…I…" Cammie stammered.

"I asked you a question."

"Well…yes. I took off my skates right before the test to give my feet a rest."

"And? Where did you leave the skates?"

"In…in the locker room."

"Why did you leave the locker room?"

Cammie didn't understand a thing. Why was Coach Ferguson asking her all those questions? "I…I came here to watch other skaters getting tested."

"Idiot girl!" Coach Ferguson said through her clenched teeth.

"W-what?"

"You heard me!" Coach Ferguson sighed gravely. "Cammie, I thought you were brighter than that. How could you even think of leaving your skates unattended?"

"I...I don't understand," Cammie stammered.

"You left your skates in the locker room, walked away, and somebody tampered with them."

"Tampered with my skates?" Cammie must have said the last words out loud because two girls in the front row stared at her.

Coach Ferguson led her away into the locker room where no one could hear them. "Take off your skates. Now see?"

Coach Ferguson ran her finger along the deep scratches that ran across the blades. The edges were no longer sharp and even; they were rough, with small bumps and indentations all over the surface.

"But...but who did it?" Cammie asked weakly.

Coach Ferguson looked her straight in the face. "And this is the question you should ask yourself. Who is the person that hates you so much that he— or she—was willing to jeopardize your test? Ah?"

Cammie swallowed hard, but the lump in her throat didn't dissolve. "I...I don't know."

"I wish you did." Coach Ferguson stood up. "Anyway, that's not the issue now. What we need

to do is to get you ready to take the test. I've spoken with the judges. They have agreed to change
the order. You can still be tested after the last skater
in your category is done. So we'll take your skates
to—"

"Mel Reed," Cammie said quickly.

Coach Ferguson curved her lips. "There's no
time to go to Mr. Reed. You only have half an hour.
So I'm going to ask Mr. Sullivan, the Silver Rink
Zamboni driver, to smooth out your edges the best
he can so you can take the tests today. It won't be
the best sharpening job you can possibly get, but it
would have to do. And then after the test, you can
take your skates to Mr. Reed. Is that understood?"

"Yes." Cammie sniffed.

"And you'd better pull yourself together if you
want to pass those tests."

Cammie nodded, trying to keep her tears from
pouring out of her eyes. She still didn't quite understand what had happened. Someone had messed up
her skates. But why? And who was it?

Coach Ferguson left the locker room with
Cammie's skates in her hands. Cammie leaned
against the wall and closed her eyes for a moment.
She was tired—even before she took her tests. *So
much for a perfect performance*, she thought bitterly.

The door to the locker room creaked open, and Cammie saw Sonia peer in.

"Hey, she's alone," Sonia said to someone behind her, and then Jeff walked in, looking sad.

"Are you all right?" Jeff asked.

Cammie shrugged. It was a dumb question. "Coach Ferguson will ask Mr. Sullivan to fix my skates so I can still take the tests. She says someone has tampered with my blades. Can you believe it?"

Jeff looked even more uncomfortable. "Actually, we can."

"Cammie, I saw her, and so did Jeff. We both did."

Cammie looked up at both of them. They were avoiding her look.

"Who are you talking about? Who did you see?"

"It was Isabelle," Jeff said. For some reason, he looked guilty, as though he was the one who had messed with Cammie's skates.

"Isabelle?" Cammie frowned. She still couldn't believe it. Or rather, she didn't want to.

"Isabelle took your skates and did something to them," Sonia said.

"How do you know it was her?"

"We saw her carry a pair of skates. First we thought they were hers," Jeff said.

"But then we realized she had her own skates on," Sonia said. "And one more thing…"

"What?"

"There was a woman with her. Tall, big with long hair, dressed in white."

"Auntie," Cammie said automatically.

"Is that what you call her? Well, never mind. Cammie, we think she's a witch."

"What?" Cammie stared at Sonia. "What a crazy idea!"

"Not as crazy as you think. Don't forget, Jeff and I were attacked by witches. We know what they are like."

Cammie smirked. "Big deal! Alex and I, we fought them."

"Still, it's not the same as being attacked."

Before Cammie could say anything, Coach Ferguson returned with her skates. Jeff and Sonia were out of the locker room within a split second.

"Here they are, as good as Mr. Sullivan could get them," Coach Ferguson said. "Now hurry. There is only one skater left in your group, so you are next."

With trembling hands, Cammie put on her

skates, slipped the skate guards over them, and walked outside. Coach Ferguson was right: the last girl in her group was just coming off the ice. Cammie closed her eyes, trying to cast the thoughts about Isabelle and witches out of her mind. She had to concentrate on her moves; she had to ace that test. Wasn't it what she had been working for? She was ready.

"Cammie Wester!" her name came out of the loudspeaker for the second time today.

Cammie opened her eyes and skated to the center of the rink to do her first move: forward perimeter power crossover stroking. Her legs shook a little, but when she began to skate, she forgot about being nervous, and bad thoughts no longer bothered her. Now it was just her and the ice.

Cammie completed the pattern. She knew she had done well; perhaps her timing wasn't as perfect as during practice, but it was okay. She did the rest of the moves equally well. Her blades didn't feel sharp enough, not the way Cammie liked them, but it didn't bother her.

She stepped off the ice and looked into Coach Ferguson's impassive face.

"You did fine," the coach said without a hint of

smile. "I think not all the lobes of your three turns were equal, but it wasn't bad altogether."

"Thank you!" Cammie forced out a weak smile and sank on a bench, trying to catch her breath. She buried her head in her hands. She realized things could have been worse. She could have missed the test altogether, and then what?

Someone slapped her on the shoulder. "You did great, don't you worry!"

Cammie raised her head. Alex stood by her side, grinning.

"You think so?"

"Sure."

"Coach Ferguson said my three-turn lobes weren't equal."

Alex whistled. "I didn't notice it. Come on, three turns have always been your strongest move."

"Yeah, right!" Cammie couldn't suppress a giggle. She knew Alex was kidding. If she hadn't had to do all forward three turns to break the curse of pride two years ago, she might have never mastered them at all.

"All right, you've passed. Congratulations!" Coach Ferguson said. Cammie hadn't seen her come back.

"Good." Cammie sighed with relief. Now she only had her free skate test left, and that was easy.

"I'll be watching you from the stands," Alex said with an encouraging smile as he moved away.

"How are the blades, by the way?" Coach Ferguson asked.

Cammie lifted her left leg and gave the blade a critical look. "Not quite the way I like it. But I can skate."

"You may want to take them to Mr. Reed's shop after you're done testing," Coach Ferguson said. "Mr. Sullivan isn't the best skate sharpener; it was only a temporary solution."

"Pre-juvenile free skate test is next!" the familiar voice boomed from the loudspeaker.

"You're second in this group," Coach Ferguson said. "I hope you're not too tired."

Cammie shook her head.

"All right. Good luck, then."

The coach walked away from her, and Cammie moved up to the edge of the rink to watch the first girl skate. The girl was short and slightly overweight, but she looked very secure as she completed the moves. Her jumps were high, and when she did her combination spin, she seemed to go around forever.

A group of screaming girls clapped from their front row seats whenever the girl completed a required move. Cammie wished she had a group of friends to cheer for her. *But Alex is here*, she reminded herself. She squinted, trying to locate him among the spectators. He hadn't told her where he was sitting. Cammie scanned the first row, moved up to the second, the third... oh, no! Right in the middle of the third row, next to a tall woman in a white fur coat, sat Isabelle. Cammie's best friend looked as gorgeous as always. She had taken off her blue skating dress—probably because she had finished her tests—and was now wearing white leather pants and a matching jacket. Both Isabelle and Auntie had paper cups in their hands—probably filled with hot skate shake—and Isabelle's eyes were fixed firmly on Cammie. So they had come to cheer for her after all.

Cammie felt her lips spread into a wide smile. Isabelle hadn't abandoned her. Cammie rose on her toes and gave her friend a cheerful wave. For some reason, Isabelle didn't wave back. She sat looking somewhat rigid and uncomfortable, sipping her shake, listening intently to what Auntie was telling her. Yet Isabelle must have seen Cammie because Auntie turned her face from Isabelle's and looked at Cammie. Her bright red lips twisted in a sugary smile, and she waved at Cammie. Auntie, not Isabelle.

But they're both here to watch me, Cammie thought. *It means Jeff and Sonia were wrong. Isabelle didn't tamper with my skates. Because if she had, she wouldn't be here trying to support me.*

"Don't you hear, Cammie? It's your turn!" Coach Ferguson pushed Cammie in the direction of the ice.

Oh, no! The man must have called Cammie's name, and she hadn't even heard it. She pulled off her guards and took the ice. Her blades felt fine, and it was all that mattered. Somehow the very fact that Alex was in the stands cheering for Cammie and now Isabelle and Auntie were there too gave extra spring to Cammie's legs and filled her with the desire to do her best. When she jumped, she felt as though she was flying across the ice, and her spins were quick and effortless.

Cammie walked off the ice, her cheeks burning with excitement. She had done well. Now Alex would have no reason to think that she had made a mistake moving to Skateland. And after seeing what a good skater she was, Isabelle would surely want to be her best friend again.

"That was nice," Coach Ferguson said, this time giving Cammie a real smile. "I'm sure you passed. Now you can relax. It's been a rough day for you."

Cammie smiled back and went to the locker room to get out of her skating dress. She quickly changed into jeans and a sweatshirt. When she walked into the Sport Center lobby, Alex was already there waiting for her.

"You passed," Alex said excitedly. "I just saw your coach. All the judges passed you and were actually happy with your skating."

"I can't believe it!" Cammie squealed. "Wow!"

"So where do you want to go now?"

"How about getting something nice to eat at Sweet Blades first?" Cammie said. "And then, if you don't mind, I need to go to Mel Reed's shop. See, even though Mr. Sullivan fixed my skates, the blades are still not perfect. I don't even know how I was able to pull off those moves in the field."

"Oh, you did fine," Alex said. "And you know what? I think my skates need sharpening too. I heard about Mel Reed. They say he's the best sharpener in the area."

"He is!" Cammie said proudly. "The first time he sharpened my skates, I knew I didn't want to give them to anybody else."

"Wow!" Alex seemed impressed. "I'm not sure Dad would want to drive me to Skateland each time my skates need sharpening. But I can come with you now and check out that guy."

Self–Spinning Boots

Cammie and Alex went to Main Square, and as both of them were ravenously hungry, they stopped at a small restaurant called *Figure Skater's Finest Food*, where they ordered grilled chicken with lots of rice and vegetables.

"Best food for figure skaters," the petite, curly haired waitress said. "I skate myself, and I eat a lot of meat and vegetables."

The food really tasted good, and when they left the restaurant, they felt pleasantly full and strong. But they couldn't skip Sweet Blades, especially because they absolutely had to reward themselves for passing their tests. Just like a year ago, they ordered two skate pastries: black and white boots with hard candy blades. They split them and had the time of their lives.

When they left the bakery and headed in the direction of the Icy Park, where Mel Reed's shop was located, it was already getting dark. The display windows of the stores around the rink were brightly lit, and the multicolored reflections formed intricate patterns on the light gray ice, making the rink look like a kaleidoscope. Alex glided forward, did a mohawk, got on the left forward outside edge, and sprung into the air. A split second later, he landed on his right backward outside edge.

"That was some axel!" Cammie said.

"I'm sure yours is pretty good too."

"Okay, let me try one." Cammie picked up speed and jumped.

"Good!"

"Not as high as yours."

"Well, you're a girl."

Cammie gave Alex an angry look. "So what? Most of the top skaters are girls."

"What? Go ahead, try to catch me." Alex skated forward across the rink, along the icy path, farther and farther down the street past the small houses with shimmering windows. Cammie glided after him trying to stay close. They passed several passersby, who weren't in any hurry, turned to the right, then to the left, and finally slowed down in front of a flashing sign that said *Icy Park*.

"I don't think we can race there; the paths are two windy," Cammie said.

Alex squinted at her. "So you give up, huh?"

"What?" Cammie gave him a light punch on the shoulder. "I never give up."

"I know you don't. Still let's go slower. This place is creepy in the dark. I was only here during the day."

They skated past the statuette of a skater holding a flower-shaped Skateland directory. Alex looked at the multicolored petals with interest. "I didn't realize there were so many rinks in Skateland. Have you skated at all of them?"

"Not really. I practice at the Green Rink; that's where they assigned me. And outside my rink, I've only seen the White Rink—that's where we practiced this afternoon; and the Silver Rink, of course."

"I see. It would be cool to try all of those rinks; what do you think?"

"I guess. Maybe, they would let us visit other

rinks if we asked. Not the Black and the Purple ones, though."

"Why not?"

"That's a good question." Cammie thought for a moment. "For some reason, the Black Rink and the Purple Rink are restricted. They say witches skate at the Black Rink. Do you know what poem they made so little kids would stay away from it?

Children, never think of skating
In the Icy Park,
For there are wicked witches waiting,
Lurking in the dark.

But few people really believe in witches here. Can you imagine? I mean, they talk about them all the time, but if you mention a witch, people will laugh at you."

Alex smirked. "They wouldn't if they got attacked the way we did. Have you ever shared it with anyone here?"

"Oh, a thousand times. But all I hear is that I have overactive imagination. Wait." Cammie bent down to tighten the lace on her right boot.

"Well, that's what I get when I share our experiences at our home rink," Alex said.

"Yes, people are like that."

They skated in silence for a while, passing huge trees covered with snow so thick that they could barely see the branches. It had gotten colder, and the ice under their blades felt harder. It wasn't easy to get deep on the edge. Cammie kept slipping, which soon made her tired. It hadn't been an easy day, after all.

"Slow down!" Cammie said, feeling that she couldn't catch up with Alex. "It's hard to skate fast on this ice."

"I know. Do you want to take a break?"

"Sure."

They found a log on the side of the road and sat down looking into the dark sky, where the first stars had already appeared and were now winking at them from between the snow-glazed limbs.

"So the Black Rink is for the witches, right?" Alex thought out loud. "How about the Purple one? Who skates there?"

"Mr. Reed does," Cammie said.

"Does he skate?" Alex pulled his hat down to cover his ears better.

"Oh, he's terrific. He can do quintuple jumps. I mean, it's not that he can actually do them." Cammie grinned at the sight of Alex almost falling off the log when he heard her mention quintuple jumps.

"So he can or he can't?" Alex asked, a bewildered look on his face.

"It's his boots. He invented self-spinning boots that throw you up in the air and help you to do the jumps."

"Cool! Have you tried them?"

Cammie rubbed her hands against each other. "I don't think he lets anybody else skate in those boots. Isabelle wanted to buy them, but Mr. Reed said she wouldn't be able to use them in competitions. It's illegal."

Alex laughed appreciatively. "I bet it is.

Everybody would be doing quintuple jumps then."

"So for now, they're for practices only."

"I still want to try." Alex got up. "I'm cold. Let's go."

They skated for another ten minutes until finally they saw the dark silhouette of Mr. Reed's log cabin against the sparkling moonlit snow.

"Here you go," Cammie said nervously. "You know what? I just remembered we don't have an appointment."

"What's the big deal? We'll pay him."

Before Cammie could say something, the cabin door opened wide, and out stepped Mr. Reed, wearing black ski pants and a matching jacket. He had the familiar self-spinning boots in his hands.

When Mr. Reed saw Cammie and Alex, he stopped abruptly. "Hi there. I don't think I have any customers scheduled for tonight. Today is the testing day. Correct me if I'm wrong."

Cammie and Alex exchanged sheepish looks.

"So I'm right," Mr. Reed said. "Well, it must be an emergency, or you wouldn't have come all the way here at this late hour."

Cammie gave Mr. Reed a pleading look. "I'm sorry to have come without an appointment, but it is really urgent. Someone tampered with my blades right before the test."

Mr. Reed fixed his deep blue eyes on Cammie. "So you didn't get tested?"

"I did. Mr. Sullivan sharpened them and—"

Mr. Reed snorted. "No offense to Mr. Sullivan, but I don't think he knows much about sharpening. Driving a Zamboni machine—that is his area of expertise. Skate sharpening, however, is an old and noble art that only few of us have managed to master."

"That's right," Cammie said eagerly. "That's why my coach told me to take my skates to you after I got tested."

"Okay, I see you have a pressing need. How about you, young man?" Mr. Reed was now talking to Alex. Even though Alex wasn't a short boy, Mr. Reed towered over him as a giant over a dwarf. The man had to be at least six feet three inches tall.

Alex flinched. "I guess I don't really have a bad problem with my skates. I just thought I'd come with Cammie to keep her company. But if you don't have time, it's all right."

Mr. Reed gave both of them a penetrating look. "Well, actually, I *am* pressed for time. I was about to go skating. But as soon as you're here, I'll do my job. Come inside, both of you, and take off your skates."

"Thank you; oh, thank you so much!" Cammie exclaimed, hopping with joy.

"And I wouldn't try those uncontrolled hops outside a skating rink," Mr. Reed said. "The ice on those narrow paths isn't really good for jumping."

Cammie nodded in agreement and followed Mr. Reed up the steps to the patio. The man unlocked the front door. "After you, young people."

Cammie and Alex walked into the brightly lit lobby.

"Cool!" Alex must have seen the display of antique figure skating boots and blades.

"You can look around while I'm working on your skates," Mr. Reed said. He gave Cammie's blades a critical look. "I can tell somebody has tampered with them. What a barbarian! Any idea who it is?"

The question made Cammie uncomfortable. Even though Sonia and Jeff had insisted it was Isabelle's fault, Cammie still couldn't quite believe it. Why would Isabelle do such a horrible thing? They were still friends. She was the one who had brought Cammie to Skateland.

"I don't know," Cammie said, feeling blood rush to her cheeks.

"Do you have enemies in Skateland?" Mr. Reed's blue eyes studied her hot face.

Cammie shrugged without saying a word. She let her eyes wander away from Mr. Reed's piercing look to the shelves filled with skating books and the display of skate guards on the counter.

"In this case, I suggest you look among your friends," Mr. Reed said. He carried Cammie's skates in his office and turned on his grinding wheel.

Cammie sighed with relief and joined Alex, who was studying Mr. Reed's skating trophies, his medals, and photos of him with skating celebrities.

"Hey, here's a picture signed by Michelle Kwan.

And this book has been given to Mr. Reed by Brian Boitano," Cammie said excitedly.

"He must have been a terrific skater," Alex said, looking through Dorothy Hamill's autobiography.

"He still is," Cammie said. She was looking at a silver skating pin in the shape of a spinning skater. A diamond glittered in the middle of the skater's waist. "Alex, do you know what it is?"

"What?" Alex asked absentmindedly. He had already put Dorothy Hamill's book down and was now turning the pages of the last issue of the *Skating* magazine.

"This is one of Mr. Reed's good-luck pins. They have magic powers. He says they bring out the best in you, helping you to skate perfectly."

"They do?"Alex's eyebrows shot up. He put the magazine down. "Hey, let me look at it."

Cammie handed him the pin. Alex twisted it in his fingers. "Looks pretty, but what's so magical about it?"

"Mr. Reed won it at a big competition. He says all hard work and effort paid off, so now when you have this pin with you as you compete, you skate your best." Cammie sighed deeply. "I wish I could have it. But Mr. Reed won't sell any of those pins."

"Come on, *you* don't need it. You're a wonderful skater."

"My double jumps are still not there," Cammie said sadly.

"Keep practicing. You'll get them soon. I know."

"Okay." Reluctantly Cammie put the pin back on the shelf where it belonged. "He also has a bronze pin and a gold one—three altogether. Now wait a minute! Where's the gold pin? It's gone!"

"He must have sold it to someone," Alex said absentmindedly. He was looking at the toy rink with miniature skaters doing moves in the field. "Hey, that's what I really like."

"What do you mean *he must have sold it?* Mr. Reed says these pins aren't for sale."

"Anything can be sold if enough money is offered. Hey, look at that little boy! I bet you'd want his double threes, huh?"

"Alex, no! Mr. Reed says he'd never ever sell any of these pins to anybody. Come on, Isabelle begged him to sell her one. She said her father would pay anything. In fact, she offered Mr. Reed ten thousand dollars. Can you believe it?"

Alex looked back from the toy rink, an expression of shock on his face. "What did you say? Ten thousand dollars for a pin?"

"Yes!"

"And Mr. Reed still wouldn't sell it?"

"No. He said *absolutely not.*"

"Well, I don't know."

"Let me ask him."

Before Cammie had a chance to leave the room, Mr. Reed appeared carrying her skates. "Here they are." He ran his index finger against the sharp blade.

"Uh, thank you very much. " Cammie handed Mr. Reed the money.

The man nodded and put the bills into a big leather wallet.

"Now as for your skates, young man," Mr. Reed said to Alex, "they aren't too bad. But I know you'll be able to really feel the edges now." He gave Alex his skates.

"Thank you!" Alex said excitedly. "I like my blades sharp."

"Most skaters do." Mr. Reed winked at them.

"Mr. Reed, I want to ask you something. Did somebody buy your gold good-luck pin?" Cammie asked.

An expression of confusion appeared on Mr. Reed's narrow face. "What are you talking about?"

"The skating pin. The one that looks like a spinning skater."

"Ah, all right, what about it?"

"Did you sell the gold one to somebody?"

Mr. Reed's facial expression changed from confusion to anger. "Oh, how many times do I have to explain that those pins aren't for sale? You can't buy perfection. There is no monetary equivalent for glory. If you want to be a good skater, you need to work hard; there is no other way."

Cammie swallowed nervously. Getting Mr. Reed upset was the last thing she wanted. "Mr. Reed, I—"

"Forget those pins!" Mr. Reed boomed. "Did you hear me?"

"No … you don't understand. I don't want one."

"Good."

"All I was saying is that the gold pin is missing."

"What?" The lines on Mr. Reed's face deepened as he gave Cammie a look full of sarcasm. "It's not missing, young lady, because I never sold it to anyone. Is that understood?"

"Yes but—"

"Those pins are part of my life—a reflection of

all hard work and effort I put into my skating. Do you understand?"

"Sure, but—"

"Those pins are priceless."

"Mr. Reed, I understand. All I wanted to—"

"So I will never sell any of those pins. Did you hear me?"

Cammie sighed gravely. "Yes, sir."

"Repeat what I said."

"You'll never sell those pins. But—"

"No buts. Anyway, your skates are ready. Now if you will excuse me, I want to use the last hours of my day off to do some skating."

Alex cleared his throat. "Mr. Reed, do you mind if we watch you practice?"

Mr. Reed tilted his head. "And why, may I ask, would you want to do that?"

Alex smiled mischievously. "People say you're a good skater."

Mr. Reed laughed. "Don't give me that, young man. There are plenty of good skaters where you come from. I'm not even talking of the Olympic division skaters you can watch on television. So if you don't tell me why you're so adamant about watching an old man make a fool of himself, you'll be out of here. Do you hear me?"

"Yes, sir," Alex muttered. His face was bright red like a fresh tomato.

Cammie really felt sorry for him.

"I'm listening, young man."

"I wanted to see your self-spinning boots," Alex said, and the red color on his face deepened. Now his cheeks looked almost burgundy.

"That's it?" Mr. Reed said lightly. "I don't see why not. Follow me."

He left the room without giving Cammie and Alex another look. They exchanged nervous glances and hurried to put on their skates. When they walked out of the cabin, Mr. Reed was turning the lights off. The multicolored sign *Melvin Reed's Skate Sharpening Shop* flashed before Cammie's eyes, and then everything turned dark.

"It's my day off, so I really don't want any more skaters infringing on my privacy without an appointment," Mr. Reed said.

They followed the man along the icy path to the huge circular-shaped rink. Deep purple ice glittered in the light of the moon.

"The Purple Rink!" Alex breathed out.

"Welcome to the Purple Rink!" Mr. Reed said without looking at them. "Let me change into my boots first. See, these boots are very powerful. I didn't want to try them on the narrow path. You need to learn to control the speed."

"What do you mean?" Alex asked.

"In a minute." Mr. Reed took off his mountain-climbing boots and changed into self-spinning boots. In the light of the moon, Cammie could see that both the boots and the blades were made of silvery metal. In fact, it was almost impossible to say where the boots ended and the blades began.

"Now watch me." With the energy uncharacter-istic of an older man, Mr. Reed sprung off the snow, stepped on the purple ice, and glided to the mid-dle of the rink. He went around in incredibly fast strokes, turned around, did a couple of backward crossovers, glided on the forward outside edge, and flew into the air.

"One, two, three … four?" Alex muttered at Cammie's side. "A quad axel?"

"Yup." Cammie watched Mr. Reed ride out of the quad axel easily, as though he had done nothing but a waltz jump. He did a series of double threes at blinding speed and shot into the air again, this time spinning around five times.

"I can't believe it. A quintuple salchow," Alex said. He sounded shocked.

"I told you."

"You did, but until I saw it myself... oh, man!"

Mr. Reed did a quintuple toe loop and a quintuple loop. It must have been more than Alex could handle because he jumped to his feet.

"Mr. Reed, it's unbelievable; it's great!" Alex yelled waving both arms. "Could I try them? Just once. Could I?"

Mr. Reed skated to the edge of the rink, where Cammie sat on a small wood bench. Next to her, Alex was hopping with excitement. As Cammie looked Mr. Reed in the face, she couldn't help noticing how happy the man looked.

"You can try them," Mr. Reed said. "Easy, though. Wait."

He took off the skates, and Cammie saw him do some adjustment to the boots. "You can do doubles, I presume?" he asked Alex.

"I can do a triple salchow and a triple toe loop," Alex said, sounding proud.

"Not bad. Then I think you can try some quads."

"Not quintuples?" Alex sounded a little disappointed.

"Not yet. I don't think you're ready. "

"All right," Alex grumbled, though Cammie saw

that his hands were shaking with excitement as he buckled the boots.

Mr. Reed gave Alex a critical look. "Ready?"

"I'm ready."

"Go!"

Without wasting another second, Alex jumped on the purple ice and glided around the rink at what seemed to Cammie fifty miles an hour. Alex was going so fast that Cammie closed her eyes for a moment and let out a weak shriek.

Mr. Reed put his hand on her shoulder. "Don't worry, he'll be fine. He looks like a good skater to me."

Alex got on the backward outside edge, picked with his left foot, and went up. He performed four perfect revolutions in the air and landed securely on his right foot.

"A quad toe!" Cammie jumped to her feet. "He did it!"

Mr. Reed grinned appreciatively. "See how easy it is with self-spinning boots?"

"Yeah!" Cammie couldn't take her eyes off Alex, who had just landed a perfect quad salchow. "Mr. Reed … hmm … do you think—"

"I presume you want to try the self-spinning boots too." Mr. Wood didn't sound as though he was asking a question; apparently he knew Cammie's answer.

Cammie's heart raced excitedly in her chest. "Can I? Really?"

"Okay, young man!" Mr. Reed shouted. "Your time is up. Let the lady get her share of fun."

Alex didn't look too happy, but he obeyed. He took off the self-spinning boots and handed them to Cammie.

"It's unbelievable." Alex was panting, but his green eyes shone with joy.

"Okay, young lady." Mr. Reed did something to the boots. "Do you have your double jumps?"

"Pretty much," Cammie said undecidedly.

"All right. The reason I'm asking is that it's not advisable to go up more than one level from what you can do in your natural strength," Mr. Reed said. "It means if you have only mastered single jumps, I wouldn't recommend trying triples. Do you understand?"

Cammie nodded. "Sure. But I do have most of my doubles, except the lutz. Well, perhaps, not all of them are consistent, but—"

"That's good. So we'll have you try some triple jumps."

As Cammie was putting on the self-spinning boots, her hands shook with anticipation.

"Don't get too excited," Mr. Reed said. "Too much adrenaline may throw you off. Now this is what you do. Once you're on the ice, skate naturally, the way you always practice. I have to warn you, though; you'll go much faster. Don't get scared; the extraordinary speed is the combination of the power of the boots and the quality of the ice. Do you understand me?"

Cammie wrinkled her forehead. "Ah?"

"Never mind. Jump in the air the way you always do. The self-spinning boots will help you to make an extra revolution. Ready?"

Cammie inhaled then exhaled quickly. Her legs shook slightly, but her whole body was filled with excitement. She was going to do triples. Was it true? She was going to do triples!

"Go!"

As Cammie approached the ice, she was hesitant for a moment. She shot a quick look at Alex. He was watching her with shining eyes.

"So what are you waiting for?" Mr. Reed gave Cammie a gentle push in the back.

She didn't understand what happened next. The moment her blades touched the ice, she sped across the rink with such breathtaking speed that for a moment she thought she had gone blind. The only time in her life she had gone that fast was on the declining road that led to the castle of the Witch of Fear. To break that speed, Cammie had had to do a salchow that had thrown her on a patch of soft snow. That had saved her life. But what was she supposed to do now? She was going so fast that she couldn't even see any patches of snow around her. Of course, there was snow around the rink, but where did the rink end? Her eyes couldn't discern anything.

"Try a jump!" Mr. Reed's voice came from somewhere.

Ah, a jump. What jump? How could she even think of jumping? She would break every bone in her body.

"Don't be afraid!" Now it was Alex's voice.

Yes, it was easy for him to say *don't be afraid!* He wasn't the one gliding across the ice, not seeing where he was going.

"A salchow, Cammie! Try a salchow!"

A salchow. Cammie's favorite jump. The one that saved her life a year ago. Well, if it had helped her then, it would probably help her now. Okay, how was she supposed to do a salchow? All of a sudden Cammie forgot how she had to get into the salchow.

From the backward outside edge? Now it was the loop. Forward outside? That was the axel. Boy, what was wrong with her?

"Do a mohawk, then a three turn!" Alex's voice reached her ears again.

Okay, she would do what he had said. A mohawk—okay, that was easy; a forward outside three turn—wasn't it great that they had spent several hours practicing those a year ago at the Witch of Pride's rink. Now she was on her left backward inside edge, so the most natural thing in the world was to bend her skating knee, whip the free leg around, and…

Before Cammie could understand anything, she was spinning in the air faster, faster, and faster. *But I'm not doing a spin; it should be a salchow,* a weird thought crossed her mind. A split second later, she was gliding on the ice, her arms spread, one leg behind her.

"You did it!" Alex yelled. "A triple salchow."

A triple salchow? She had just done a triple salchow! She couldn't believe it. So that's what it was like to land a triple. It meant going up high and spinning fast in the air. It was kind of scary, but at the same time, it was…great. Incredible.

"I'm going for another one!" Cammie shouted

and went through the same routine. This time it was easier; the movements were familiar. Cammie landed securely on her right foot and laughed with joy. She had done it!

"Now that's enough!" This time it was Mr. Reed calling her. Oh, no! She wasn't done yet.

"Come back!"

She had to obey. The boots weren't hers after all. Reluctantly, Cammie moved to the edge of the rink, the boots carrying her gently. Alex stretched his hand to help her off the ice. Panting, she sank down on the bench.

"It was awesome!" Cammie whispered. Her lips could barely move.

"I would buy these boots," Alex said excitedly. "How much do you want for them?"

"I already explained everything to her!" Mr. Reed pointed to Cammie. "You can't use these boots in competitions; it's illegal. And if not, what's the point?"

"To have fun!" Alex said defensively.

"That's what I thought," Mr. Reed said. "And I was also sure I could help skaters to get a hang of their jumps. I meant those boots to be sort of a harness. Yet most coaches disapprove of them. Anyway, you need to ask your coach's permission. If your coach says *yes*, I'll make you custom boots like these. I promise."

"Great!" Alex exclaimed. "I'll talk to Coach Louise."

"And I'll talk to Coach Ferguson," Cammie echoed.

Mr. Reed gave them a sad smile. "Do you want my opinion? I don't think you're getting these boots."

"He's a weird guy, isn't he?" Alex asked after the two of them had left the Icy Park and were on their way to Skateland parking lot, where Alex was to be picked up by his father.

Cammie agreed silently.

"I wish I could get those boots, though," Alex said dreamingly.

"I'd rather get the good-luck pin," Cammie said. "The boots are great, but if you can't compete in them, what's the purpose?"

"But the feeling of landing a quad!" Alex spread his arms. "I haven't experienced anything like that in my life. And that little pin? What does it really do? Have you even tried skating with it?"

"Of course not. You heard the man. He says he

never sold it to anyone. But the pin is missing. And you know what I think?"

Cammie blocked Alex's way, looking into his green eyes. "I think it was Isabelle who bought it. Her father must have offered Mr. Reed a million dollars, but Mr. Reed won't tell us because he doesn't want to sell the other pins."

Alex rubbed his forehead. "Isabelle? You know what? You may be right. She would do anything to win, though she's a lousy skater."

"She's not!"

"Of course, she is. Stop worshipping her, Cammie. She can't even land an axel!"

"She's working on it."

Alex gave Cammie a sympathetic look. "I don't want to hurt your feelings, Cammie, but I don't think she's a good friend for you. I wouldn't be surprised to find out it was she who tampered with your skates this afternoon."

Cammie stopped in her tracks. "What makes you think so?"

Alex shrugged. "Just a guess."

"Why do you all pin it on Isabelle?" Cammie cried out in desperation.

Alex gave her a curious look. "What do you mean *you all?* Who else thinks it was her?"

"Oh, what difference does it make? Jeff and Sonia—you know, the kids we rescued from the Witch of Injuries and the Witch of Fear. They say they saw Isabelle carrying a pair of skates. But they don't know if the skates were mine or not."

"Did anybody else's skates get damaged today?"

"I don't think so."

"There's your answer then."

"Oh, no!" Cammie moaned. "I still have no proof. And Isabelle was always so nice to me."

"Just be careful, Cammie."

They already stood in the brighly lit parking lot. Alex's father waved at them from his beige Lexus.

"Don't forget the poem you told me about," Alex said, winking.

Cammie gave him a blank look. "What poem?"

"*For there are wicked witches waiting, lurking in the dark*. You know what I think? Your friend Isabelle is a witch."

"Oh, come off it!"

"I've got to go." Alex smiled at Cammie and got into his father's car. The car took off, and it looked as though its red taillights flashed Cammie another warning: *be careful*. Feeling slightly upset, Cammie turned around and skated to the dorm.

PERFECT JUMPS

Though Cammie was really impressed with Mr. Reed's self-spinning boots, it took her three whole weeks to finally approach Coach Ferguson. What caused her enthusiasm to wane a little was her roommate's complete lack of interest in Mr. Reed's incredible invention.

"But it's crazy," Sonia said after Cammie shared the wonderful experience of spinning high in the air. "Mr. Reed told you that you couldn't use those boots in competition. So what's the point?"

"It's hard to explain. But I know that if you tried

them once, you'd want to jump in them more and more."

"Yes, so maybe that's the reason self-spinning boots are illegal in Skateland," Sonia said, wise and mature as always.

It was funny, but Cammie often had the impression that Sonia was much older than she was, though in reality, Sonia was three and a half months younger.

"Coach Ferguson won't let you use those boots. Don't even ask," Sonia said.

That was something Cammie didn't want to hear. Why did Sonia always think she knew everything?

"Well, what if she does?"

Sonia shrugged her bony shoulders. "I doubt it. But if it makes you feel better, go ahead; ask her."

"I will." Cammie put on her skating clothes and left the room without giving Sonia another look. What was wrong with her roommate? Surely Cammie wasn't going to use the self-spinning boots in competition if they were illegal, but why not have some fun? Cammie knew she would never forget the wonderful sensation of the boots carrying her up in the air, higher and higher, and then making her go around several times smoothly, effortlessly. She also felt incredibly secure in Mel Reed's boots, knowing that her landing would be perfect; she would never slip off the edge or land hard on the toe pick. Without the magical boots, Cammie still found double jumps a little scary—even though she could land most of them. But so many things could go wrong; you never knew. Cammie remembered her last geometry lesson, where the teacher had explained to the students the laws and principles underlying the successful landing of multirevolution jumps.

"First of all, your body needs to be perpendicular to the ice when you take off," the teacher had said. "It is best if the skater's body forms a perfect ninety-degree angle to the surface of the ice."

The teacher drew a right angle on the blackboard and waited for the students to copy it. "And how can you achieve this perfect position?"

There was a moment's silence as the students looked at one another. The teacher expected them to know the answer, but it looked as though nobody, including Cammie, had any idea of what he was talking about. Even Jeff was quiet, staring at the blackboard.

"You make the entrance edge longer and deeper," the teacher said.

The class let out a loud sigh. Of course they all

knew that, but they also realized that getting on a good, deep edge wasn't always easy, especially when you entered your jump at high speed. And if your edge wasn't good enough, you didn't get enough height, or your body was tilted in the air and then, instead of landing gracefully, riding on your backward outside edge, you crashed on the ice. You blew the jump. End of the story.

Yet with self-spinning boots, you didn't have to worry about any technique. You could enter a triple jump riding on the flat; your body could be crooked—it didn't matter. The magic boots let you float in the air and carried you down to the ice, making even a beginner look like a pro.

I have to get those boots, Cammie thought. *Oh, I need them so badly.*

"Absolutely not!" Coach Ferguson said even before Cammie could finish her passionate description of the wonderful qualities of the self-spinning boots.

"But why? I wouldn't compete in them, I'd only—"

"Exactly. You can't compete in them, and I won't let you ruin your technique with some kind of…" Coach Ferguson paused, apparently thinking of the best way to express her indignation. " ...*cheater boots!*"

Cammie's cheeks got so hot that she had to cover them with her hands to cool them down a little. "But I wouldn't cheat, I—"

"End of discussion. Let's get to work now. Show me your double loop."

With a deep sigh, Cammie skated away from the coach to the middle of the rink. Angry tears pricked her eyes. What was Coach Ferguson's problem? Why couldn't she understand that Cammie's desire to get self-spinning boots had nothing to do with cheating? She only wanted to experience the wonderful feeling of flying and spinning in the air again.

"Faster!" Coach Ferguson barked from the boards.

Cammie clenched her teeth and picked up speed. Faster and faster she went. *Okay, so you think I'm a cheater? Fine, I'll show you I'm not.* She did a quick three turn, got on the backward outside edge—*hold it, hold it,* she reminded herself—and propelled herself up into the air. She knew her body was perpendicular to the ice, it wasn't tilted, and when her foot touched the ice, she had no doubts any more. She had just landed a beautiful—perfect—double loop.

"Yes!" Coach Ferguson clapped her hands.

Smiling, Cammie skated up to her.

"See? You can do it. Ready to try a double flip?"

Cammie nodded and went back to the middle of the rink. Miraculously, she landed her double flip, too—easily, flawlessly.

Now if only I could do the double lutz, Cammie thought after Coach Ferguson congratulated her on the job well done. *But it probably won't happen. Three jumps in one practice—it would be too good to be true.*

But everything seemed to work that day. Cammie landed her double lutz with equal ease.

"That's my girl!" Coach Ferguson said. The funniest thing was that she didn't look surprised at all. "I knew you could do it. You just needed more confidence. Now I want you to try a double loop in your program."

Cammie felt her heart beat faster and faster. She remembered her last disastrous competition when she had messed up all of her jumps. Could she really skate her program without a single fall?

Coach Ferguson went to the sound booth to turn on Cammie's music. Cammie took her starting position in the middle of the rink. Her hands were clammy. She clenched her fists and looked around. The huge rink was almost empty; the rest of the students were practicing their routines closer to the boards. Because Cammie was supposed to skate her program, she had been given the right of way. Cammie looked up in the stands. She would pretend that there were hundreds of people watching her—like at a competition. So if she managed to land all of her jumps now, she would also be able to do them in a competition. She knew it.

And then ... No, it couldn't be true. There wasn't enough light in the stands, so perhaps, Cammie was imagining things. She blinked and looked up again. Nothing changed; the person she had just seen was still there; and the person was Isabelle—bright and pretty in dark pants and a white sweater. Cammie's eyes slid to the left and right of Isabelle, expecting to see Auntie sitting beside her, but no, the older woman wasn't there. *Finally, she's alone*, Cammie thought, but at the same moment, a wave of bitterness swept over her. So Isabelle had come to watch her skate. Why? She hadn't been talking to Cammie for a month. She had probably ruined her skates. She had cut her off in public sessions several times. So what was she here for? To pull another prank? To destroy Cammie's confidence? Well, Cammie wouldn't let her. She had just landed three of her most difficult jumps, and now she would skate a clean program.

The familiar chords of "Moonlight Sonata" poured from the speakers. Cammie moved ahead letting the music carry her. Everything was easy: the steps, the spins—even the jumps. Cammie didn't make a single mistake, and when she skated up to Coach Ferguson after she was finished, she knew she had done a good job even before the coach could say a word.

"Excellent; that was excellent, Cammie," Coach Ferguson said. "Now I know that you're ready for the competition and you won't let me down."

As much as Cammie tried to look cool, she couldn't suppress a happy smile. Instinctively, she glanced up in the stands. Isabelle must have noticed that Cammie was looking at her because she gave her a cheerful wave with her hand. Cammie turned away.

"Just keep up the good work the rest of the week, and you'll do fine," Coach Ferguson said.

The rest of the week. Wow! Cammie had almost forgotten that Skateland Annual Competition would take place in only a week.

"Only a week," Cammie said, feeling a little nervous.

Coach Ferguson patted her arm. "Nothing to worry about. You're ready. Now you may go home and rest. Take good care of yourself. Don't catch a cold. I know how vulnerable we skaters are before big competitions."

Cammie nodded. She knew what the coach was talking about. She had heard of skaters spraining their ankles or getting stomach viruses right before the biggest events of their lives. But it wasn't going to happen to her. She would be extra careful.

When Cammie was leaving the locker room, Isabelle caught up with her. "Hi, how are you?"

Cammie noticed that Isabelle looked different. Gone was the worried, insecure look that she had had for weeks. Now it was the old Isabelle—smiling, radiant, and pretty.

"You must have landed your axel," Cammie said. Of course! What else could have made Isabelle so happy? Isabelle laughed excitedly and brushed a stray lock off her face. "Sure. And not just the axel. You can't believe it, Cammie. Everything clicked. Just like that." She snapped her fingers.

Cammie stared at Isabelle. "What're you talking about?"

"Well, don't you know how it can be? You work on some move, and it won't happen. You try your

best—it's still not there. And then one day…"
Isabelle spread her arms. A tiny diamond ring sparkled on her middle finger.

"What?"

"One day you can do it, and not only that particular move, but many more. Do you know what
I'm talking about?"

"Sure." Of course Cammie knew. She had just
landed three of her most difficult jumps. And it had
taken her so long—more than a year, actually.

"So believe it or not, but I'm doing triples now,"
Isabelle said triumphantly.

Cammie's mouth dropped open. "Triples?"

"And why are you so surprised?" Isabelle smirked
proudly. "I'm a solid skater. I have all the basics.
And besides, I'm older than you. I'll be seventeen
next month. Dad is going to throw a huge party. By
the way, you're invited."

"Thanks," Cammie said automatically. She was
still thinking of what Isabelle had just said. Triple
jumps? Isabelle was doing triple jumps? But how
was it possible? Only three weeks ago she couldn't
even land a single axel, and now she was doing triples? It was unheard of. Impossible.

Cammie must have said the last word out loud

because Isabelle's pretty face contorted. "Why are you so sure?"

"Sure of what?"

"That it's impossible," Isabelle demanded.

"Oh, no, I..." Isabelle was making Cammie very uncomfortable. She knew her reaction wasn't quite what Isabelle had expected. Normally when Cammie heard of another skater's progress, she was always happy for her, screaming with her, hopping with delight. But now there was a feeling in the back of Cammie's mind that something was wrong. A skater who could barely do a single axel three weeks ago couldn't have graduated to triples that fast.

"There are people who started taking lessons when they were teenagers, and now they are Olympic-division skaters," Isabelle said angrily.

"I know, but triples? In three weeks?"

"So you don't believe me?"

Cammie flinched. She couldn't look Isabelle in the eyes.

"Okay, you know what? I'll let you see for yourself at the competition this coming weekend," Isabelle said. "Then you'll know I wasn't lying. Deal?"

Cammie sighed. "Deal."

"All right, what're we doing here? Do you want

to hang out a little? You're done practicing for tonight."

"Yes, but…" Actually, Cammie had a lot of homework to do. But wasn't spending time with Isabelle something she had been looking forward to for months?

"Let's go." Isabelle hadn't even waited for Cammie's answer. She took Cammie by the hand, and together they left the Green Rink. They headed in the direction of Main Square.

"We could have a couple of skate shakes with ice cream or cookies and then take a walk or something," Isabelle said excitedly.

Cammie didn't recognize her friend. Isabelle really looked happy. She joked with Cammie, asked her about all the details of her life in Skateland— her roommate, her classmates, her coach. She even apologized for cutting Cammie off during public sessions.

"You probably think I did it on purpose, but it's not true." Isabelle sucked on her hard candy made in the shape of a blade.

"It's all right. I knew you didn't mean it," Cammie said quickly.

It was Cammie's best day in Skateland. She had just landed three of her most difficult jumps. She had skated her program without a single mistake. And now—finally—she was with her best friend again, sipping a delicious strawberry flavored skate shake, taking small bites off a huge chocolate-covered snowflake pie. Life was good!

"Of course, all of my hard work has finally paid off," Isabelle said and took another swig of her orange flavored skate shake. "See, if you land one difficult jump...well, the rest of them will follow. The axel was like a turning point for me. I landed it, and the following day I tried a double axel, and it worked. And once you have your double axel, triple jumps are nothing but a formality; what do you think?"

Cammie gave Isabelle an uncertain look. "I don't know."

She still didn't quite understand. Okay, so following Isabelle's logic, she too was ready for triple jumps because she had most of her doubles. Except for the double axel, of course. *Well, who knows?* Cammie thought. *Maybe I can try that double axel tomorrow.*

"But I wouldn't recommend trying it without your coach." Isabelle must have read Cammie's thoughts. "You don't want to get hurt, do you?"

"Of course not." Cammie remembered Coach

Ferguson's warning about skaters getting hurt right before big competitions. "I don't think I want to try any of those new jumps before the competition anyway. Perhaps afterward I can talk to Coach Ferguson about it."

Isabelle nodded. "Smart decision."

They spent the rest of the evening chatting excitedly; then they went to the movies to see *Ice Princess*. Cammie had already seen the movie before, but she had liked it so much that she didn't mind seeing it again.

"I wish we could hang out more often, but I'm really busy," Isabelle said when the two of them walked up the steps to their dorm rooms.

"Oh!" Cammie remembered a very important thing. "I see you are spending a lot of time with Auntie. What are the two of you doing?"

Isabelle looked away. Cammie could tell her friend felt uneasy.

"What do you mean?" Isabelle asked in an unnaturally high-pitched voice.

"You and Auntie." Cammie shrugged. "She must be a great woman."

Isabelle wrapped a long lock of hair around her finger. "Well, yes, she's kind of cool. So what?"

"Nothing. I was only wondering what you did together all the time."

Isabelle narrowed her eyes. "What do you mean *all the time?* I don't even see her that often."

"I thought…I see the two of you together almost every night. She brings you home in her icemobile."

"So? If she brings me home, it doesn't mean we are up to something. I work very hard, you know. I skate more than you do. I stay at the rink long after the official practice time is over."

Cammie looked at Isabelle in amazement. Her friend was a dedicated skater! Perhaps Cammie should do the same? Her afternoon practice was over at six o'clock; perhaps she should stay at the rink and practice some more? But even when Cammie thought of that, she decided she wasn't going to do it. She was already too tired, and she was way behind in her schoolwork.

"But when do you have time for homework and everything?" Cammie asked.

Isabelle snorted. "Homework? Who needs homework? I want to be an elite skater, not a scholar."

She's right, Cammie thought. *What dedication!*

I'm not a real skater because I can't make myself practice longer. I just can't.

"Look," Isabelle said as she bent and kissed Cammie on the cheek. "It's late. I'd better get going. But I'll see you around, okay? And I'll cheer for you at the competition."

"I'll cheer for you too." Cammie said. She watched Isabelle's slender figure as the older girl walked along the corridor, unlocked her door, and disappeared inside. Then Cammie sighed and went to her own room. The lights were already out; even Sonia was asleep in bed.

It must be late, Cammie thought. She looked at her watch. Ouch! It was almost midnight. How on earth was she going to get up at five tomorrow? Without taking a shower, Cammie quickly undressed and got into bed. Within a moment, she was asleep.

"Where were you? I was so worried?" Those were the words that woke up Cammie even before the alarm clock went off at five.

Cammie groaned and rolled to the other side. "Ugh, what time is it?"

"It's almost five," Sonia said as she wrapped her

bathrobe around her slim body. "Did anything happen to you last night?"

Cammie sat up and rubbed her eyes. She felt as though she hadn't slept at all. "Nothing happened to me. I just hung out with Isabelle, that's all."

Sonia dropped her tights. "Isabelle? You spent all that time with Isabelle?"

"Well, yes." Cammie got out of bed. Her body hurt; her legs wouldn't cooperate. She should have gone to bed earlier. How was she going to skate this morning?

Sonia put on her tights and reached for her T-shirt. "Cammie, you know Isabelle isn't your friend. She's just up to something. If I were you, I'd stay away from her."

"And you're wrong!" Cammie exclaimed. "And if you don't have any friends yourself, it doesn't mean—"

Sonia looked away. Cammie must have hit her tender cord. Cammie knew Sonia really never hung out with any other girls; she was too focused on skating and school.

"Look, I didn't mean—" Cammie said.

"It's okay," Sonia said quickly. "Let's not talk about Isabelle. The morning is too nice."

Cammie groaned again. Sonia must have thought

the morning was nice, but she didn't remember ever feeling worse.

"So how is Coach Ferguson? Did she allow you to buy those self-spinning boots?"

Self-spinning boots? Cammie had completely forgotten about them. She waved her hand. "No. But it's okay. You know I landed all of my double jumps yesterday. And then I skated my program and didn't make a single mistake. Can you imagine?"

Sonia squealed with delight and rushed to hug Cammie. "That's awesome! Why didn't you tell me?"

"When could I tell you? I didn't get home till midnight. Yes, and by the way, Isabelle saw me skate, and she was really, really happy for me."

"Oh!" Sonia appeared to be thinking about something. "You know what? That must be it."

Cammie gave her a questioning look.

"The reason Isabelle is talking to you again is that she saw you skate and got jealous. Be careful now, Cammie; she may try to tamper with your skating again."

"That's silly!" Cammie took a pair of skating tights from the closet and pulled them on. "Isabelle doesn't have to be jealous. For your information, she's doing triples now."

Sonia's eyes turned huge and round, like two blue saucers. "Isabelle is doing triples?"

"Yes, she is!" Cammie said triumphantly. "Now, you see, she has no reason to be jealous of me. She's a much better skater."

Sonia gave Cammie a look that strongly reminded Cammie of her mother's facial expression when she rebuked her for not doing something right. "Isabelle can't be doing triples. She's not ready for them."

"Well, I couldn't quite believe her myself at the beginning," Cammie said. She put on a green sweater over her long-sleeved T-shirt. "But she explained everything to me. She got all the basics nailed, so the jumps are easy now."

Sonia shook her head slowly. "Something isn't right there, Cammie."

Cammie ran a brush through her hair. "Why would she lie? Anyway, the competition is less than a week away, so we'll see what she can do."

"I guess." Sonia still didn't look convinced. Deep in her heart, Cammie knew that Sonia was right, but she didn't see why Isabelle would want to lie about something so obvious. She could either do triples or not. Either way, the competition would show.

They ate a quick breakfast in the dining room. Cammie noticed that Isabelle wasn't there again;

there was nothing strange about it because Isabelle had explained to her that she hated Mrs. Page's food.

"Back home, we always had terrific cooks," Isabelle had said. "I can't eat that junk. So Auntie usually takes me out to eat."

"Who's Auntie to you?" Cammie had been wondering about it for quite a while.

"Just a friend of the family," Isabelle said nonchalantly.

Why don't my parents have friends like Auntie? Cammie thought but didn't say anything.

Still, Cammie wasn't as picky as Isabelle, and she didn't mind Mrs. Page's cereal and toast. Besides, it wasn't the woman's fault that she couldn't serve something more nutritious to the young skaters.

"I wish you could try my brownies some day," Mrs. Page said. "I could give them the shape of blades or snowflakes—whatever you like."

"So where are they?" Dana grunted as she finished her toast.

Mrs. Page sighed. "Regulations. Your coaches want you girls to stay skinny."

"So why is she telling us about those brownies if we can't have them?" Liz said angrily.

Dana giggled.

Cammie finished her breakfast and got up.

Mercifully, the food had revived her; or perhaps she was still excited from the previous night.

Her morning practice was good. Coach Ferguson didn't even suspect Cammie hadn't got enough sleep last night. Things even went well at school. For the first time in a month, Cammie won their spelling bee. And the word Mr. Rocker had given her was hard enough: *choctaw*.

C-h-o-c-t-a-w. And Cammie spelled it right!

And when it was time for the afternoon practice, Cammie could land every jump again—solidly, securely. She skated her routine twice, and again there were no mistakes. Cammie felt completely happy. There were still five days before the competition, but she was ready. In fact, she was better prepared than at any time in her life.

When Cammie stepped off the ice, she thought she saw Auntie's bulky figure in the stands. She squinted, trying to see better. No, it was ridiculous. Why would Auntie want to come and watch Cammie's practice? She was a friend of Isabelle's family, not Cammie's. Cammie scanned the bleachers again. She didn't see Auntie, but somehow she felt uncomfortable. Cammie didn't like the woman. Perhaps it was good that her own family didn't have friends like Auntie!

Annual Competition

"Are you nervous?"

"Do you have to ask? Oh, what if I don't land my lutz?"

"Me too. You know, I'm still having problem with that combination."

"I do everything well in practice, but I know I'll freeze up in front of the judges. What am I going to do?"

When Cammie entered the dining room on the day of Skateland Annual Competition, those were the first words she heard. From the looks on the skaters' faces, Cammie knew they were nervous.

Even Dana and Liz weren't their usual cheery selves. They looked worried talking about shaky places in their programs. Sonia didn't seem much different from what she normally was—still calm and reserved—but the moment Cammie looked into her roommate's pale face, she knew Sonia was also scared. *How come I'm not afraid?* Cammie asked herself. When she thought of the moment she was going to step on the ice and skate her free program in front of the judges, all she felt was joy, not fear. She knew she had never been so well prepared. During the whole week, her practices had been great. Her jumps had never been better. She had been landing them so consistently, she couldn't believe it; in fact, she had never missed a jump the entire week. For the first time in her life, she didn't worry that she might fall from a jump or land on both feet. And because the fear was gone, Cammie could finally skate her heart out, actually enjoying what she was doing.

"Good luck out there!" Mrs. Page said as she handed Cammie a cup of hot tea.

"Thank you!" Cammie took a mouthful of her oatmeal and smiled gladly. She thought of her parents, who were going to come and watch her compete, and of Alex. He would be competing today, right before Cammie, and when he was done, of course he would come and cheer for her. How wonderful! Cammie knew she would skate well, without mistakes.

In her room, Cammie got dressed slowly, carefully, making sure she had thought of everything. Her new skating dress—very light pink with sequins—was already in her skating bag. She would go to the Sport Center wearing jeans and a sweatshirt, and she would change there. Cammie put her hair up in a bun and fastened it with a matching pink band.

There was a knock at the door.

"Cammie, can you get it? I'm still in the shower!" Sonia shouted.

"No problem." Cammie opened the door and stepped back instinctively. Standing in front of her was Isabelle, bright and sparkly in a light blue sweater, her black hair flowing down her shoulders.

"All ready for the big event?" Isabelle asked cheerfully.

"Sure. When is your competition?"

"Three o'clock. Right after yours." Isabelle smiled and tossed her hair back. "So I wanted to wish you luck and tell you I'd be there cheering for you."

"Thank you! I think I'm really well prepared," Cammie said.

"Yes, I know. I saw you skate. Still…" Isabelle looked around as though she didn't want to be overheard. "Do you want to step out of your room for a moment? I want to give you something."

"What?" Cammie looked at Isabelle's hands but didn't see anything.

"It's sort of a secret," Isabelle said. "Come on."

That was interesting.

"Cammie, who is it?" Sonia called from the bathroom.

"It's for me!" Cammie shouted back and closed the door behind her.

"Here it is!" Isabelle took something out of her jeans pocket and put the little object into Cammie's hand, closing her fingers tight around it.

Cammie unclasped her hand. "Oh no!" A small gold pin in the shape of a skater doing a perfect scratch spin sat in her palm. As Cammie turned the pin around, the diamond caught the light of the lamp on the ceiling and sparkled like a tiny rainbow.

"The good-luck pin? The one from Mel Reed's shop?" Cammie still couldn't quite believe what she saw.

"Exactly!" Isabelle smiled, and Cammie saw

that she had already applied lipstick, which made her look even prettier. "This pin brought me luck. I aced my test. Now I want you to have it when you compete."

"But … " Cammie ran her finger against the diamond. It felt cold and hard, like a piece of ice. "How about you? Don't you need it?"

"It's okay. I want you to do your best today. You're a great skater, Cammie. You deserve it."

"Thank you!" Cammie couldn't take her eyes off the sparkling pin. How nice was it of Isabelle to give it to her! She was a good friend, after all. Now Cammie knew that she would win the competition. Not only was she in the best possible shape; she also had the good-luck pin.

"But there's one thing," Isabelle whispered.

"What?" Cammie said also in a whisper. She looked around, but the long corridor was still deserted. There was nothing unusual about that; all the skaters were in their rooms, putting the last touches on their costumes and hair.

"Let it be our secret—yours and mine," Isabelle said. "Don't show the pin to anybody."

"Why not?"

"Well … you know … do you want people to tell

you that you only won because you had the good-luck pin with you?"

Ugh! That was something Cammie had never thought of. "You mean … do you mean I can't win without it?"

"Oh, no, no! That's not what I wanted to say. The good-luck pin doesn't give you extra skills; it only brings out the best in you, whatever you have already. Come on, don't you understand? Every skater can have good days and bad days."

"Ah!" Well that was something Cammie could definitely relate to. She remembered certain practices where she couldn't land a single jump, and she could never figure out why. Maybe she was tired. Perhaps she was upset or, on the contrary, too excited. And competitions were even worse—really nerve wrecking. Even the best skaters, who had been doing their best in practices, often choked when they faced the judges. Even in Cammie's last competition back home … Cammie's stomach tightened when she remembered the scary feeling of being unable to land on one foot, to keep her balance. And her practices had been pretty good—that Cammie remembered well. The same could easily happen today. If Cammie had been landing her jumps during practices, did it mean that she wouldn't make any mistakes in competition? Not necessarily. Perhaps Isabelle's pin could really help her.

"So what are you thinking about?" Isabelle shifted her feet, looking impatient.

"No, it's ... nothing." Cammie forced a smile. "Where did you get this pin?"

Isabelle's already huge eyes widened. "What do you mean? I bought it from Mel Reed, of course."

"But he said he'd never sell it to anyone."

"Ah, that!" Isabelle laughed, and for a split second, her facial expression and her posture strongly reminded Cammie of Auntie's. "Look, Cammie, you're probably too young to understand it, but everything can be bought. Ever heard the expression *money talks?*"

"Well—"

"Okay, you know what? Are you taking the pin or not? I need to get ready. In case you forgot, I'm competing today too."

Cammie saw that Isabelle was getting upset.

"Sorry, Isabelle! Of course, I'll take it. And thank you so, so much!" *Are you stupid?* she told herself. *Isabelle is trying to help you, and instead of being grateful, you ask her all kinds of unnecessary questions.*

"Then I'd better go. I'll see you at the rink."

Isabelle hugged Cammie and sprinted back to her room, her long hair flowing behind her like a scarf.

Cammie cradled the pin in her hand and looked at it again. How beautiful! And it would go well with her new skating dress. Although...Hadn't Isabelle told her not to show the pin to anyone? Well, then where was she going to wear it? *I'll pin it to my camisole*, Cammie decided. *This way, I'll still be wearing it while I skate, and yet no one will be able to see it.*

"Where have you been all this time?" Sonia asked when Cammie returned to their room. Her roommate looked as though she was ready to go, dressed in jeans and a warm green parka, her skating bag in her hand.

"Oh, it was nothing. I was just talking to...Isabelle."

"And why would Isabelle want to talk to you right before the competition?"

Caught in her last moment's preparation, Cammie wasn't exactly looking at Sonia. Yet she knew that her friend wasn't happy.

"And why shouldn't she? We're friends, you know." Cammie zipped up her skating bag and pulled on a pair of thick gloves that she always wore outside. "I'm ready. Let's go."

As they walked down the steps, Cammie thought

she could hear Sonia mutter *friends—yeah, right,* but she ignored it. She had better thoughts on her mind.

Competition. Competition. Of course, Cammie wasn't the only skater whose mind was on the most important event of the year: Skateland Annual Competition. The area adjacent to the octagonal building of the Sport Center looked even busier than usual. Skaters' parents gave the last-minute instructions to their children. Judges pressed through crowds of people looking serious, not talking to anyone. Cammie and Sonia used the computer built into the front door to enter their names. The automatic door opened to let them in. In the brightly lit lobby, Cammie looked around at the food stands and vendors selling skating clothes, books, and accessories. She wished she could hang around and explore the area.

"Don't. It will ruin your concentration." As usual, Sonia knew what was best for Cammie.

"We need to get changed and be ready for practice," Sonia said as she turned in the direction of the locker rooms.

She was right. If Cammie wanted to win today, she couldn't neglect her last-minute practice.

Cammie took her time applying makeup and getting into her new skating dress. She wanted to look really pretty today. Skating your best wasn't everything; it was also important to make a positive impression on the judges with your appearance. Normally, Cammie didn't use makeup—her mother wouldn't let her—and Cammie herself realized she was too young. Perhaps when she was in high school... But competitions were different. Even the youngest competitors were allowed to use a touch of lipstick and mascara to make their eyes and lips pop.

Cammie looked at herself in the mirror. *Wow!* She was almost as pretty as Isabelle. And today her parents would see her skate her best, and Alex too.

Someone knocked on the door.

"No!" several girls squealed in unison. Apparently they were not fully dressed yet.

"I'll get it." Cammie cracked the door open. "Mom!"

Cammie's mother smiled at her. She wore her warm winter coat—ready to watch the competition from beginning to end. "So how have you been, sweetie? Ready to do your best?"

"I'm ready." Cammie hugged her mother.

"A little nervous, huh?"

"Well…I guess." But honestly, Cammie didn't feel very nervous, just excited. And happy. In fact, she couldn't wait to get on the ice. "Where's Dad?"

"Up in the stands saving us seats." Mom smoothed Cammie's bun. "This competition is quite popular. We wanted to get good seats so we could see your every move. What're you going to do now?"

"I'm going to the White Rink upstairs to practice."

"Okay. Good luck!"

Humming her program music, Cammie rushed to the White Rink to do her moves one more time before she showed her newly acquired skills to the judges. She had just pulled off her guards when Alex ran into her.

"There you are!" Alex said slightly out of breath. "Are you going to watch me skate?"

"Oh! When is your competition?"

"My warm-up starts in twenty minutes."

"No problem, I'll make it. The practice is only half-an-hour long."

"Good." Alex smiled, and Cammie noticed how handsome he looked in his dark green skating outfit. "So how is your program? Ready to show the judges what you can do?"

Cammie laughed. Alex always put her at ease with his positive attitude.

"All right, I've got to go. Do your best, remember?" Alex patted Cammie on the shoulder and clomped away in his guard-covered skates.

Cammie jumped on the ice and circled the rink several times in fast energetic strokes. She didn't want to waste any time. All she had to do was get her body ready for difficult moves, practice her jumps and spins, and be out at the Silver Rink to cheer for Alex.

The practice went as smoothly as Cammie had planned. She felt strong and rested, and both her spins and jumps were perfect. Cammie walked off the ice three minutes before the official practice end, figuring that little time wouldn't make a lot of difference, and she really wanted to see Alex skate his new program.

When Cammie appeared at the Silver Rink, Alex's group of skaters had just finished their warm-up. The first competitor—a short, somewhat stocky boy in a gray outfit—already stood in the center of the arena waiting for his music to start. Oops! She had almost missed the beginning. Well, never mind.

The important thing was that Alex hadn't skated yet.

Cammie looked around for a vacant seat, but there was none.

"Cammie! Over here."

Cammie turned around and saw Jeff in the third row motioning her to come up.

He took his bottle of water from the seat next to his. "I saved this seat for Sonia. Where is she?"

"Still practicing, I guess."

The boy on the ice had just fallen from his double axel.

"He was too tilted in the air and couldn't achieve a perfect ninety-degree angle," Jeff said, sounding very much like their math teacher.

Cammie giggled but calmed down as she saw an older woman next to her give her a look of reproach.

"Anybody can make a mistake," the woman hissed.

"I'm sorry." Cammie hung her head. *The woman must be the boy's grandmother*, she thought. The boy was finally done, and he skated to the boards, looking disappointed. The older woman sighed and leaned back in her seat.

"Our next competitor is Alex Bernard!"

"Go, Alex!" Cammie and Jeff squealed in unison.

The older woman gave them a nasty look. Cammie ignored her.

Tall, blond, and graceful, Alex looked his best. He started his program with a flawless double axel followed by a triple-toe-loop-double-toe-loop combination.

"Yes!" Cammie and Jeff applauded enthusiastically.

Alex landed several double jumps effortlessly. As he moved across the ice in straight-line footwork, Cammie and Jeff cheered without stopping. Even the older woman joined them.

"Good skating," she grumbled.

The only mistake Alex made was a misstep on his twizzle, where he had to put his free foot down. Other than that, his program was perfect.

"I'm sure he's going to win," Jeff said excitedly.

"Alex has never left a competition without a gold medal," Cammie said. She had been clapping so hard that her hands hurt.

"I'd better get ready," Jeff said. "I'm in the next group. How about you?"

"The girls are skating right after the boys."

"Okay, I'll see you then. I know you'll skate great today."

Cammie nodded. "I think so too."

From the corner of her eye, she saw the woman's jealous look.

"We'll see how *you* can skate, missy," Cammie thought she heard the woman whisper, but she didn't even look at her. She knew today was her day.

Cammie didn't watch the rest of the boys skate. She thought she'd better go back to the locker room and relax a little before her warm-up started. Sometimes watching other skaters got her too excited, and she knew she had to stay focused.

As Cammie walked in the direction of the locker room, Coach Ferguson approached her.

"Here you are. Good. I couldn't see your practice. How did it go?"

"It was fine. I landed all of my jumps. I don't think I made any mistakes."

"All right, now all you need to do is skate a clean program. Think you can do it?"

"Of course."

When was her warm-up going to start? Cammie was ready to show the judges what she could do.

"Go to the locker room and relax a little." For a split second, Coach Ferguson's gray eyes slid down Cammie's joyful face. "I'll see you on the ice."

"Thanks."

In the locker room, Cammie took off her skates for a while to give her feet some rest. She looked in the mirror again. Everything looked good. Except... *Oh, the good-luck pin,* Cammie remembered. *I forgot to attach it to my camisole.*

Cammie reached for her skating bag, where the gold pin was still clasped to the side pocket. She unzipped her skating dress, pulled down the sleeves, and pinned the gold spinning skater to her white camisole. Now she was all set.

She looked at the big clock on the wall. Five minutes till her warm-up. Okay, it was time to put on her skates. She laced her boots and walked out of the locker room and then onto the shiny silvery ice—the smoothest ice in Skateland.

Cammie went through her usual warm-up routine. Everything was fine until she tried to land her first double: the toe loop. For some reason, it didn't happen. When Cammie shot in the air, she felt all right but then, for no apparent reason, she crushed on the ice with a loud thud. Huh? What was wrong? Had it really happened to her? Had she just fallen?

Her head down, Cammie forced herself to get up. She brushed the shaved ice off her tights. She had to try again.

Her second attempt was as bad as the first.

"Cammie!" Coach Ferguson beckoned her to come up. "Don't try a toe loop again."

"But—"

"Did you hear me? You're too worried about it now. Stop it. You'll land it well once you skate to the music."

"But I think I—"

"Now forget about jumping. Just circle around the rink; do a couple of spins. You'll be fine."

Reluctantly, Cammie skated away from the boards. She did exactly what coach Ferguson had told her. She tried several mohawks and three turns. Went into a sit spin. It wasn't low enough—at least, that was what it seemed to Cammie, but it would have to do.

I must be tired, she thought. *I've just had a practice, and I did fine. There's nothing to worry about.*

"Nothing to worry about," Coach Ferguson said when Cammie walked off the ice. "Listen to the music. Concentrate on one step at a time, and you will skate great. I know it."

Cammie nodded. The coach was right. She had never been better prepared in her life. And now she would show everybody what a good skater she was.

Absentmindedly, Cammie watched the first girl in her group skate her program. The skater was all right, pretty good actually, but Cammie would do better. She knew she was a stronger skater.

"Our next competitor is Cammie Wester!"

"Go!" Coach Ferguson gave Cammie an encouraging smile and gently pushed her in the direction of the ice.

Cammie skated to the middle and raised her arms above her head waiting for her music to start. She scanned the rows of seats trying to spot her parents, but there were too many people. Still she knew Mom and Dad were there, and it made her feel good. Alex had to be somewhere in the stands too, wishing her the best. And as though knowing what she was thinking about, Alex shouted from somewhere, "Go, Cammie!"

Cammie smiled happily and thought of waving at her friend, but it was too late. The first chords of her music filled the arena, and she pushed off the ice into her beginning three turn and then into backward crossovers.

Her first jump was easy—a single axel. Cammie bent her knee, got on her forward outside edge, and sprung in the air. Bang! She landed heavily on her rear. Huh? She quickly got up, feeling her legs get cold in wet tights. Had it really happened? Had she just fallen from an axel? A single axel? But that was her best jump, the easiest. Why? What was wrong with her?

It's not a good time to think about it, Cammie told herself. *Go on! Concentrate!* She tried to forget about the fall and focus on doing the rest of the program well. Her first combination spin was coming. Cammie stretched her right leg behind her for the camel spin. For some unknown reason, she leaned forward too much, got on her toe pick, and fell forward. Her knee responded with dull pain. Cammie clenched her teeth and blinked, trying to keep tears from running down her cheeks. She got up. Where was her music? She was way behind.

"Okay, that's it!" Cammie muttered. "I'm not making any more mistakes." She swung her right leg around and went up in the air. She had never had problems with her double salchow; in fact, it was the first double jump she had landed. But this time something was definitely wrong with her because the jump was under-rotated, and Cammie landed clumsily on both feet. Her head spun. She couldn't remember her next move. Was it supposed to be the spiral sequence? Yes, that was probably it. Cammie got on the right outside edge and raised her left leg behind her. The blade scratched the ice. She wasn't on the edge; she was on the flat. Cammie tried to lean more into the circle and tripped. Luckily, she managed to break her fall, but she touched the ice with both hands, and that was a definite no-no.

Cammie's brushed her wet hands against her dress. All she wanted now was to get off the ice. But her music was still playing, so Cammie picked up speed in preparation for her double loop. Even before she jumped, she knew she was on the flat. But she could still land the jump if only... No, she fell again, and this time, she didn't even get up right away.

What's the use? Cammie thought, trying not to hear the encouraging clapping from the audience. *I've lost already.* But she knew she had to go on. There was an unwritten rule in figure skating stating that no matter how badly you might have done, you had to keep going. Not finishing your program was much worse than falling ten times. So Cammie got up. She fell three more times: from her double toe loop, her flip, and her lutz. But yet she didn't give up, and she even managed to finish her program with the music. The last chord sounded, and there was Cammie Wester standing in her finishing posture—her arms raised gracefully above her head, her chin up, and a smile on her face.

The audience clapped as though she had done a

good job. It wasn't something unexpected; Cammie knew that people always wanted a skater to do her best. So she bowed first to the judges, then to the audience, trying not to think of Mom and Dad watching her from the stands. She kept her head high, and she never stopped smiling. She smiled even when she left the ice, and even when Coach Ferguson grabbed her hand and hissed, "What happened?" Cammie was still smiling.

"Cammie, do you hear me? What's wrong with you? Are you sick?"

"Ah?" Cammie looked into her coach's gray eyes knowing that the silly smile was still on her lips, and she couldn't erase it.

Coach Ferguson let go of Cammie's hand. There was an expression of concern on the woman's face. "Okay, you're not in the condition to talk now. We'll save it for later. Go change."

Cammie nodded and strolled in the direction of the locker room.

"Cammie!"

She recognized Alex's voice even before she saw him. She kept walking.

"Cammie, come on! Talk to me!"

Cammie looked around. Alex looked worried, his green eyes searching her face for an answer, for some kind of an explanation. Only Cammie didn't feel like talking; she didn't even want to think of what had just happened. Her only desire was to fall asleep and forget everything. And then perhaps she would wake up and find out that the whole competition had been nothing but a bad dream. A nightmare.

"Cammie!" Alex took her hand and squeezed it tight. "I know something is terribly wrong. You looked great in practice. You—"

"Alex!" Cammie freed her hand. "I…I really don't feel like talking about it now."

"But—"

"Later." Cammie tried to smile, but her upper lip twittered, and she had to look away for Alex not to see tears in her eyes.

"Look, I don't think it's a good idea for you to be alone now."

"I'll be fine."

"Cammie, perhaps it would be better if we talked about it."

"No, please, Alex; some other time."

Alex sighed deeply, and Cammie saw that he was hurt. But there was nothing she could do. Cammie was drained out by her disastrous performance. She had no strength for talks, explanations, even encouragements. All she wanted was to forget what had just happened.

"All right." Alex stepped back. He looked very disappointed.

Cammie faked another smile. "We'll talk later. Really, I..." She couldn't even finish the sentence. Tears clouded her eyes. Cammie turned away from Alex's green eyes, his concern, his golden performance this afternoon, and ran to the locker room. Luckily, it was empty; everybody was out at the arena watching the competition. Without taking off her skates, Cammie fell on the bench and burst into tears.

MYSTERIOUS TRIPLES

C ammie didn't remember how long she cried. The locker room was still empty and quiet, except for the distant sound of applause from the arena that reached Cammie's ears from time to time. Other skaters were probably doing their best, and there she was—humiliated and defeated.

"Honey?"

Cammie raised her head. Her parents had just walked in. Through the tears that clouded her vision, Cammie could see how sad her mother's face looked. That made her feel even worse, and she bit her lip hard not to start bawling like a baby.

"Cammie, are you all right?" Cammie's mom sat beside her on the bench and touched her forehead.

Cammie jerked away from her. "What do you mean?"

"Do you have a stomach problem? What did you eat this morning?"

"Ah, I get it. You think I skated badly because I'm sick. Well, it could be a good excuse, but no, that's not what happened. I just couldn't do it."

Cammie grimaced and picked another Kleenex from a box beside her. There were always boxes of Kleenex in the girls' locker room during competitions—perhaps because someone always cried there. Having always placed high, Cammie had never realized that there was always a girl who came in last. This time, it was probably her.

"Am I in last place?" Cammie asked, hoping that maybe she was tenth or eleventh out of the field of twelve. After all, she hadn't seen the other girls skate. Perhaps, someone had done even worse.

Her mother looked uncomfortable. She twisted her pocketbook in her hand and gave Cammie's father a questioning look. He made a funny face imitating someone who couldn't care less.

"Cammie, you're a champ. Does that little piece of gold really matter that much to you?"

"So I *am* last," Cammie said, looking straight into her father's green eyes—so much like her own.

"Oh, well, you are last. So what?" Cammie's father spread his arms.

"Just don't let it get to you, sweetie," Mother said quickly. "Your father and I have been talking about it. Maybe now is not the best time to make this decision, but…you know, I've always thought that your moving away from home was a little premature. After all, you're not old enough, and all the pressure of testing and competing may have been too much for you."

Cammie stared at her mother in disbelief. Had she heard her right? Was her mother going to make her come home?

"Dad?" Cammie glanced at her father, expecting him to say something wise.

"Well…" Her father shifted his feet, looked around, and sat on the edge of the bench next to Cammie. "We aren't going to put any pressure on you, but honestly, do you like it here? Maybe you would really do better living at home, practicing at your own rink."

"No!" Now Cammie really felt panicky. No

matter how hard her practices might have been, she had never thought of leaving Skateland. She had been working hard and getting better. Even if she skated badly today, it didn't mean she was going to give up.

"Coach Louise has been asking about you," Mom said. "And you have always been the best skater at your rink. You were probably too nervous today, so you made all those mistakes."

Cammie ran her finger along the run on her tights. She must have ripped them when she fell from her lutz. "I'm not coming home,"

"Talk to her!" Mom said to Cammie's father, who looked concerned.

"Cammie, we're not going to put pressure on you, but—"

"But this is exactly what the two of you are doing—putting pressure on me!" Cammie exclaimed.

Mom winced and put her hands against her ears.

"So now you're shouting at your parents," Dad said. "I don't know, Cammie. We—"

"I don't want to hear another word!" Cammie grabbed her sweatshirt. "I'm out of here."

As she was running out of the locker room, she

heard her mother's voice. "I think we need to talk to her coach."

"Definitely," her father said and added something, but Cammie didn't hear anything else because she had left the locker room already and slammed the door hard behind her. There. She wouldn't allow anybody—even her parents—to boss her around. The good thing about having picked a fight with her mom and dad was the fact that her tears had dried up. She was no longer upset; she was mad. What had happened to her? How had she allowed herself to skate so badly? Why had she lost her concentration? Well, there was only one answer: she hadn't worked hard enough. But she wasn't giving up. She would stay in Skateland, and she would practice even harder. And finally, finally she would skate a perfect program, and she would become a good skater.

Once the decision was made, Cammie felt that she was strong enough to walk back into the ice arena and face people's shrugs, smirks, and compassionate looks. Cammie appeared in the stands, her head up, her eyes dry. She sank into a seat in the back and let out a deep sigh. She looked around. Surprisingly, no one was watching her. Instead, everybody's attention was on a group of girls finishing their warm-up on the ice. Cammie looked at the skaters, and her heart skipped a beat. Right in the middle of the rink Isabelle was doing a perfect layback spin, her back arched, her free leg parallel to the ice. Like the very first time Cammie saw her, Isabelle had a classy black dress on. Her black hair was pulled up in a bun, and a red rose sat on the back of Isabel's head. She looked like perfect Carmen.

Cammie couldn't believe that she could have forgotten about Isabelle's competition. Of course, her own poor performance had gotten her so upset that she had completely lost track of things. Well, at least she had gotten to the arena in time.

Hey, what was that? Cammie rose from her seat unable to believe what she had just seen. Isabelle had landed a solid double axel. A double? How could she do that? Cammie knew how hard her friend had been working to get her single axel. And now she could do doubles perfectly well. For crying out loud, Cammie hadn't even started working on the double axel!

Another double axel. And another one. Cammie shook her head, amazed.

"This is the end of junior girls' warm-up," the announcer's voice came from the speakers.

Cammie gasped. Junior girls? *Junior?* Isabelle

was competing in the junior division. But juniors could do triples. What was her friend doing among those experienced skaters?

Before Cammie could give the matter another thought, the first competitor skated to the middle of the rink and took her starting position. The music began—something jazzy—and Cammie saw that she was right. The girl could land all the triples easily. The only mistake she made was on her triple lutz that she had turned into a double. Other than that she was flawless.

Cammie watched the rest of the girls with mixed feelings. Normally when she saw someone skate better than her, she always wondered how much time it would take her to get to that level. She respected and admired skaters who were more skilled and more experienced than her. This time, however, she couldn't fully enjoy what she saw.

First of all, she had just come out of the worst performance of her life, which didn't leave her much hope of ever competing against such qualified skaters. And second…Cammie sighed deeply and pulled her sweatshirt tighter around her. The second thing that bothered her was the fact that Isabelle was competing against such strong skaters. Isabelle, who had come to Skateland almost at the same time with Cammie. Isabelle, who had never been a great jumper, who had been struggling so much with her single axel, must have found a way to learn all of the triple jumps within a month. How was it possible?

Cammie didn't know what to think. She would have to watch Isabelle skate; then she would know. Just to test her patience, Isabelle was the last in the group of ten to skate.

Now finally, finally—

"Our last competitor is Isabelle Alvarez!" the announcer's voice boomed from the speakers, and Isabelle appeared on the ice, looking so glamorous that the audience started applauding even before the girl began to skate.

Cammie waited, her hands clasped firmly on her lap.

The first chords of Bizet's *Carmen* sounded in the arena, and Isabelle floated across the rink—so graceful, so composed. She went into fast backward crossovers, picked up speed…

Cammie held her breath. She squeezed her hands so hard; her fingers hurt. There! Isabelle landed a flawless triple lutz. Cammie jumped to her feet. No! But Isabelle wasn't done yet. She bent her right knee and launched herself in the air again.

A triple toe loop. Huh? Cammie's mouth opened wide, and she sank back into the seat, shaking her head. Isabelle had landed a triple-triple combination. But how was it possible?

Before Cammie could pull herself together, Isabelle landed a triple salchow-triple loop combination, a triple flip, and a triple lutz.

I must be asleep, Cammie thought. *Things like that don't happen in real life.*

Now Isabelle was doing circular footwork. Her feet moved on the ice in perfect harmony with the music. The audience was going crazy. The applause was so loud that Cammie wondered how Isabelle could even hear her music with all that noise around her. Cammie looked around. Two teenage boys that sat three rows in front of her cheered and whistled. A gaggle of girls in the front rows clapped and squealed. As Cammie looked closer at the second row of seats, she recognized Auntie's familiar stocky figure. The woman brought her palms together following Bizet's rhythm and nodded. Her thick auburn hair swirled around Auntie's shoulders.

Cammie leaned against the back of her seat. Had Isabelle been hiding her true skating skills all along? But it didn't make sense. She had been so excited about going to Skateland just to land her single axel.

And now… Cammie grabbed the back of the seat ahead of her as Isabelle performed a perfect double axel. Maybe everything had suddenly come together, and Isabelle had finally become the skater she was meant to be.

Isabelle finished her program with a blurry scratch spin. People jumped to their feet. Isabelle was the only competitor who received a standing ovation. From where she sat, Cammie could see Isabelle skate to the barrier and hug her coach—a tall, slender man with snow-white hair. He seemed to be really excited about Isabelle's perfect performance, smiling and patting Isabelle on her back.

"This concludes junior girls' free skate," the announcer's voice said. "Our next competition is—"

Cammie didn't hear what the announcer said next. She sprinted down the steps to the exit from the arena, where Isabelle still stood chatting with someone who looked like a reporter. Cammie squinted to have a better look at the woman, who seemed to be taking in Isabelle's every word. She was short, very business looking, and there was a microphone in her hand that she now held close to Isabelle's mouth.

Cammie waited for the interview to be over;

then she rushed to her friend. "Isabelle! You were incredible!"

Isabelle's dark eyes sparkled. "Did you see me? I landed all those triples! And you know ... " Isabelle lowered her voice and looked around. "The reporter says with all those jumps, I'll probably get a pass to the nationals. Can you believe it?"

As confused as she was, Cammie couldn't contain her excitement. The nationals. Her friend was going to the nationals. "Congratulations! But how ... I mean, how did you do that?"

Isabelle stepped back, looking down at Cammie. Now that Cammie didn't have her skates on, the difference in height was even more obvious.

"What kind of question is that? Naturally, I worked hard on my jumps, and all that hard work has paid off."

"But the triples ... A month ago you couldn't even land your axel."

"Hush! What do you have to shout for?" Isabelle looked around, but no one was listening to them. "Of course I could land my axel. Single axel—big deal. Actually, I had it when I was about eleven."

"W-what?" Cammie wrinkled her forehead. "But you only started skating at thirteen. You told me."

"Be quiet! What's the matter with you?" Isabelle hissed. "Oh, hi!"

Cammie looked back to find out who her friend was greeting and saw another reporter accompanied by a group of people who looked like a TV crew.

"How about a little interview for the local channel?" a plump, cheerful man asked.

Isabelle gave him one of her best smiles. "Sure."

"But Isabelle…" There were so many things Cammie wanted to ask Isabelle. But her friend wasn't paying any attention to her anymore. The TV interview was more important, of course. Disappointed, Cammie took a step back.

"Can you please wait a minute?" Isabelle asked the reporter. "I want to say good-bye to my friend."

"Ah, your friend." The short man turned his attention to Cammie. "Are you a skater too?"

Cammie could feel blood rush to her cheeks.

"Oh, yes, she's a wonderful skater. Unfortunately, she's had a bad day today," Isabelle sang.

Cammie looked down. She was sure her face was red like a ripe cherry.

Isabelle took Cammie by the hand and led her away from the reporters. "Listen, we'll talk later.

I'm sorry about your performance, but you'll do better next time. All right? Now go home; you need your rest."

Before Cammie could say a word, Isabelle let go of her hand and rejoined the TV crew, who appeared to be very happy to see her.

Cammie felt tears well up in her eyes again. Today had been the worst day of her life. Not only had she skated her worst; now Isabelle, who had just given the performance of her life, didn't want to talk to her. Well, fine. She didn't need friends anyway.

Cammie turned around to walk away from the arena and almost ran into two teenage girls in skating dresses. "Oh, I'm sorry."

"It's okay," the girl in a yellow dress said and then addressed her friend. "I can't believe the results aren't up yet. We never had to wait so long."

The other girl, a petite brunette in a red dress, smirked. "They're probably waiting for Isabelle to be done with her interview, and then they'll take her picture with a gold medal around her neck. Where did she come from anyway?"

The girl in a yellow dress shrugged. "Don't ask me."

Cammie stopped short. The girls were talking about Isabelle. And it looked like the results of

Isabelle's competition hadn't been posted yet. So had Isabelle won the gold medal or not? The other girls had skated great, too.

"Attention, everybody!" the familiar announcer's voice came from the speakers. "The president of Skateland is here to make a statement."

Immediately it became quiet in the arena. The friends and relatives of the competitors stopped talking. The girls who were in the middle of their warm-up froze in the middle of the rink. Cammie looked in the direction of the rows of seats behind the judges' table. The president of Skateland? She had never seen the president of Skateland; she didn't even have the slightest idea who he or she was.

And then a short, very old woman stood up from a wheelchair, and Cammie recognized her right away. It was the lady Alex and she had met at the Main Square rink when they came to Skateland for the first time. The woman was a former champion; and even though she had a bad case of arthritis, she could still do wonderful spins on ice.

"Wilhelmina van Uffeln, president of Skateland!" the announcer's voice thundered again.

Wilhelmina bowed her head slightly and waited for the rest of the sounds at the rink to melt in the air. Now it was quiet—so quiet that Cammie could hear herself breathing.

"I'm afraid I'm a bearer of bad news," Wilhelmina said in a deep raspy voice.

There was a quick outburst of *oh's* and *what's*, and then silence fell again.

"It has just come to my attention that there was a case of cheating at the current competition."

"What? Cheating?" A girl's voice came from the front row.

Wilhelmina hung her head and cleared her throat. One of the judges, a short, bald man, handed her a glass of water. Wilhelmina took a sip and gave the glass back to the man.

"It grieves my heart to even talk about this. I have always believed that honesty is the key ingredient to any competition. You are here to learn the intricate art and technique of figure skating, and unless you do it with a pure heart, we—coaches and judges—are wasting our time."

The silence was even deeper now. Cammie found herself short of breath. She inhaled and let the air out slowly.

"If you are trying to get the judges to believe that your skills are higher than they naturally are, you are only deceiving yourselves. Deception has never made anyone a better skater," Wilhelmina said.

A wave of questions and exclamations rolled across the rink. From where she stood, Cammie could see people turning to each other looking confused.

"Cheating is disgraceful to our sport, and I am afraid we have to be hard on those who break our code of ethics."

People stirred in their seats again. "But who?"

"What happened?"

"Does she mean…someone really cheated?"

"That's exactly what I mean," Wilhelmina said gravely. "And the person who cheated is a girl whom we accepted as our student hoping that one day she would become a good skater. However, instead of pouring her energy into perfecting her moves, the person in question has been trying to come up with the most perfect ways of getting the judges to believe that she can land triple jumps."

Wilhelmina took a pause, looking at the audience with her heavily lidded eyes. The skaters and the parents still looked as though they didn't have a clue, but Cammie suddenly knew. In fact, she had always known.

"The cheater's name is Isabelle Alvarez," Wilhelmina said.

"What?"

"I can't believe it!"

"No!" Auntie barked, and as Cammie looked at the woman, she saw her shaking her head violently and throwing her fists in the air.

"I knew it!" the girl in a yellow dress said to her friend.

"But how did she do it?" a high-pitched voice asked from the stands.

Wilhelmina's wrinkles deepened. "Normally I wouldn't elaborate on the cheating technique. But I am also here to discourage all of you skaters from ever trying to deceive those who trust you and want the best for you. Be sure: your sin will find you out. Isabelle Alvarez! I want you to step on the ice, please."

It was only at that moment that Cammie saw Isabelle hiding behind one of the reporters. Now that she had become an object of humiliation, Isabelle didn't look smug and confident anymore— just a scared, confused girl.

"Isabelle!" Wilhelmina gestured for Isabelle to step on the ice. Isabelle stepped back and shook her head. Stray locks had come out of her bun, but Isabelle wasn't trying to tuck them back in.

Poor Isabelle! Cammie thought. *How horrible it must be to be accused of cheating in front of everybody.* Still, Cammie didn't understand how Isabelle had managed to land those triple jumps.

At that moment, Isabelle made a quick move as though trying to run away from the arena.

"Don't even think of it!" The old woman's voice sounded surprisingly strong.

From where she stood, Cammie saw the reporter behind whom Isabelle was lurking push her gently in the direction of the ice. Isabelle looked around, hung her head, and skated to the middle of the rink.

"Look at her boots!" Wilhelmina said.

Cammie stared at the woman, then at Isabelle. The girl's boots looked perfectly normal; there was nothing wrong with them.

"The boots Isabel Alvarez is wearing were invented by Melvin Reed exclusively for training purposes and are not allowed to be used in competition. I have just contacted Mr. Reed, and he assured me that he had warned Isabelle of the possible consequences of breaking the law. It is sad to admit that Mr. Reed was aware of the temptation young skaters might fall into trying to bypass the law. That is why the self-spinning boots look nothing like regular figure skating boots. They are made from metal and are therefore easily identified."

Cammie stared at Isabelle's boots, feeling confused. What was Wilhelmina talking about? All Cammie could see was white leather—just like on regular figure-skating boots.

"What Isabelle did is another proof that she deliberately broke the law. Isabelle covered the self-spinning boots with pieces of white leather. She must have glued them on top of the metal. However, as Isabelle was landing her gorgeous triple jumps..." Wilhelmina squeezed her face in mocking admiration.

The audience giggled.

Cammie cringed.

"A piece of leather came off. Isabelle, would you please raise your right foot."

Looking like a startled deer, Isabelle obeyed.

The people, including Cammie, gasped. The front of Isabelle's right boot looked exactly like a regular figure skating boot. The back of it, however, was shiny silver.

"So what do you want to say for yourself,

Isabelle?" Wilhelmina asked. "Are you going to confess or deny your transgression?"

Isabelle lowered her head. She looked as though she was going to cry.

"Then the case is clear," Wilhelmina said. "I'm afraid we have to be strict with Isabelle. I have already discussed the issue with the panel of judges, and it is our unanimous decision that Isabelle Alvarez be disqualified from all competitions for a year. For the same period of time, she will not be allowed to skate at any of Skateland's official practice rinks. Case closed."

Wilhelmina lowered herself back into her wheelchair. Isabelle hurried away from the rink. She looked as though she was trying to get out of the public eye as soon as she could. As Isabelle approached the exit, the same reporter grabbed her by the hand. He said something to Isabelle.

He probably wants to interview Isabelle about what has just happened, Cammie thought.

Isabelle shook her head, pulled her hand out of the reporter's grasp, and ran out of the arena.

BLACK RINK

"**I** still think Isabelle had something to do with your poor performance," Sonia said as she climbed into bed.

Cammie sighed. Her eyes hurt from crying too much, and the last thing she wanted was another conversation about the competition. "I did badly, okay?"

"I saw you in practice. You were ready." Sonia pulled the covers up to her chest and fixed her bright blue eyes on Cammie.

"I probably got nervous. It can happen to anybody."

"Exactly, but you're not the nervous type. No, Isabelle must have jinxed you or something."

As frustrated as she was, Cammie couldn't

help laughing. "Jinxed. There's no such thing as jinxing!"

Sonia turned to the side. "Look who is talking! And how about Jeff and me? We were cursed by witches, remember?"

"Well, Isabelle isn't a witch."

"No, she isn't, but who is her lady friend?"

"Auntie? I told you before she's a friend of the family."

"If she's a friend of Isabelle's family, it doesn't mean she isn't a witch."

Sonia's conclusion sounded as reasonable as everything she had ever said. And yet Cammie didn't want to give in to her. If she started blaming someone else for her disastrous skating, it would mean she was a sore loser.

"Now Isabelle is in real trouble herself," Cammie said to change the subject, although Isabelle's cheating had been the topic of everybody's conversation all day long after the end of the competition. No matter where Cammie had gone—to the Sport Center lobby, to the dining room, even to Main Square—she had seen people with rounded eyes, quick nervous gestures, and abrupt questions like, "Did you know her?"

"I heard she couldn't even skate, is that true?"

"She deserved it," Sonia said angrily. "And Cammie, please, I told you that before: stay away from Isabelle. She isn't a good friend for you. She'll get you in trouble."

"She won't!" Cammie said confidently. "I would never agree to cheating. Ever."

"Whatever." Sonia pressed her lips, showing her disappointment, and turned the light out. "Have a good night."

"Good night!" Cammie turned on her back and stared at the dark ceiling. She remembered it was Sunday tomorrow, so she wouldn't have to get up early to be in time for the morning practice. It would be nice to have a day off. She needed it. It was only then that Cammie realized how tired she was. Her muscles hurt, and her legs felt heavy. She closed her eyes. Perhaps if she fell asleep right away, she would forget about what had happened today.

Cammie lay quietly for several minutes, but she couldn't go to asleep. She turned to the side then flipped around on her stomach. Nothing helped; sleep wouldn't come. Not only was she tired, there was something bothering her in the back of her mind. Something was telling her she had done something wrong. But what was it?

The pin! Cammie remembered. Of course! The

gold good-luck pin that Isabelle had given her, the magic thing that was supposed to make Cammie skate her best. Was that cheating too? Just like Isabelle's self-spinning boots?

No, of course, not, Cammie said to the mysterious somebody who had planted that weird idea into her mind. *I didn't cheat. I never tried any jumps I wasn't capable of.*

Yes, but you did use the pin! the still, small voice said.

Okay, but it didn't help me to win. I came in last, Cammie objected.

But good-luck pins are as illegal as self-spinning boots.

"No they aren't!" Cammie said angrily.

"What's that?" Sonia muttered from her bed. From where she lay, Cammie could see Sonia's head rise from the pillow. Cammie quickly put her hand against her mouth. Had she actually said the words out loud? How stupid!

"Cammie? Are you all right?" Sonia asked.

Cammie took a deep breath. "I'm fine. Just can't sleep."

"Forget about what happened," Sonia said softly. "You're a terrific skater. You'll win next time."

"Easy for you to say. You got the gold," Cammie whined.

"Stay away from Isabelle, and you'll be fine."

Cammie saw Sonia's head dive under the covers again. She switched sides again, trying to get more comfortable. It was easy for Sonia to talk. *Stay away from Isabelle, and you'll win the gold.* Cammie surely wished things were as simple as that. But really, could the good-luck pin have had something to do with Cammie's poor skating? Cammie thought about it for a moment and shook her head. Of course not. If she had won, that would have been a different issue. *Perhaps it's even good I lost,* Cammie thought. *What if I had won, and then somebody had come up and said that he had seen me with that gold pin? Just like that judge who had noticed Isabelle's partially exposed self-spinning boot.* Cammie felt her body tighten at the very idea of being caught cheating during a competition. But no, that was ridiculous. *Isabelle's good-luck pin didn't work,* Cammie thought. *I didn't skate any better than I normally would have. In fact, I've never skated that badly.*

Cammie felt her eyes moisten again, though she had thought there were no more tears left in her body. *No, I shouldn't cry,* she told herself. *What's the use? It's not going to make me skate any better. On*

Monday I'll come to the rink, and I'll work hard—harder than I ever worked. And I'll get better. Now I'm going to sleep.

Cammie turned on her back again. The room was quiet except for Sonia's rhythmic breathing.

Ding! The familiar sound of bells outside told Cammie that Auntie had brought Isabelle to the dorm. This time, Cammie stayed in bed. She didn't need to look outside to figure out who it was. *I wonder what Isabelle is going to do now,* Cammie thought. *She has been banned from all practice rinks. So what's next? Is she going back home? Or will she stay? And if she does leave, how about me?*

Cammie wrapped the covers tighter around her body. No, she wasn't going to leave Skateland. And perhaps Sonia was right about Isabelle. If Isabelle was leaving, maybe it was for the best. Cammie would concentrate on her skating and become really good. And then in a year, maybe Isabelle would return and then…

Cammie was asleep before she could make plans for the next year.

When she opened her eyes, it was late morning, and Sonia was gone.

Cammie stretched in bed and smiled happily. She didn't have to be in a hurry. Now she would take a nice hot shower without rushing anywhere and then go to the dining room. Breakfast was over, of course, but on Sunday, Mrs. Page always had something for skaters who wanted to sleep in.

Cammie got dressed slowly, enjoying the feeling of not being in a rush. When she left the room, it was unusually quiet in the lobby. Of course, the other skaters were out somewhere celebrating the end of the competition. Cammie was happy to be alone. She didn't have anything to brag about, and the last thing she wanted now was to answer questions about her poor performance.

The delicious smell of pancakes greeted Cammie in the dining room. Mrs. Page stood by the dishwasher, loading plates and cups into the machine.

"Hi, Mrs. Page. Sorry I overslept. Do you have anything left for me?" Cammie asked.

Mrs. Page turned around, and her face brightened. "But of course, sweetheart. I'll serve you and Isabelle in just a moment."

Isabelle? Following the direction of Mrs. Page's hand, Cammie looked at the table by the window where Isabelle sat alone with a somewhat nervous smile on her lips. Cammie's heart hit hard against her ribcage as she approached her friend. "Hi."

Isabelle picked up her fork and drew a circle on

the napkin. "You're the only one who's talking to me. Other girls won't even come near me."

"Oh!" Cammie didn't quite know what to say. She looked down then at Mrs. Page still working on the dishes—*I'll be with you in a minute, girls!*—then back at Isabelle. "We're friends, you know."

"Thanks." Isabelle bit her lip hard. Angry tears appeared in her eyes. "I mean … How could it happen? I thought I had everything taken care of. It was Dad's fault, you know. If he had used enough glue on those boots … And I told him that. But no; he said too much glue would leak, and it would look suspicious. Suspicious, yeah right. And now what? I can't even go to practice rinks!"

For a moment, Cammie thought Isabelle was going to cry. But as the older girl raised her head, her eyes were dry. "I won't let it get to me. I'll become great one day anyway."

Mrs. Page approached their table with a steaming plate filled with pancakes. "Strawberry preserves, raspberry jam, and maple syrup—whatever you like best. Enjoy."

"So what are you going to do?" Cammie asked carefully as she ladled some strawberry preserves on her pancake.

"I'm not going home, if that's what you mean."
Isabelle sipped her tea.

"But…where are you going to practice? You're
not allowed at any of the practice rinks."

"That's what I first thought. But it's not quite
that bad."

Isabelle smiled mischievously, which made her
look like the Isabelle Cammie knew—smug and ar-
rogant. "Fortunately for me, the judges as well as
the old brat—"

Cammie gave her a questioning look.

"The president. Wilhelmina, oh, my…" Isabelle
snorted. "Who cares that she was a world champion? I bet she wouldn't even be able to do a waltz
jump now."

"I saw her spin one day. She's really good,"
Cammie said.

Isabelle helped herself to another pancake.
"Whatever. Anyway, Wilhelmina the ballerina forgot about the restricted rinks."

"Restricted rinks?"

"Sure. There are two restricted rinks in
Skateland: the Purple Rink—well, that's old Mel
Reed's private area reserved for skating research."
Isabelle pronounced the last two words in a really
deep, almost manly, voice.

Cammie smiled.

"So the Purple Rink is off limits. But then there is the Black Rink, and..." Isabelle lifted her fork in the air. "This is where I'm going to practice from now on. And then in a year, beware Wilhelmina. Here comes Isabelle Alvarez!"

"Wait." Cammie put her half-eaten pancake on the plate. "The Black Rink? But it's dangerous. Don't you know what people say? That's where witches hang out."

"Oh, pu-lease!" Isabelle pouted and made her voice sound almost like a baby's. "*Children, never think of skating in the Icy Park.*"

"They are real, Isabelle," Cammie said firmly. "Please, you've got to believe me. Alex and I, we saw them. We fought them."

"Alex Bernard, yes," Isabelle said dreamily. "A charming young man. Too young for me, though."

"Isabelle." Cammie stomped her foot. "You don't know what you're talking about. The Black Rink is dangerous."

"Maybe for you," Isabelle said haughtily. "You know what it is really like? Auntie told me all about it. You see, she knows everything about Skateland. The real reason they don't want skaters to go to the Black Rink is that the ice there is super hard and smooth. It makes you skate really fast. So not every skater can handle it. You have to be really qualified. Your technique has to be perfect—edges and every-thing. Coaches go there a lot, though."

Cammie stared at Isabelle. "They do?"

"Sure. Auntie just told me she saw your Coach Ferguson there several times."

"Ah, I didn't know that."

"Of course, she wouldn't tell you. Coaches and judges have special ice time there. But there are also public sessions. In fact, there's one this afternoon at one o'clock. And I'm going." Isabelle looked at her tiny gold wristwatch.

"I guess you'll have fun."

The Black Rink, wow, Cammie thought. Wouldn't it be fun to skate there once? The ice there was probably fantastic.

As though overhearing Cammie's thoughts, Isabelle spoke up again. "Do you want to come along? Unless you have other plans for Sunday, of course."

Plans? Cammie didn't have any plans. Except for catching up on her homework, which she really didn't feel like doing. It was sad how everything had turned out. Originally Cammie thought that she would go home with her parents, where they would have a nice party celebrating her great performance at Skateland Annual Competition. Now, of course, there was nothing to celebrate. Cammie's Mom had still wanted Cammie to come home, perhaps take a couple of days off. But Cammie had refused. No, no, she had to practice. She also had school, and she couldn't lose any of her ice time. The truth was, however, that Cammie simply didn't feel like celebrating, and the thing she really dreaded was meeting some of her old friends and telling them what had happened to her. No, even spending a lonely Sunday in Skateland would be better. And now Isabelle was inviting her to the Black Rink.

"So? Or maybe you're not a good enough skater to handle the Black Rink ice," Isabelle said.

Cammie wiped her lips with a napkin and stood up. "So what are we waiting for? I thought you said the public session started at one o'clock. I still need time to change and put on my skates."

Isabelle patted Cammie on the shoulder. "That's the spirit. Go change. I'll meet you downstairs."

The Black Rink was nothing like the rinks Cammie had visited before. It wasn't rectangular, like most of the arenas, but oval and big—very big. The ceiling vaulted high above the rink like the dark sky on a rainy night. Bright lamps hanging from the ceiling lit up the arena fairly well, but for some reason, the whole place looked gloomy, even a little eerie. The walls and the bleachers were painted black, and the ice was of the same color: coal black but shiny, as though covered with lacquer.

Cammie and Isabelle entered the arena and took their seats in the bleachers to re-lace their skates. Cammie looked around, surprised to see how many people were at the rink. Of course, back home she had skated at public sessions a lot. But here in Skateland, she had already gotten used to free-style sessions, where there were rarely more than fifteen skaters on ice. The Black Rink, however, was jam-packed. Cammie also noticed that most of the skaters looked nothing like her friends from the Green Rink. The people who laced their skates next to Cammie and Isabelle, as well as those who already zoomed around the shiny black surface, looked as though they were in their late teens.

Cammie guessed there was nobody under sixteen except for herself. The most unusual thing, however, was the clothing that all of the Black Rink skaters had adopted. Girls and boys skated in black leather jackets and matching pants. To complete the look, most of the skaters had decorated themselves with chains, pins, pendants—anything made from silvery metal. For Cammie, who was used to spandex and rhinestones, public session at the Black Rink was a real eye-opener.

"Ready to go?" Isabelle said excitedly. She pulled off her parka, and Cammie was shocked to see that her friend was also wearing a black leather jacket with metal clasps and zippers and tight black jeans.

"Is there a dress code here?" Cammie asked.

Isabelle laughed. "No, silly, it's just the style we like."

We? Cammie wondered if Isabelle had skated at the Black Rink a lot before. Before she could ask, Isabelle took her hand. "Let's not waste time. I know you'll like it here."

Stepping on the ice that was black like Isabelle's father's BMW was a little scary. Cammie hesitated, watching her friend drop her skate guards on top of the barrier.

Isabelle turned to her and winked. "Come on!"

She skated off. Boy, was she going fast!

"Ah, all right!" Cammie jumped onto the ice and moved forward. Wow! Immediately she felt how smooth and hard the surface was under her blades. She was gliding at blinding speed even though she really wasn't putting too much effort into it. Cammie went into a mohawk and skated around the rink in backward crossovers—faster, faster, and faster. It was amazing how she hardly pushed off the ice; it seemed as though the black surface was moving by itself under her feet. Cammie was sure she could skate like that for hours and never get tired.

"So how's it going?" Isabelle approached Cammie, her black hair flying, her cheeks burning.

"It's awesome!" Cammie shouted over loud rap music.

"Just wait; after this, you won't want to skate anywhere else!" Isabelle skated away and executed a fast succession of turns in perfect timing with the blasting song.

Cammie laughed happily. Isabelle was right. She wondered why Skateland authorities wouldn't make ice surfaces at other rinks equally good. Wouldn't it be fun to skate her program here? Well, she was going to try it.

Cammie glided on her right backward outside edge, stepped forward with her left foot, and went up into an axel. Perhaps it was due to the smoothness of the ice surface or the fact that Cammie was under no pressure, but the jump felt really good—high and easy.

"Yes!" Cammie gave herself a thumbs-up and kept going. She repeated the steps, this time planning to do a salchow, when a huge black shape appeared from nowhere. Bang! The blow was unexpected, which made it even harder. Cammie collapsed on the ice. Her thigh hit the hard surface. "Ouch!"

The big black figure approached her and turned into a tall guy who looked about twenty.

"Hey, you all right?" His jaws never stopped moving as he chewed on a piece of gum.

"I'm fine." Cammie rubbed her thigh.

"Gotta watch what you're doing. It's not a tot class at the Pink Rink, huh?" The guy chuckled and skated away from Cammie.

She scowled. "Yeah, that was really nice."

Okay, so what was she going to do next? Ah, the salchow. Cammie prepared herself for the jump again. But before she could leap in the air, another black figure, this time short and bulky, cut her off.

"Oh, no!" Cammie stopped short. Unable to stop the rotation, she went forward, almost falling on her face. Fortunately, she managed to stay on her feet. She turned around at the intruder. It was a pimpled bulky girl about Isabelle's age. Instead of apologizing, the girl merely smirked and skated away.

Cammie made an evil face, even though the nasty girl wasn't looking at her. Perhaps the ice at the Black Rink was good, but the people surely weren't.

But I'm going to land that salchow anyway, Cammie decided. *If those idiots think I'm afraid of them, they're wrong!* She went forward, did a mohawk... Hey, what was that? Two tall girls were skating right at her. There was no time for her to turn; they were too close. *That's it,* a thought flashed through Cammie's mind. *This time, I'll probably get injured.*

Cammie expected to go down any time, when another skater appeared from nowhere with an out-stretched arm. He stepped between Cammie and the tall girls, forcing them to turn, which they did, shouting cuss words at the brave skater.

The boy turned to Cammie. "You may want to be careful here," he said softly.

The boy had a baseball cap and sunglasses on. Sunglasses at the Black Rink? The light wasn't even bright. There was something familiar in the skater's posture—even in the tone of his voice. But before Cammie could think of where she could have seen her helper, the boy skated away.

Cammie took a deep breath. Perhaps, the nice guy was right; the Black Rink wasn't safe. Maybe it would be better to leave now?

Cammie turned into the direction of the exit, but before she could step off the ice, Isabelle caught up with her. "Hey, where are you going?"

Cammie pouted. "Out. I don't like it here that much. Well, I mean, the ice is terrific, but the people are really nasty. They keep cutting me off."

"Hey, hang in there. The public session is almost over. All these people will be off the ice in five minutes. And then…" Isabelle winked at Cammie. "That's when we'll really have fun."

"What do you mean? Will they let us skate after the session is over?" Cammie couldn't believe it. At her home rink, Mr. Walrus came to resurface the ice right when the official skating time was over, practically on the dot. He never let anybody add even a minute to the practice. No pleading or whining ever helped. And here in Skateland things were the same. If the official practice was over at three, that was it. Cammie remembered once begging Coach Ferguson to let her do another layback spin—just to feel she could do it well.

"No, Cammie, your time is up," the coach had said. "You need to learn to discipline yourself."

Apparently here at the Black Rink people didn't worry much about discipline.

"Well…" Cammie scanned the rink. The black-leathered guys were chasing each other.

"Three more minutes," Isabelle said.

Reluctantly, Cammie skated away from the boards. She tried a couple of forward power pulls. Did a few cross rolls. Glanced at the skaters again. They didn't look ready to leave the ice.

"A minute!" Isabelle shouted, whooshing past her.

As though overhearing Isabelle, the huge clock on the wall came to life, striking three.

Immediately the skaters stopped in the middle of what they were doing and skated to the exit. Cammie glanced at Isabelle.

"Stay where you are!" Isabelle shouted.

Aren't they going to kick us out? Cammie thought. Isabelle probably knew what she was doing. Besides, the rink looked really nice now that the aggressive skaters had left. The ice was amazingly smooth, as though it hadn't been torn up by fast skaters for the last two hours. *This is what black ice is like*, Cammie thought excitedly. She watched the teenagers as they filed out of the rink. The lights dimmed.

Cammie looked at Isabelle.

"It's all right. Keep skating," Isabelle said.

Cammie shrugged and hurried across the rink. Wow, even though the Black Rink customers were nasty, skating on the black ice was really worth all the trouble. *Finally I'll do that salchow*, Cammie thought. She went into her three turn and launched herself in the air. One, two, land! Great! It was a perfect double salchow.

Cammie went for her double toe loop next and then her double loop. She landed every jump nicely, securely. *I wish I had done it at the competition*, she said to herself but forgot the thought immediately. Who cared about the past competition when she was skating so fast, the wind whistling in her ears, and every jump came out nicely? She was really, really happy.

Cammie didn't remember the exact moment Isabelle left the rink. She was so busy practicing her jumps that she didn't notice what was going on around her. She only realized that at some point she was on the black surface alone, and for a split second, she wondered where her friend was. *Perhaps, in the bathroom*, she thought and picked up more speed. All she wanted was to skate, skate and never stop.

The lights dimmed even more, flashed, and finally went off. The music stopped, and Cammie found herself in complete darkness.

"Hey, the lights!" she shouted, hoping that someone would turn the lamps back on.

Nothing happened. Everything was pitch dark around Cammie—so dark that she couldn't even see the ice. For a second, she thought she had gone blind, for when she raised her hand to her face, she couldn't see her fingers.

"Help!" she shouted.

No answer came. The arena felt deserted. Everything around Cammie was black, and no sound could be heard. Cammie went forward, totally unaware of the direction she was taking. Even though she wasn't trying to move fast, her speed was still high. As scared as she was, Cammie made herself stop. She realized that, not seeing anything around her, she could easily slam into the boards, and at high speed, it could really result in a bad injury. No, she had to stay where she was and wait for somebody to come and turn on the lights. After all, somebody had to be in the building. They couldn't have left without making sure there was no one on the ice. And besides, Isabelle was still there. Isabelle couldn't have left without Cammie.

"Isabelle!" Cammie shouted. "Where are you?"

Her voice bounced against the walls of the rink and came back to her in resounding echo. Cammie shuddered. It was scary.

"Isabelle!" Cammie called again, this time not so loudly. Nobody answered. Her friend either didn't hear her or didn't want to answer. No, that was absurd. Why wouldn't Isabelle want to answer her? Why would she leave Cammie at the Black Rink by herself? Perhaps Isabelle had gone to the restroom, and when the lights went out, she couldn't find her way back to the ice. She probably didn't know Cammie was stuck there.

"Isabelle, do you hear me?" Cammie tried to stay calm, but she felt her knees buckling under her. She hated being in the dark all by herself. When she was younger, she had always asked her parents to let the light on in her bedroom. It had really taken her mom a while to get Cammie to fall asleep in the dark room by herself.

A faint noise came from somewhere on Cammie's left, as though somebody was hiding in the dark.

"Who is it?" This time Cammie's voice wasn't as loud as before. For some reason, she didn't feel like shouting anymore. "Isabelle?"

There was no answer. Cammie sighed and stared

at the darkness, trying to discern at least something, but all was in vain.

Finally, when Cammie was about to give up and start crying, she heard the clanging sound, as though a door somewhere ahead of her had opened and closed. The next thing was the sound of female voices, and the voices were coming closer and closer.

Oh, good! Cammie thought. Finally somebody was coming to her rescue. But before she could say a word, a faint shimmering light that looked like a candle pierced the darkness around her, and a cold, high-pitched voice said, "Everybody ready? Candles on, then."

More candle lights appeared in front of Cammie, like stars in the dark sky, and Cammie saw a group of weird-looking women wearing floor-length dresses and skates.

"Step on the ice now, witches!" the cold voice said. "Let's do some warm-up."

Witches? Had she heard right? Had the woman really said *witches?* Unable to move, paralyzed with fear, Cammie stared at the women, and to her horror, she recognized the one in the front. She hadn't forgotten her bony fingers with long, sharp fingernails and the high-pitched voice. Of course, it was her, the Witch of Fear, the one who had held Sonia captive for almost a year. And the women behind her…oh, no, all of them were witches too. And they were about to step on the ice now. They were about to see Cammie. And what would they do once they saw her? Nothing good. They wouldn't let her walk away; they would probably attack her, just like they had attacked Sonia and Jeff. And Cammie had no one to help her. Alex was long gone. She would have to face the wicked witches alone.

WITCHES' PARTY

I'm not giving up, Cammie thought as she moved to her right carefully, trying to make as little noise as she could. None of the witches was looking at her. It meant that Cammie had a chance. All she had to do was get to the exit, and from there, she could sneak out without being noticed. Even though each of the witches had a lit candle in her hand, there wasn't enough light at the rink, and it was really difficult to get around. Cammie stared at the blackness ahead of her. The lights from the witches' candles cast faint reflections on the black ice without really bringing anything into focus. Cammie took several tentative steps to the right. To her relief, she saw the faint outline of the boards. Good. Now if she stayed close to it, she would eventually get to the exit. Cammie grabbed a hold of the boards and moved along. Yes! Her hand slid over a latch. There was the exit. She had made it.

Trying to be quiet as a mouse, Cammie lifted the latch. It clanged softly, and the door creaked as Cammie pulled it. She froze in place, trying not to breathe. No, the witches hadn't heard her—they were too loud.

"What kind of dance are we doing for a workout today?" a squeaky voice asked.

"How about *Smack and Attack?*" a low croaky voice suggested.

"No, we did it yesterday," the squeaky voice said. "I want to do *Scare and Tear!*"

"Not that one; it's too strenuous for my broken limbs," someone whined. Cammie raised her head, listening in. She could swear she had heard that voice before. And she was sure it belonged to someone whose arms and legs were bandaged; someone tall and scrawny—oh yes, there she was! The woman who had just spoken up lifted the candle to her face, and this time Cammie recognized her. It was the Witch of Injuries, the one who had attacked Jeff a year before.

"So what do you suggest?" Someone in the group laughed sarcastically. "Would you rather perform *Weep or Sleep?* It's for beginners!"

That voice sounded familiar too. As much in a hurry as Cammie was, she couldn't help looking back.

"Oh, no!" she whispered and bit on her finger, trying to keep herself from screaming. The woman who had mocked the *Weep and Sleep* dance was none other than Auntie. Yes, Auntie, a friend of Isabelle's family. So she was a witch, and Sonia was right after all.

I need to get out of here, Cammie thought as she closed the door carefully behind her and stepped into the darkness. Ouch! Her knee hit against something hard. What was it? She stretched her arms in front of her. A bench. Oh, no! She had walked through a wrong door. What she had found wasn't the exit from the ice but the door to a small, enclosed area where skaters usually went for a short break or to re-lace their skates. Cammie had to get to the exit as soon as possible, before the witches started dancing.

Too late. The witches looked as though they had come to a decision.

"We are doing *You Can't Hide from Pride*. My dance!" Auntie said happily.

"Why does it always have to be your dance, Witch of Pride?" the Witch of Injuries whined.

Now wait a minute! The Witch of Pride? Was that who Auntie was? The Witch of Pride? Almost breathless, Cammie collapsed on the bench. So that was the reason Auntie's appearance had always looked familiar to her. But why hadn't she recognized the Witch of Pride earlier? Well, probably because Alex and she had only seen the woman in the dark cave, so they couldn't really discern her features. And then, of course, they had seen her again at her rink, but they had been so busy practicing their three turns that they had had no time to study the woman's appearance.

Jeff and Sonia had recognized their attackers—the Witch of Injuries and the Witch of Fear—right away. Sure enough, they had seen them many times. But the Witch of Pride had been attacking fat kids, the ones who had got so full of themselves that they had stopped practicing and kept filling up with junk food. Cammie hadn't seen the fat kids for the whole year; they were probably still eating and not skating.

"Everybody take your starting position!" the Witch of Pride shouted.

The witches spread themselves around the rink.

"Hang on! Where's Isabelle?" The Witch of Fear skated to the middle of the arena and frowned at the rest of the witches.

"I'm here!"

The witches stepped to the sides to let Isabelle pass, and Cammie's friend skated up to the Witch of Fear.

Isabelle was with the witches! Was she one of them? Why had she brought Cammie to the rink? Did she want Cammie to be attacked?

"You're late!" The Witch of Fear looked at Isabelle reproachfully.

"She had an important errand to attend to," the Witch of Pride said.

"Yes, I—"

Before Isabelle could say another word, the Witch of Fear cut her off. "We have no time for excuses. We'll deal with the situation later. Now everybody ready? Music, please. And…"

The air filled with music that sounded like a triumphant march. The witches began to skim across the ice, performing a footwork sequence that was supposed to portray a skater who was incredibly proud of her achievements. The Witch of Fear whooshed past Cammie, shaking her fist above her head. The Witch of Injuries raised a crutch in the air, smiling as though she had just been given a birthday gift. Two ugly women dressed in what looked like black rags skated by, flailing their arms, kicking their feet. Altogether, the dance looked pretty stupid to Cammie, although she had to admit it matched the title—what was it?—ah, *You Can't Hide from Pride*. Of course, the Witch of Pride seemed to be enjoying herself the most. She was performing the solo in the group number, executing a difficult combination spin in the middle of the rink. Camel spin, sit spin, scratch spin. And again layback spin, and oh, Biellmann spin. Cammie had to admit Auntie—no, the Witch of Pride—was a terrific skater.

The music stopped as suddenly as it had begun. On the last beat, the Witch of Pride went into an axel, sharp and precise. Silence fell, and there was Auntie in the middle of the rink, frozen in the position of a winner, her arms above her head, one leg directly behind the other.

"Applause, everybody!" the Witch of Pride shouted, still holding her ending position.

The rest of the witches scowled and brought their hands together.

"Okay, that will do!" The Witch of Fear skated to the center of the rink and gave the Witch of Pride a meaningful look.

Auntie gawked at her. Apparently she hated the idea of moving away from the center.

"Now, cut it out, Pride!" The Witch of Fear pinched Auntie's side.

The Witch of Pride groaned disapprovingly but finally relaxed and skated away from the middle.

"The first thing on our agenda tonight is the plan of attack," said the Witch of Fear, who seemed to be presiding over the meeting. "As you all know, last week I asked the Witch of Control to prepare a list of the most promising skaters in Skateland who deserve our undivided attention. So Witch of Control, if you please."

The witches let a very rigid-looking woman skate to the middle.

The Witch of Control ran her hand against her perfectly buttoned military jacket, took a piece of paper out of her pants pocket, and cleared her throat. "The current Skateland residents that show

the biggest potential are Cindy Jackson, Dwayne Mc
Kingley, Dana Winston, Elizabeth Stone, Jeffrey
Patterson, Sonia Harrison, Cammie Wester…"

Cammie gasped. The witch had just called her
name. And not only Cammie's name, she also had
mentioned Jeff and Sonia, as well as Dana and Liz.
And the witch wasn't even done yet. On and on she
went; more names were mentioned; and each time
the Witch of Control gave the name of a skater, the
rest of the women nodded in perfect agreement.
Cammie's head spun, although deep in her heart
she even felt proud. After all, the Witch of Control
had picked her out as one of the promising skaters in Skateland. That was good. Maybe there was
still hope for Cammie. So what that she had skated
poorly at the last competition? If she was talented,
she would definitely improve.

Finally the witch's presentation was over.
Cammie hadn't been counting the names, but it
looked as though the Witch of Control had mentioned about thirty skaters.

"Good job!" the Witch of Fear said. "Our next
speaker is the Witch of Destruction. If I'm not mistaken, she has come up with a perfect strategy for
knocking the above mentioned skaters out of the
run."

"And you're quite right!" a deep, almost male, voice spoke from the crowd, and as the witch skated to the middle, Cammie saw that she was very tall and muscular. In fact, if Cammie had seen the woman from the back, she would have been sure it was a man.

"As I was thinking of the best way to distribute assignments among all of you, honorable witches, I thought of a perfect criterion for assigning a witch to a skater," the Witch of Destruction said. "Let me see if you can guess what it is."

The witches exchanged puzzled looks.

"Okay, I'll tell you what it is. It's the skater's main weakness."

The witches still looked mystified.

"Take Jeffrey Patterson, for example," the Witch of Destruction said.

Jeff! Oh, no! Cammie hugged herself, trying not to shake. They were going to do something bad to Jeff.

"He's an incredibly daring skater who will always go for a new move. However, our records show that he's pretty vulnerable. A year ago, our honorable Winja, aka Witch of Injuries, did an incredible job of getting Jeffrey out of the skating scene. For the entire year, the boy kept getting one injury after another. Until, of course, two brats appeared from nowhere and broke the curse."

The witches groaned. Seated on her bench, Cammie smiled. She knew exactly what brats the Witch of Destruction was talking about—Alex and her, of course.

"Therefore, I was thinking, why can't Winja attack Jeffrey again? The boy looks like a perfect target to me."

The Witch of Injuries raised her crutch in the air. "And I'll be only too happy to do it. The rascal has been injury-free too long. It's time to take care of him."

"So be it!" The horde of witches roared.

Behind the boards, Cammie shook her head in unbelief.

"Good," the Witch of Destruction said. "The same, of course, goes for Sonia Harrison. A year ago, she was so paralyzed with fear, she could barely stroke. And yesterday, the little monster managed to land a perfect triple toe loop in her program. How about that!"

"Atrocious!"

"Totally unacceptable!"

The witches shook their fists in the air, looking annoyed.

"Ready to do your job, Witch of Fear?" The Witch of Destruction turned to the intimidating-looking chairwoman. "From what I can see, Sonia is a skater who can be easily scared."

The Witch of Fear curved her thin lips. "Consider it done. I won't have that chicken of a skater move up to the novice level. "

"Excellent. Now how about ... "

The Witch of Destruction kept going over her list assigning a witch to each skater. Cammie shook her head in bewilderment. So that was what those witches did at the Black Rink—planning attacks against residents of Skateland. And nobody—not even coaches and judges, not even Wilhelmina, the president—believed that there really were witches in Skateland. Although ... Wilhelmina probably knew. Cammie remembered how a year ago Wilhelmina had talked about witches with Alex and her.

"Skaters don't like to do their basics anymore," the old woman had said. "No wonder they are an easy prey for witches."

Back then Cammie and Alex had only laughed at the woman's words. They couldn't believe she was serious. And even after Cammie had moved to Skateland, she still had had no idea that the witches attacked skaters on a regular basis. Jeff and Sonia's situations hadn't been isolated cases.

"Next on the list is Cammie Wester," the Witch of Destruction said.

Cammie leaned forward. She'd better find out what evil plot the witches had against her.

"Wait!" a weak voice came from the crowd of the witches.

The Witch of Destruction lifted her eyes from her paper, looking annoyed. It was clear that she hated being interrupted. Unable to believe what she saw, Cammie watched Isabelle skate up to Auntie and whisper something in her ear.

"What?" Auntie squealed. "What are you talking about? Stop! Everybody stop!"

Auntie waved her arms at the crowd of startled witches; then she turned to the Witch of Destruction. "You are laying out the whole strategy here, and there's a spy at the rink. For crying out loud, Isabelle, why didn't you mention it before?"

Isabelle dropped her arms and shifted her feet. "I tried to. You wouldn't listen."

"What's going on here?" the Witch of Fear shouted. "Can anybody explain?"

"That girl, Cammie Wester, is here. The one against whom you're planning an attack. Now she knows everything. She knows what skaters we have targeted, and she will blab out our strategy to the whole land!"

The Witch of Fear looked around. "I don't see anybody here."

"Perhaps she's gone," the Witch of Destruction snarled.

"She's here," the Witch of Pride said. "She came to the public skate with Isabelle, and she never left the rink. Isabelle talked her into staying after the official end of practice, and she did."

Auntie's voice turned into a shout again. "Why didn't you warn us, Isabelle?"

"Search the rink!" the Witch of Fear said coldly. "If she's here, we'll find her."

"Now wait a minute! How about my brilliant strategy?" the Witch of Destruction said crossly. "Does it mean I will have to do the whole thing over again?"

"You might have to," the Witch of Control said. "The girl will definitely warn her friends about what we have planned."

The Witch of Fear guffawed. "Not after we catch her. Now where is she?"

The witches looked around. Cammie slid down to the floor. She knew trying to hide behind the boards was useless. It would probably be the first place the witches would search.

There came a scratching of the blades; it got louder. Someone was approaching Cammie's hiding place. She buried her head between her knees and wrapped her arms around her body. *Oh please, let them not see me*, she prayed silently. The scraping stopped; Cammie heard someone breathing hard right over her. As scared as she was, she couldn't resist the desire to look up. Two dark figures leaned over the boards, apparently trying to see if someone was behind—

"There! I got her!" One of the rag-covered witches climbed over the boards and grabbed Cammie's hand. "Now I need a special reward, Witch of Fear. Don't forget about me!"

"And you'll get it," the Witch of Fear said. "I always keep my promises. Now bring the girl to the middle."

The rag-covered witch lifted Cammie off the floor.

"Let me go." Cammie tried to set herself free.

"You'd better obey me, baby, or I'll pinch your hard," the witch said in a mocking voice.

Cammie jerked away from the dumpy-looking woman, and the witch did pinch her.

"Ouch!" Cammie grabbed her thigh. The witches' fingernails were sharp as claws.

"Faster! We don't have all day!" the Witch of Fear called from the middle of the rink.

Ignoring Cammie's protests, the rag-covered witch carried her to the middle of the rink and positioned her on the ice next to Isabelle.

Cammie stood up straight and tried to catch Isabelle's look. The older girl grimaced and stared away.

"How could you do that, Isabelle?" Cammie asked softly. "How could you lie to me like that? I thought we were friends."

Isabelle pulled her leather jacket down, still not looking at Cammie. Cammie was waiting for her friend to say something, maybe to apologize. There had to be an explanation; there was to be a reason for everything that had happened. What Isabelle had done was without excuse.

"What have I done wrong?" Cammie asked softly.

An excited laughter followed. Cammie looked in the direction of the laughing person and saw that it was Auntie holding her stomach. "*Friends ... What have I done wrong?* Come on, girl, are you from a different planet?"

Cammie stared at Auntie. She couldn't understand what was going on.

"If you're a figure skater, all you want to do is to win. That's it. And if you think too much about friendship and honesty, you are going to lose. Like *you* have lost," the Witch of Pride snapped.

"I haven't, but..." Cammie forgot what she was going to say next.

"Sure you have. How about yesterday's competition?" Auntie put her hands on her wide hips. "But you still haven't found out why you lost, have you?"

"I...I didn't skate well. Perhaps I wasn't ready."

"Huh! You were perfectly ready. And you would have done your best if only—"

"Auntie, please!" Isabelle whined.

Cammie looked at the girl and saw that her eyes were full of tears.

"Don't tell her. I'll be in worse trouble; don't you understand?" Isabelle wailed.

The Witch of Destruction let out a croaky laughter. "You're in a deep pit already, girl. You might forget about skating forever."

Isabelle stomped her foot. "I'll never give up skating. I've only been suspended for a year and then—"

"And then what? You're almost seventeen. Even now it's too late. You still haven't even landed an axel. Without self-spinning boots, you're a nobody." Auntie was grinning.

Isabelle buried her face in her hands and cried. No matter how upset Cammie was, she felt sorry for Isabelle. Whatever she might have done, it was cruel to tell somebody that she was never going to skate again. So what that Isabelle was older? Not everybody had to go to the Olympics. But there were ice shows…something.

"Don't cry, Isabelle," Cammie said. "You'll skate in a year. Just be patient."

Auntie slapped her thigh. "Look at this little idiot. She's still trying to protect Isabelle. Okay, missy, let me tell you why you skated poorly yesterday. It was because of the gold pin you wore."

Cammie felt her eyes widen. "The pin?"

"That's right, the good-luck pin. Isabelle stole it from Melvin Reed's shop. Or, to be more exact, we did it together. Isabelle was the lookout; and I did the actual stealing. Pretty smart, huh? So the very thing that had given luck to the owner brought a curse on you."

Cammie felt her toes freeze in her skating boots.

It seemed as though the Black Rink was colder than all the other rinks in Skateland.

"But why did the pin work as a curse?" Cammie whispered.

Auntie waved her hand dismissively. "You'd have to ask old Mel about it. I'm not good at all that cursing and blessing. The point is, girl, Isabelle isn't your friend. And it's about time you understood it."

"But Isabelle didn't know about the pin!" Cammie said weakly. "She only gave it to me because she wanted me to skate my best."

"Huh! And why do you think Isabelle failed her test? She was ready, you know."

"You…" Confused, Cammie stared at Isabelle, who looked defeated.

"It's true. The gold pin brought me bad luck," Isabelle said. "So I gave it to you because…"

Isabelle waited a second then shouted at the top of her lungs, "Because I got tired of being the worst, you know? It was all about you. Cammie, Cammie, and Cammie; everybody in Skateland kept telling me how talented you were and how great it was that I had brought you to Skateland. But I wanted to be a skater myself. I wanted to do my best, do you understand?"

"But…of course…" Cammie stammered.

She tried to think of a good answer but couldn't. Everything was too weird.

"Keep going!" Auntie said, giving Isabelle a stern look. "Tell her everything. How you cut her off in public sessions. How you tampered with her skates."

"So it was you!" Cammie cried out.

So Sonia and Jeff were right. How sad! They had been right, and she, Cammie, was a fool. And Sonia and Jeff had also said that Isabelle was a witch. And now Isabelle was really at the Black Rink in the company of witches.

"Are you a witch, Isabelle?" Cammie asked.

Isabelle didn't say anything. She looked down, playing with a chain on her leather jacket.

"Oh, no, she's not quite there yet." Auntie giggled. "But she's...how can I put it? ...oh, yes, a witch-in-training—that would be a good way of putting it."

From that moment on, Cammie didn't hear anything else. Tears rolled down her cheeks, blurring her vision, separating her from the witches, from Isabelle, everybody. She was aware of the activity around her, of the Witch of Fear shouting orders at the rest of the witches, and the orders concerned Cammie, of course. Perhaps she needed to listen because the witches were obviously deciding what they were going to do with her.

"Our time is almost up," the Witch of Fear said coldly. "I think we will lock her up here for tonight, and tomorrow we will see how to handle her better. Any objections?"

The murmurs from the witches could mean nothing but approval.

"There's one thing, though," Auntie said. "Somebody would have to guard her tonight. And I suggest that Isabelle do it. Let's make it part of her training."

"Excellent!"

"Wouldn't have thought of a better guard!"

The witches clapped their hands, exchanging excited glances.

"All right, Isabelle, now you'll be spending the night in the lounge," the Witch of Fear said. "You can watch television; you can help yourself to the food in the refrigerator—anything. Just make sure the girl doesn't escape. Do you think you can handle the job?"

Isabelle shrugged, still looking down. "I…yes, I think I can do it."

"It's settled then." The Witch of Fear put her bony hand on Isabelle's shoulder and winked at the two witches dressed in rags. They skated up to Cammie, lifted her in the air, and carried her back to the bench behind the boards where they had first found her.

"Have a very scary night, super skater!" They giggled and exchanged quick high fives.

Cammie looked away.

"That brings our meeting to a close. Everybody is free to go," the Witch of Fear said.

The witches stepped off the ice, still talking loudly. One by one, they walked out of the rink through the exit door, extinguishing their candles. Gradually, the arena plunged into deeper and deeper darkness. The last thing Cammie saw was Isabelle getting off the ice and walking through the door to the right of the exit. Bang! The heavy door clanged shut behind her, and at the same moment, the light of the last candle died. Cammie looked in all directions around the rink, but she could only see just exactly what its name suggested—nothing but black.

THIRTY-FOOT WALTZ JUMP

"Isabelle!" Cammie called weakly.

Dead silence. Cammie couldn't even hear the sound of television in the lounge; the door had to be soundproof.

Okay, she had to get out of this evil place. But now, when the lights were out, Cammie wasn't sure she could find the exit. It had to be directly across from her bench. But she wasn't sure she could skate in the right direction without careening to the right or to the left. Why hadn't the witches left at least one small light on?

Cammie clenched her teeth and opened the

door. She raised her right leg, ready to step on the ice. *Come on, you can do it!* she told herself. *You do it every day.* Her leg hung in the air, but Cammie hesitated. Gliding on the fast black ice in the unknown direction could be really dangerous. What if she slammed into a board and got hurt? Then her last hope of ever getting out of this place would be gone. Cammie shook her head. No, that was ridiculous. She couldn't stay at the Black Rink overnight. Sonia would be worried about her. Well, maybe Sonia would tell the authorities that Cammie hadn't returned to the dorm, and they would come here looking for her? *But I didn't tell Sonia where I was going,* Cammie remembered. *Oh, why didn't I leave a note?* Feeling helpless, Cammie looked around, trying to discern something, but the darkness was equally deep on every side.

"Isabelle!" Cammie shouted. "I-sa-belle!"

No use. Isabelle was probably seated comfortably in the lounge watching a rerun of the Grand Prix Final or something equally exciting. Angry tears pricked Cammie's eyes. She had to get to Isabelle somehow. Isabelle was the only person who could help her.

"Isabelle!" Cammie yelled again as loud as she

could. "Isa—" She coughed, unable to contain her tears.

"Cammie, Cammie!"

She froze; she couldn't believe her ears. A human voice, and it wasn't Isabelle's! For all Cammie knew, Isabelle was in the lounge, and besides, the voice she had just heard didn't belong to a girl. The person who had called her had to be a boy, and the voice sounded familiar, though she wasn't sure—

"Cammie, it's me, Alex!"

"Alex!" Cammie squealed, looking frantically around her. "But...where are you? What are you doing here?"

"Hang on, I'm coming! Keep speaking so I can move in the direction of your voice. Keep it down, though—we don't want the witch to hear us."

"But all the witches are gone."

"I mean Isabelle!" Now Alex sounded really angry.

"Yeah, can you believe it? She's in that—what did they call it?—witches' program."

"All right, here it is."

Cammie could hear Alex breathing heavily right next to her.

"Where's the stupid latch?"

"It's open." Cammie stretched her hand. "Here's my hand, can you feel it?"

Their hands met.

Alex grasped Cammie's palm hard. "There you are. Now move to the right, maybe, a couple of inches...yes!"

Alex was inside, and Cammie moved a little to give him room on the bench. "Oh, Alex, I'm so happy you're here! How did you know where I was?"

Alex groaned. "I followed you to the Black Rink. I knew Isabelle had something bad planned. Of course, I didn't realize she was a witch."

"You were the guy with sunglasses on!" Cammie cried out.

Next to her in the dark, Alex grinned. "And you didn't recognize me, huh?"

"How could I? You normally don't wear those black outfits with chains."

"What couldn't a figure skater wear?" Alex said as he gave Cammie a playful shove on the side.

A moment later, both of them were laughing. Nothing scared Cammie anymore. Even the creepy atmosphere of the Black Rink seemed almost friendly as soon as Alex was with her. A minute before, Cammie had been lonely, deserted, humiliated. Now it was enough for Alex to come to her rescue, and there she was roaring with laughter, and the whole ordeal wasn't a nightmare anymore; it was an adventure.

"All right, that's enough," Alex finally said. "We need to find a way out of here."

"I think the exit is across from where we are." Cammie pointed forward, although Alex obviously couldn't see her hand. "And Isabelle is in the lounge on the right. She'll let us out."

"What? Don't tell me you're going to plead with the witch!"

Even though Cammie couldn't see Alex's face, she knew he was upset.

"Well, what else can we do? And Alex, Isabelle isn't that bad. She's just—"

"Now stop it!" Alex's voice sounded harsh. "We'll find the exit without her. I know it's across from us. So let's go."

Cammie tightened up. "What if we get lost? I can't see a thing."

"We won't. Give me your hand."

Cammie felt Alex's long fingers clasp tightly around her hand. She followed her friend to the ice.

"Ride on the flat. Straight line," Alex said.

That was a good idea. *As long as she didn't get on*

her edges … and the moment Cammie thought of it, she felt her knee buckle and her body twist slightly to the right.

"Look straight ahead. Don't turn your head," Alex hissed. "Don't you remember what Coach Louise said about the position of the head? You'll go in the direction you're looking."

"Yes, but Coach Louise hated it when we got on the flat," Cammie griped. She straightened her knee and stared at the blackness ahead of her. They were moving fast, but this time it looked as though she was directly behind Alex.

"Ouch! Cammie, slow down, the ice ends right here—"

Bang! Cammie slammed into the boards, but before she got scared, her right hand felt emptiness, and she realized it was the exit from the ice.

"Are you all right?" Alex's voice was full of concern.

Cammie rubbed her knee. It hurt slightly; she was sure there would be a bruise tomorrow.

"Cammie!"

"I'm fine; I'm fine." She crawled away from the ice.

"Are you hurt?" Alex's strong arms picked her up.

"Nothing but a small bruise." Cammie rose to her feet. "Where do we go from here?"

"Straight ahead."

They wobbled in the direction of the exit—at least that was where Cammie thought it was. Another moment and their bodies were pressed against the tightly closed door. Cammie ran her hand against the hard surface, and her fingers glided on something metal. "Here's the lock."

"Do we need a key?"

Cammie kicked the door with her skate guard. "Looks like it."

"Hmm. I was afraid of that."

They stood in silence, trying to decide what to do next. Now that they were close to the lounge, Cammie could discern the vague sound of television. She recognized the music from the *Four Seasons* by Vivaldi. Isabelle really was watching a figure skating competition.

"We don't have a choice; we have to talk to her," Cammie said.

"No!" Alex snapped, and Cammie could feel his soft hair brush her cheek. "We don't need the witch's help, I already told you. We'll find a way out of here ourselves."

Cammie sighed and sank on the floor. She

couldn't possibly think of anything else rather than talking to Isabelle.

"Yes!"

Cammie stood up quickly. "What?"

"This is where the witches keep their candles. Hey, there's a whole box of them. And matches. Hang on!"

Cammie heard the sound of a match scraping against a box, and then a small light flickered in front of her. Dark shadows stepped away from the circle where Cammie stood, and she finally saw Alex's excited face.

His green eyes flickered mischievously. "See? What did I tell you?"

Cammie clapped her hands. "Brilliant!"

"Thank you. Now let's look for another exit. Remember how we couldn't get to the Sport Center last time? There is always a back door."

Cammie laughed, thinking of how much time it had taken them to get to the competition a year ago.

"Here, take a candle. The more light the better." Alex lit another candle for Cammie, and the two of them walked around the glass-enclosed ice arena. There were several doors on their right, but each of them was locked.

"Hmm, no luck here," Alex said.

They walked in the opposite direction and finally came across a door that wasn't locked. They went inside and flipped the light switch. Miraculously the light went on, and Cammie and Alex found themselves in a big locker room. Cammie couldn't help wondering why it was so dirty inside. The floor was littered with gum and candy wraps; two mismatched dirty socks hung from the side of a trash can, and three beer bottles perched on the bench. The room smelt of sweat.

"Ugh!" Cammie wrinkled her nose and turned to Alex.

Her friend was opening lockers—one after another.

"What're you doing?"

"I don't know yet," he said without looking at her.

From where she stood, Cammie could see that most of the lockers were empty. "Hey, there's nothing in there."

"You never know; you never know," Alex muttered. "Yes!"

Alex had a pair of skates in his hand—regular women's figure skates, except one of the sides of the right boot that was metal, not white.

Cammie gasped. "These are … these are Melvin Reed's self-spinning boots."

"See?" Alex looked at Cammie, his eyes shining. "You simply have to look well; you can always find something."

"These are Isabelle's, of course," Cammie said. "The ones she cheated in. You don't want them, Alex. Isabelle was disqualified, remember?"

Alex narrowed his eyes. "I'm not going to compete in them. But they may prove handy. Okay, let's leave them here for a while."

They searched the rest of the lockers but found nothing. As they walked out of the locker room, the ice arena seemed even darker.

"This Black Rink is getting to me," Cammie said nervously "I really want to get out of here."

"Don't worry," Alex said without looking back. He walked ahead of Cammie leading the way. "Okay, a little farther … there is something here … yes!"

"What—"

Before Cammie could finish her sentence, Alex pushed a small door hard and cold winter air rushed through the opening.

"It must be an emergency exit," Alex said. "The alarm may go off. Come on. You first."

Alex stepped away to let Cammie walk out first.

She obeyed, half expecting the siren to shatter the silence, but nothing happened. Everything was quiet.

Cammie laughed happily and turned to Alex. "We are free!"

"Hmm." Frowning, Alex stared at something ahead of him.

"What?" But Cammie already knew what Alex had seen. Yes, they were outside the Black Rink, but the whole area was bordered with stone walls, both on the right and on the left. Straight ahead of them stretched the Icy Park separated from the Black Rink by a deep and wide ravine. Even the cold winter air hadn't allowed the foamy water to freeze, and now it was hitting hard against huge, sharp rocks.

"Isn't it the same ravine we crossed last year?" Cammie asked. "We did waltz jumps, remember?"

"Yeah, I think it's the same, but this time waltz jumps won't help," Alex said. "Back at the Zamboni parking lot, the ravine was only six feet wide. Here it's much wider—at least thirty feet. Nobody can do a waltz jump that big—not even a world champion."

"So what are we going to do?"

"Let me think. Could we build a bridge or something?" Alex looked around.

"Maybe we can go down and try to walk on those rocks," Cammie said.

Alex bent down staring at the fast rapids. He made a snowball and threw it into the rapids. The small white ball plunged into the water and quickly reappeared as the waves tossed it around. Alex shook his head. "The water looks deep to me. We may drown."

"What can we do?" Cammie looked to the right, to the left, then back at the emergency exit through which they had just walked. "You know what? I think I have an idea. The self-spinning boots. Remember what Mr. Reed said? I'm sure we can program them to do a waltz jump, and the magic power will give us more distance."

Alex's face brightened. "Cammie, you're a genius! How come I haven't thought of it? I'll get the boots."

"Be careful, you don't want Isabelle to see you. She doesn't even know you're at the rink, remember?"

Alex straightened up. "You think I'm afraid of the witch? You know what? I even wish the two of us would have a nice long chat."

"Alex, please! The only thing that matters now is to get out of here. What if Isabelle has a way of contacting the witches? Then they'll come back and attack us."

"Then we'll defeat them again!" Alex said, shaking his fists. "What can they do to us? We're strong skaters."

"Don't be too self-confident. Did you hear what the Witch of Destruction said? They are about to play to the skater's weakest point."

Alex put his hands on his sides. "And what's that supposed to mean? Are you calling me a show-off?"

"Alex, that's not important." Cammie didn't know what else to say to persuade Alex that it would be best to stay away from Isabelle now. She understood that all Alex wanted was to punish the girl for what she had done to Cammie. But Cammie didn't want Isabelle to summon the other witches to the rink. No matter how brave Alex was, Cammie knew that the two of them didn't have a chance against the horde of evil women.

"Look, I'll get the boots, okay?" Without waiting for Alex's answer, Cammie turned around and walked in the direction of the emergency door.

"No!" Alex pulled her away. "You stay here. Isabelle knows that you're at the rink. You're the first one she'll be looking for. I'll go. And … okay,

okay, I won't try to confront her!" Alex shouted before Cammie could give him another warning.

Alex disappeared through the emergency door. Feeling nervous, Cammie paced the small area that separated the building from the deep ravine. *Oh please let him be safe. Let him not get caught*, she prayed.

When Alex's reappeared carrying the self-spinning boots, Cammie yelped with excitement and rushed to his side. "You got them!"

"Now there's a problem," Alex said, frowning slightly.

"What?"

"How are we going to get to the other side of the ravine with only one pair of boots?"

"Ah!" That was something Cammie hadn't thought of. "How about searching all the lockers? Maybe the witches have another pair of self-spinning boots?"

Alex shook his head and sat down on the snow, placing the boots next to him. "I think Mr. Reed only had one pair in the first place. He told us he could make them for us if only our coaches allowed us to use them in practice. But Coach Louise wouldn't hear of them. Now I wish she had said yes."

Cammie smiled sadly. "Coach Ferguson said

the same thing. How come coaches never think of emergency situations?"

They were quiet for a while, listening to the sound of the water as it threw pebbles against hard rocks. The bright green color of the pine trees of the Icy Park faded slightly, which meant that night was going to settle in Skateland in no time.

"We've got to do something. And I think I have an idea," Alex finally said. He took off his own skates and slipped on Mr. Reed's boots.

Cammie watched him, her eyes wide open. "Are you going to leave me here and get help?"

Alex smirked. "Sure, if you want to be punished for going to a restricted rink, this is exactly what I'm going to do."

Cammie gasped. She had completely forgotten that by going to the Black Rink with Isabelle, she had broken one of the cardinal rules of Skateland. There were two rinks skaters-in-training weren't allowed to attend: the Purple Rink that belonged to Mr. Reed and, of course, the Black Rink. How come Cammie hadn't even thought of that rule? When Isabelle invited her to come, all that mattered to Cammie was her relationship with Isabelle. *I should have talked to Sonia first*, Cammie thought sadly. *She would have warned me for sure.*

"I watched you after the competition," Alex said. "I stayed in Skateland overnight with my parents. I told them I wanted to celebrate, perhaps get an extra practice at the Silver Rink. They believed me. But what I really wanted was to find you and talk to you. I knew you hadn't lost the competition because you were poorly trained. I was sure Isabelle had done something to your skates or to yourself. But you wouldn't talk to me. So I came to your dorm this afternoon, but before I could enter, I saw you leaving the place with Isabelle. So I followed you."

"And where did you get this jacket?" Cammie pointed to Alex's black leather jacket decorated with chains and zippers.

"I borrowed it from Kevin."

Cammie gave him a puzzled look. "Kevin?"

"One of the fat guys we met last time we were in Skateland."

"Ah, Kevin." Now Cammie remembered. Last time Alex and she were in Skateland, they had stopped by the house of four fat kids, who had served them junk food. One of the boy's name was Kevin.

"By the way, do you know who skates at the Black Rink?" Alex asked.

That was an interesting question. Really, if skaters-in-training weren't allowed to go to the Black Rink, who was it for?

"Rebels and outcasts. The ones who didn't make it in figure skating for some reason. Some of them were disqualified, like Isabelle; some quit on their own. No wonder they hate good skaters like you. That was the reason they tried to hurt you."

"Oh, okay." Now Cammie understood why everybody at the Black Rink had been so nasty to her. And now that Isabelle was disqualified, she skated at the restricted rink too.

"Anyway, I have an idea," Alex said. "I'm not sure it'll work, but we'll give it a try."

He fumbled with the self-spinning boots, changing the controls on the inside. Then he laced the boots and stood up. "Now, Cammie Wester, you're going to see the biggest waltz jump a human being has ever landed."

Before Cammie could say a word, Alex skated forward, did a mohawk into backward crossovers, got on his left forward outside edge, and soared in the air. When Alex called the jump the biggest waltz jump ever, he surely wasn't exaggerating. Cammie had really seen nothing of the kind in her whole life. Floating about eight feet from the ice, Alex flew across the ravine fast as lightning. His tall figure passed the pine trees and disappeared in the thicket.

Cammie screamed. "Alex!"

No answer followed.

"Alex!" Cammie jumped, trying to see beyond the row of trees of the Icy Park. Alex had to be somewhere there. Why didn't he answer her? Was he hurt?

"I'm here!" Alex walked from behind the trees, a huge grin on his face. "I'll tell you, Cammie, that was some feeling. I thought I'd never stop."

"Oh!" Cammie's knees buckled and she sank on the snow.

"Now watch me."

It was only then that Cammie saw Alex carry two heavy logs about three feet long.

"What are those for?"

Without further explanation, Alex got out of his boots, stuck the logs inside, and tied his scarf around the logs to keep them together. Now the whole construction looked like the lower part of a skater's body—with legs and a waist; only the top was missing.

"What're you going to do with it?" Cammie shouted.

Without answering, Alex weighed the structure

in his hands. "Feels heavy enough. It could probably pass for a small skater." He bent down and checked the boot settings.

"Now Cammie, I'm going to send this thing across the ravine. Be sure to catch it in case it decides to fly above the walls, okay?"

Now Cammie got it. She nodded and positioned herself on the edge of the ravine, her arms and legs spread to make sure she didn't miss the self-spinning boots with the logs stuck inside.

"One, two, three, go!" Alex let the structure out of his hands, and it flew up in the air and across the ravine. It passed Cammie on the left and hit hard against the wall of the rink. Alex's scarf untied, and the boots fell on the ground within three feet from each other. Cammie ran to the wall and picked up the boots.

"Terrific! It worked!" Alex shouted from the other side.

Cammie lifted the boots the air. "Yes, they look fine. Nothing is broken."

"Now let's see Cammie Wester's waltz jump!" Alex cheered.

Cammie grinned. Alex was really something. Now that he was teasing her, she really had no time to get scared. As quickly as she could, Cammie got out of her own skates and put on the self-spinning boots.

"Don't forget to take your skates!" Alex yelled. "You'll need them."

"Thanks!" Cammie put her skates into the skating bag and straightened up. She looked at the other side of the ravine. It seemed so far away.

"Don't think of it; just jump!" Alex shouted. "Do your normal waltz jump. It feels great; believe me."

Cammie closed her eyes for a moment, trying not to think of the cold water and the huge rocks at the bottom of the ravine. She skated forward, first tentatively, then faster and faster. As she went into her mohawk, she wasn't afraid any more. *Deep edge, bend your knees,* she told herself. *Hold it and...jump!*

It was the most wonderful sensation. Cammie went up and up and up and then forward faster and faster. Her eyes were still closed; she didn't know where she was going...

"Hey, it's time to land!" Alex's voice came from her left side, and it was really close.

Cammie opened her eyes. Oh, no, the pine trees were directly in front of her. She'd better land.

The self-spinning boots didn't let her down. The moment Cammie thought of ending her jump, she felt her body going down and down until her right toe pick touched the ice, and then she glided backward.

"Yes, you made it!" Alex clapped his hands. "So how was it? Cool, huh?"

Before Cammie could say that the sensation was indeed cool, they heard a horrible scream from the other side of the ravine. "No!"

Startled, Cammie looked back and yelped. Standing on the other side next to the emergency door was Isabelle. The girl looked disgruntled, shaking her fists. "How could you! You stole my boots! They are mine!"

"You were already disqualified for using them, cheater!" Alex shouted back. Unlike Cammie, he didn't act scared at all.

"What does it have to do with you, Alex Bernard? You're not allowed at the Black Rink anyway. I'll call the police now, and you'll get arrested."

Alex narrowed his eyes. "Oh, really? And do you want the police to know what you and your charming friends did to Cammie?"

"Give me my boots back!" Isabelle wailed.

"I don't think you'll need them again. Come on, Cammie." Alex turned around and motioned Cammie to follow him.

The two of them skated in the direction of the

trees. Cammie didn't even look at Isabelle. The very thought of the girl whom she had once considered her best friend made her sick.

"Cammie, come back! You're not allowed to leave the Black Rink!" Isabelle's voice reached Cammie's ears.

Cammie winced and kept skating. She felt Alex squeeze her hand. "Don't even talk to her. She's not worth it."

"We'll get you anyway, jerks! Just wait!" Isabelle shouted.

Alex did a half turn and squinted as he looked back at Isabelle. "She's calling somebody on her cell phone. I bet she'll get the witches to come after us. We must hurry."

"Oh!" Cammie tripped in her self-spinning boots. They weren't good enough for skating along the narrow paths of the park.

"You'd better change into your own boots," Alex said.

That seemed like a good idea. As Cammie was changing, Alex kept looking behind him. "Hurry up; we don't want those witches chasing us."

"I'm ready." Cammie stood up. "Where're we going anyway?"

"Well, I think we need to get to Mel Reed's place

to give him back the self-spinning boots. And then I'll walk you to your dorm, all right?"

Cammie nodded. "Sounds good."

"And stay away from Isabelle."

"I know. Now that I know who she really is, I will never trust her again."

PURPLE ICE

They skated in silence for about twenty minutes. After a long day at the Black Rink, Cammie was tired. The pine trees that stood on both sides of the path were so tall that Cammie could barely see the sky, but it was clear that the short winter day was already gone, and night was slowly covering Skateland with a huge black blanket.

"How far are we?" Cammie asked.

"I think we are really close," Alex said, checking his map that he had pulled out of the pocket of his jeans. "Just ten more minutes, and we're there."

"Wait! I hear something!" Cammie grabbed Alex's hand.

Alex stopped listening in. "Those must be birds."

"If those are birds, they are really huge," Cammie said. Now that the sound was approaching, it no longer reminded Cammie of the birds' wings flapping in the air or the wind whistling in the trees. It was more like a pack of wolves rushing through the thicket. Or perhaps those weren't even wolves but…

"It wasn't I who put Isabelle in charge!" A shrilly voice pierced the cold silence of the park.

"Shut up, you stupid Pride!" a lower voice barked.

"It's them, the witches!" Cammie hissed. From where she was, she saw Alex's eyes round in panic.

"Hurry!"

Scared, Cammie obeyed. They darted forward, trying to get as much speed out of their tired legs as possible. That was when all the cardio lessons Cammie had attended came in handy. She remembered to bend her knees, to make her edges deeper. She glided faster and faster. The good thing was that the witches hadn't seen them yet, and that was the reason the wicked women weren't in any particular hurry. Even though they were definitely pursuing Cammie and Alex, they didn't skate very fast, and within the next five minutes, Cammie and Alex were way ahead of them.

They were approaching an open area, and through the branches of the trees, Cammie could already see the bright purple surface of Mr. Reed's private rink. She knew that the sharpening shop was on the other side, so all they needed to do was to circle the pond, and they would be safe.

"There they are!" a familiar voice screamed behind them.

Cammie looked around. Auntie, the Witch of Pride, stood on the icy path, her long dark hair disheveled, her eyes gleaming angrily in the dark. Cammie didn't really have time to see which of the other witches were following the Witch of Pride, but she could easily discern the dark outline of tall female figures in the back.

"Cammie, don't stop!" Alex called. He sounded scared, and Cammie raced after him, ignoring the nagging pain in her thighs. They skated out of the thicket then unto the smooth path surrounding the lake. A silver half moon shot from behind a cloud, casting shining reflections on the deep purple ice. Now Mr. Reed's rink looked like a gorgeous skating dress decorated with rhinestones.

"A big reward to the witch who will catch these

two!" a low voice that sounded like a man's came from behind.

It must be the Witch of Control, Cammie thought.

"The reward will be mine. I'm the one who lured the girl to Skateland!" the Witch of Pride yelled.

"Catch her first!" another witch screamed mockingly.

"Oh, I will. Stop, kids! You're ours anyway!" The Witch of Pride was directly behind Cammie now; Cammie could even discern the faint smell of her garish perfume.

"Get away!" Cammie hollered, trying to pick up speed.

"Cammie, don't talk to her!" From where she was, Cammie could already see Alex approaching Mr. Reed's shop. He was close, really close. Cammie pushed harder, trying to catch up with her friend.

"There you are!" A strong hand grabbed Cammie by the hood of her parka. Cammie jerked forward, but the witch wouldn't let go.

"I caught her; I caught her. The reward is mine!" the Witch of Pride squeaked. "Come on, girl. Stop fighting me."

"No!" Cammie yelled, pulling herself forward as hard as she could. She felt the fabric stretch tight. The witch still wouldn't let go of the hood. Cammie put her best effort in trying to set herself free, but the witch was bigger and stronger. Her long fingers groped for Cammie's throat; Cammie bent her knees and raised her right blade, aiming straight at the witch's belly. Auntie careened to the left, and Cammie's skate swung wildly in the air, missing the witch.

"Yes!" The witch growled and threw herself on top of Cammie. She probably weighed a ton; Cammie found herself fighting for breath. Sharp fingernails scratched Cammie's chin; then moved lower. Ice-cold fingers clasped around Cammie's throat, robbing her of air. The sky above her blurred; everything turned dark. The witch was cackling excitedly; Cammie was probably going to die.

"Cammie, hang in there! Cammie! I'm coming!" Alex yelled as he skated hard to her rescue.

Hearing her friend's cry, Cammie began to shake her head violently from side to side to evade the full force of the witch's chokehold.

All of a sudden, Auntie's body crashed hard into Cammie, as though something heavy hit the witch in the back.

Cammie opened her eyes and realized that Alex had just crushed the witch in the back with a huge log.

"Argh!" Auntie jumped up, screaming with pain.

"Get away from her, you evil witch!" yelled Alex.

Auntie quickly bent over and grabbed Cammie's parka. Instinctively, Cammie unzipped the parka and slipped her arms out of the sleeves. She leaped forward and sprinted wildly toward Mel Reed's house.

As Auntie started to chase Cammie, she tripped over Cammie's backpack and landed hard on her fat stomach, her face buried deep in the snow. The rest of the witches ran right into Auntie, stumbled over the unexpected obstacle, and fell one on top of another.

"Ah, you prissy sissy, how dare you!"

"Hey, what the … ?"

"Get out of my way, you idiot!"

"Let me go; let me go!"

All the witches were screaming at the same time, their shrilly and deep voices blending into a cacophony of threats and accusations. Fighting the desire to look back, Cammie picked up speed. A moment later, she caught up with Alex, who already stood on the porch of the sharpening store.

"Give me your hand, and let's get inside!" Alex yelled.

Cammie stretched her arm, but before Alex could reach it, the most horrifying scream pierced the air, causing snow to slide off the lower branches of the huge pine tree on the side of the shop and two startled bullfinches to take off hastily. "No!"

"What…" Cammie turned around and froze in her spot, her mouth wide open. The horde of witches that had apparently tripped over the body of the Witch of Pride, who was the first to fall, had slid down the bank onto the rink. Now the witches whirled and squirmed on the purple ice, begging for mercy. From the way the witches shrieked, Cammie could tell they were in great pain.

"What's going on here?" In deep contrast to the scary sight, the male voice behind Cammie sounded calm and quiet.

"Mr. Reed!" Cammie and Alex shouted in unison. "Please, help us! We're being chased by witches."

A slight smile appeared in the corners of the man's lips as he watched the tight ball of witches, with arms and legs flailing in all directions, swirl on the ice. "Not anymore, my young friends, not anymore. From what I can see, justice has triumphed, hasn't it?"

Confused, Cammie and Alex looked at each other.

"Not that the wicked creatures don't deserve it," Mr. Reed said slowly, "but I don't think we need to prolong their torturous punishment much longer. If you will excuse me for a second."

The man walked in the direction of the rink. Mesmerized, Cammie and Alex followed his pace with their eyes. As Mr. Reed approached the purple surface, he stepped down on the ice and performed what looked like a complicated footwork pattern. The moment the man was done, the howling witches were separated from one another by an invisible hand and thrown into the air off the shiny ice. The evil women fell hard on the icy path—some on their butts, others on their knees.

"Ouch!" Cammie grimaced, thinking of the pain the witches felt. She knew how much it hurt to fall even from a single jump, but to be thrown about five feet in the air covering the distance of eighteen feet probably felt much worse. She expected more wailing and bawling from the witches. Miraculously, it didn't happen. The moment the wicked women were off the purple surface, they stopped screaming right away, scraped themselves off the snow, and took off in the direction of the Black Rink. Another minute, and the attackers' dark figures disappeared behind the pine trees.

Startled, Cammie looked at Mr. Reed, who was already by their side, a smile still on his lips.

"If I'm not mistaken, you expect some sort of an explanation from me," Mr. Reed said, his eyes still fixed on the spot that the witches had left a couple of minutes before.

Cammie stared at the man, then at Alex, then again at Mr. Reed.

"So I'm right. Well, let's step into the shop," Mr. Reed said, and Cammie saw that he had her backpack in his hand.

"After you!" Mr. Reed opened the front door, letting Cammie walk in first. Mr. Reed followed Alex inside and closed the door tightly behind him.

"I don't remember the two of you making an appointment," Mr. Reed said as the three of them walked in the room decorated with skating paraphernalia.

"An appointment?" Puzzled, Cammie looked at the man. "Ah, to get our skates sharpened. Um, I think mine are still good."

She raised her right leg examining her blade and ran her fingernail against the cold steel surface. "They feel fine to me."

"Yes, mine too," Alex said as he gave his blades a critical look.

"Well, let the decision be mine," Mr. Reed said. "Do you want to sit down on this stool, Cammie?"

He remembered her name! Of course, Cammie had been to the sharpening store twice, but with all the skaters who visited the place, she never expected the man to know who she was.

"You seem surprised that I recognized you," Mr. Reed said as he looked at Cammie's left blade then at the right. "I think they need some work. You have somehow dulled these blades as you were skating away from the witches. Take them off."

Cammie got out of her skates and wiggled her toes. Finally free from the tight boots, they felt pleasantly warm and relaxed.

Mr. Reed picked up Cammie's skates and took them to the adjacent room, where he kept his sharpening tools.

"I saw you at the last competition, Cammie," Mr. Reed said over top of the buzzing sound of the grinding wheel.

"You did!" Cammie felt blood rush to her cheeks. Now she wished Mr. Reed hadn't recognized her. Was her reputation as a skater completely ruined?

"And I think I know what happened," Mr. Reed said. "Okay, the right blade is done. I don't think you want it too sharp; it may affect your spinning."

What had he just said? He knew what had happened at the competition. What did he mean by that?

Cammie jumped off her stool and ran to the sharpening room. Mr. Reed was working on her left blade, humming an unfamiliar tune.

"Mr. Reed," Cammie said, not quite sure what exactly she was going to ask.

"You didn't lose because you are a poor skater," the man said without looking at Cammie.

Cammie sighed heavily. Whether she was a good skater or not, she had failed to deliver a good performance during the competition.

"Cammie, do you remember anyone giving you some kind of a good-luck charm before the competition?" Mr. Reed asked.

Cammie cringed. So the Witch of Pride had been right after all.

"Well, yes, Isabelle let me borrow her gold skating pin. She bought it from your shop. There, I have it with me." Cammie reached for her skating bag, took out the gold pin, and put it on the table next to Mel Reed's grinding wheel.

Mr. Reed turned off the wheel, picked up the pin, and examined it thoroughly. When the old man turned to Cammie, she was shocked to see how an-

gry he looked. "I never sold the gold pin to anybody. Isabelle really wanted to buy it, but I made it
perfectly clear that it wasn't for sale. Then one day
the pin disappeared from the shop. I knew somebody had stolen it, but I wasn't sure who. However,
I knew spotting the thief wouldn't be a problem. All
I needed to do was to show up at the rink on the day
of the test to see which of the kids skated poorly."

What? Cammie wasn't sure she had heard Mr.
Reed right.

"You probably wanted to say *brilliantly*," Alex
said. He had joined Cammie in the sharpening
room and was now eyeing Mr. Reed with a puzzled
expression.

Mr. Reed's light blue eyes flashed indignantly. "I
said exactly what I meant to say."

He handed Cammie her skate. "Let me have
yours now … Alex; is that right?"

Alex nodded, looking sheepish.

"The thing is that most people don't realize that
the so-called good-luck charms work in mysterious
ways. What is a good-luck charm? It is some kind of
an object associated with success in a person's mind.
The truth is, however, that there is no glory without
hard work, and success usually comes as the result
of hours and hours of tedious practicing. Here is a

skater doing a terrific program, and he gets a skating pin as a reward. So next time the same person performs in a competition, he uses the pin as a reminder of what he once did and of what he can still do. However, if somebody who hasn't worked hard toward his goal lays his hands on the good-luck pin, he gets the opposite effect. The pin that once brought luck to the honest performer will make the impostor skate worse, not better."

"What?" Cammie couldn't suppress a shriek. So that was the reason she had lost. "But...but I worked hard before the competition. I really did."

Mr. Reed tilted his head. "I don't doubt you. I saw you during the test. You did very well, even though a certain friend of yours did her best to sabotage you."

Cammie blinked, trying to cast away the unwanted tears, and looked away. With all the horrible things that had been happening to her, she wasn't even sure she wanted to skate anymore.

"But see, you clipped the skating pin to your dress expecting it to bring you luck. Let me repeat: the golden pin is a reward for somebody else's hard work. It was meant for another skater, not you. That is why in your case it worked as a curse, and your skating deteriorated."

Fearing that she might scream, Cammie pressed her hand against her lips.

"Did Isabelle know about it?" Alex asked sharply.

Mr. Reed chuckled. "It's a good question. No, when she first stole the pin, she had no idea how it worked. Actually, Cammie, she meant it for herself, not you. Isabelle used the pin during her test hoping it would help her to land her axel. As you know, she failed the test."

"Isabelle failed the test?" Cammie whispered. "But I didn't know ... I had absolutely no idea."

"Neither did I," Alex said.

"Aha! So she didn't tell you. And why do you think?"

Cammie and Alex exchanged confused glances.

"So that one day she could use the pin against you, Cammie," Mr. Reed said.

Tears streamed down Cammie's cheeks, and this time she did nothing to stop them. She couldn't understand how a girl could hate someone for being a better skater. And Cammie had really liked Isabelle and trusted her.

"Oh, stop it!" Cammie snapped at the sight of Alex smirking.

Mr. Reed shook his head. "As insensitive as Alex

may be at the moment, he is right about the whole situation. Isabelle was never your friend. She resented you from the very first day the two of you met. Even though I wasn't at your home rink, I can assume Isabelle saw that you were a much better skater right away. She also realized that no matter how hard she worked, she would never become an elite skater. And that was something she would never forgive you for."

"But it's not my fault!" Cammie exclaimed. That was so weird. What did her performance have to do with Isabelle being unable to land her axel?

Mr. Reed nodded. "Of course, it isn't. But you can't look for logic when you deal with jealousy. Envy, jealousy, excessive competitiveness—those are things that have ruined many good skaters. Remember, children, never resent someone who is better than you. On the contrary, use it to your advantage. Practice harder. Get better."

Cammie wept silently. She knew she would never be able to skate well again because each time she did her best there would be someone in the crowd hating her. Alex gently put his hand on her shoulder.

"Mr. Reed, we saw Isabelle hanging out with witches. Did the witches have anything to do with all those attacks on Cammie?" Alex asked.

"Alas!" Mr. Reed took Alex's skates off the wheel and handed them to the boy. "When the Witch of Pride saw how adamant Isabelle was about becoming the very best, yet lacking the potential, she figured she could eventually get her into the witches' training program."

"Yes, we heard of the program," Alex said.

Cammie sneezed.

"Do you know who that program is for? It's for skaters who once dreamed of glory and success but eventually dropped out either due to a lack of skating talent or simply because they didn't want to put enough effort into their practices. Instead of moving on with their lives, those skaters became bitter. They thought of revenge. They decided to ruin the careers of others, of those whose skating hopes were still alive. The witches who chased you are all former skaters. Now that they don't skate anymore, they do their best to destroy other skaters."

Cammie looked up quickly. "That's right. Alex and I happened to be at the witches' meeting, and they had the names of skaters they were planning to attack."

Mr. Reed looked upset. "Yes, unfortunately this is what witches are like."

"We need to warn those skaters," Alex said with

determination. "We need to tell them what the witches have in mind."

Mr. Reed gave Alex an inquisitive look. "And what exactly are you going to tell them? That evil witches have worked out a terrible plot against them?"

"Sure."

"Do you think skaters are going to believe you?"

Alex looked at Cammie, then at Mr. Reed and at Cammie again. "Well, it's true."

"The sad thing is that people aren't always ready to embrace the truth."

Cammie looked at Mr. Reed, perplexed.

"Most people in Skateland don't believe in witches," the man said. "They blame skaters' failures on all kinds of reasons—laziness, injuries, lack of self-confidence. Sometimes skaters get too complacent, thinking they aren't vulnerable anymore. Don't let it ever happen to you. Be cautious."

"But what about the other kids?" Alex asked stubbornly. "We don't want them to get attacked."

"They need to do their job—that's it. Unfortunately, a skater's life is full of attacks. Which reminds me … "

Mr. Reed brought Cammie's backpack from

the lobby where he had dropped them. "It looks as though you have an extra pair of skates in there."

Cammie slapped herself on the forehead. "Oh, yes! These are your self-spinning boots. We found them at the Black Rink."

"They helped us to jump over the ravine," Alex said. "Thank you very much, Mr. Reed."

The old man's eyes twinkled. "So my invention came in useful after all. Frankly speaking, I was really upset with myself when Isabelle was disqualified for cheating. Had I foreseen it, I would never have sold her the boots. But her father was really on my case. Now I believe I need to send him a refund."

Cammie and Alex put their skates back on. They knew it was time to leave. Alex's father was probably waiting for him outside the walls of Skateland, and Cammie could only imagine how worried Sonia was about her. Besides, there were a lot of things Cammie had to think about. Was she going to stay in Skateland or go home? Somehow, with all the weird stuff going on, Cammie wasn't sure she liked skating that much anymore. But before they said good-bye to Mr. Reed, Cammie had one more question to ask.

"Mr. Reed, what happened to the witches when they fell on the purple ice? They looked as though they were in pain, and then they ran away and stopped chasing us."

Mr. Reed chuckled. "Aha! I thought you would never ask. This, Cammie, is the special thing about the Purple Rink. Have you ever wondered why my rink is restricted to most skaters?"

Cammie didn't have the answer. She looked at Alex and saw that her friend was equally uncertain.

"I think by now you know what the Black Rink can do to you. When you are there, you skate with a wild crowd; the ice is incredibly fast; you feel power, and you stop caring. Eventually, you become mean. The Purple Rink is just the opposite. It brings the skater back to his original joy—the first thing he experienced when he started skating. So the Black Rink is about glory and power; the Purple Rink fills you with joy and beauty."

"Huh?" Cammie and Alex stared at Mr. Reed.

Mr. Reed smiled slyly. "As you may also have noticed, Cammie, I didn't invite you to skate at the Purple Rink when you first came to my shop with Isabelle. I didn't want that girl to come to my rink. Her motive is not right: she skates for glory, not for the pure joy of being on the ice. My rink is not for mean skaters. This is the reason the witches can't stand being on purple ice. The negative feelings that evil people carry in their hearts make it impossible for them to embrace pure joy. In fact, when a witch comes in touch with something sweet and pure, she feels strong pain."

Cammie and Alex were silent, trying to digest what Mr. Reed had just said.

"Come on!" Mr. Reed said as he cast a quick look at their confused faces.

Without asking more questions, Cammie and Alex followed the man out of the cabin to the Purple Rink. The sparkling half moon hung directly over the center of the rink. Now that the witches were gone, the whole area looked quiet and serene.

"Do you remember skating on the purple ice in self-spinning boots?" Mr. Reed asked.

Cammie and Alex nodded in unison. How could they forget? Landing multi-revolution jumps successfully—could there be a better sensation?

"Well, I have good news for you. Once you are on the purple ice, you don't need any props to experience joy and excitement. Go ahead."

Alex hesitated. "But we won't be able to land quads without the self-spinning boots."

"Who is talking about difficult jumps? Skate; simply glide on the ice. Breathe in the beauty of your sport!"

Cammie caught Alex's look and shrugged. She didn't understand Mr. Reed any better than her friend did.

"Get on the ice! What are you waiting for?" the older man said.

Figuring it would be impolite to disobey, Cammie and Alex stepped on the purple surface and glided forward. The moment her blades touched the ice, Cammie understood what Mr. Reed had been talking about. For months, skating had been nothing but tedious work, endless hours of practice, and pain in her muscles. And on top of all that, the disappointment of losing the competition, Cammie's worries about being passed by other skaters, her fear of being cut off during practices—all this made Cammie wonder whether she wanted to go on with her skating.

But now her legs felt light and strong, and her blades were sharp and fast, and Cammie glided and glided forward and around the rink with nothing but snowy trees on her sides and the lonely moon above her head. The long-forgotten feeling of joy filled her heart, growing and growing, until Cammie was sure that in another moment she would fly off the ice, join the moon, and skate in the starry sky.

Cammie skidded to a stop and gave Alex a big, happy smile.

"Alex, you know something? I think I really like skating. I like it very much!"